CR... Y0-BZM-338

CR...
J. F...

"J. F. Gonzalez is becoming one of my must read
...
...ew

"J. F. Gonzalez is a writer to watch."
—Bentley Little, author of *The Policy*

SURVIVOR

"It pushes your eyes off the page and then pulls them
back, forcing the kind of visceral relationship between
writer and reader that the best horror writing can
produce."
—*The New York Times Book Review*

"Fans of Jack Ketchum are definitely going to enjoy
Survivor. You need to buy this book."
—*Cemetery Dance*

"Quite possibly the most disturbing book I've ever read
in my life."
—Brian Keene, author of *Dead Sea*

"There's something very unsettling in the way *Survivor*
seems to prod at the slippery slope of violent entertainment; how the book…places a great deal of personal
responsibility onto the reader.…It's not enough simply
to ask why anyone would commit such horrors; we
also have to wonder why we're so fascinated by the
details."
—*Fangoria*

BEAST UNLEASHED!

The moon was a white, glowing ball. One look and Mark felt the change come so suddenly that even if he had tried to rein it in he would have failed. He bit back a scream and managed a throat-wrenching wail as the muscles along his back rippled, contorting his spine. His face was hot and burning as his nose and jaw began pulsing outward into a lupine snout. His body suddenly erupted into a fireball of pain as it was transformed, thick black hair sprouting over his body, his face, his arms and legs. His fingers and toes were white-hot lances of agony as the skin split to allow for razor-sharp claws to erupt; likewise his gums split open, blood staining his mouth as his teeth became fangs in a drooling maw of sharp, canine teeth.

As the transformation reached its climax, Mark tipped his head to the newly risen moon and howled.

Other *Leisure* books by J. F. Gonzalez:

**THE BELOVED
SURVIVOR**

SHAPESHIFTER

J. F. GONZALEZ

LEISURE BOOKS NEW YORK CITY

For Hannah Rose Gonzalez
Who arrived at the perfect time

A LEISURE BOOK®

January 2008

Published by

Dorchester Publishing Co., Inc.
200 Madison Avenue
New York, NY 10016

ISBN 10: 0-8439-5973-8
ISBN 13: 978-0-8439-5973-4

Printed in the United States of America.

10 9 8 7 6 5 4 3 2 1

Visit us on the web at www.dorchesterpub.com.

ACKNOWLEDGMENTS

Thank you: Cathy and Hannah, Mom and Dad, Del and Sue, my DarkTales pals, Pete Atkins, William Relling, Jr., Gary Zimmerman, and Bob Strauss for pointing out things in the manuscript that kept me from looking stupid.

Thank you to Cheryl Dyson for her keen editorial suggestions that made the book even better, and everybody else at XC Publishing. Additional thanks are also bestowed on Gord Rollo, Sean Wallace, Garry Nurrish, John Betancourt, Don D'Auria and the entire Dorchester Publishing team, and Steve Calcutt of Anubis Literary Agency.

Extra thanks to Dave Silva/Paul F. Olson of Hellnotes and Brian "Saten" Keene at Jobs in Hell, for producing two of the best weekly newsletters for writers I've ever seen.

The author would like to acknowledge that the town of Pueblo, California, is completely fictitious. In addition, central Missouri residents will see that he played a bit with the geography of the towns of Florence and Sedalia to suit his needs. Likewise, for those astrologers/atronomers among you, he took the liberty of manipulating the lunar cycle for his own purposes in this story. He has no idea if the lunar cycle was as described in the period of June 1990 to January 1991, when the bulk of this novel takes place. For all he knew, the lunar cycles could have really occurred weeks earlier or later. It doesn't matter. What happens in these pages is all made up. That's why it's called fiction.

SHAPESHIFTER

Prologue

It always starts out the same.

He is running. The wind whips into his face, and his hair blows back over his forehead as he runs. He is seeking something. Exactly what, he's not sure. The only thought in his brain is the pulsing need to roam. It deadens all other senses, propelling him forward. Everything else is nonexistent.

He runs through the woods, feeling the slap of branches hitting his face. Somehow he knows just where to go. He can sense that what he's seeking is just ahead, off to the left and down a slight gully. He reduces his speed as he approaches the gully that begins a slow descent down to the lake. He crests the rise, crouches at the top of the incline and sniffs the air.

There, just ahead, oblivious to his presence. He always catches them unaware. He starts down the embankment slowly, not wanting to alert his prey. Every footstep is carefully planned and executed. His body assumes a sense of total control, moving with the smooth physique of a stalker, a carnivore on the hunt. He's barely even aware of the ripple of muscles on his body as they work to move his limbs slowly with sleek-footed stealth down the embankment. His vision relays messages to his brain, resulting in the perfect maneuvering of his lithe, lean body as it snakes down the gully. Without making a sound. Without disturbing a single blade of grass.

Once at the bottom he pauses in a crouch, sniffing the air. The wind carries the scent to his nostrils as gradually as it carries the aroma of rose petals, or the musky scent of arousal. His ears perk, their radar-like sensitivity picking up movement. Around the bend, down another slight incline, and he's right on top of the target.

The breeze is blowing against him, aiding in removing all traces of his scent from the target. Nature is on his side tonight.

His breathing slows to the point where he isn't aware of the natural act of respiration. He continues his descent, past the deadfall on the right, around a slight curve, and then down the incline. He can see his target just as he tops the crest of the incline.

Tonight's target is middle-aged. Maybe fifty. Sandy hair turning gray, thinning at the top. Blue windbreaker over a slightly paunchy body. He's seated on a beach chair, looking out over the lake. A fishing pole is embedded in a stand, which in turn is impaled in the ground. The pole tilts out into the lake, the line gravitating into its depths by whatever bait the man has sunk it with. The man himself seems to be reading a magazine. *Fish and Game*? *Playboy*?

He creeps closer until he is five feet behind the man. He doesn't make a sound as he approaches; not a foot breaks a twig, or steps on a leaf. He stops and pauses, respiration low and even. His pulse quickens as the adrenaline in his body starts churning, revving his senses into action. His eyes narrow into slits, his body crouches and launches into a spring.

It happens so fast that he's hardly aware of the act. He hits the victim in the back of the neck, sinking teeth into flesh. The man falls into the shallow depths of the lake, magazine flying into the mud. He stays on top of his prey, holding him down as teeth sink into tender flesh. There isn't much of a struggle. Not even a brief flopping of limbs. There never is.

He raises his face to the moonlit sky. The horizon is turning a murky, darkened gray as the twilight becomes the dawn. The warmth of blood in his mouth doesn't even register as he gazes at the slowly descending moon and lets out an ear-piercing howl.

It is that sound, the sound of a wolf baying at the moon that awakens him. He jerks abruptly into consciousness, the bedsheets slick with sweat, his breath coming in gasps. The stillness of the air is broken by his screams as he springs up from bed, his thoughts whirling. Reality crashes in and the bedroom swims into a more familiar circle of scenery. His breathing is the only sound in the room as he struggles to calm himself. It slows to a more steady rhythm as he leans against the headboard, sweat dotting his skin. *The dream again. The goddamn dream again.*

But it's becoming less and less of a dream now.

The memories of stalking, the smell of the prey in his nostrils and the taste of blood in his mouth attest to the fact that dreams and reality can merge and become one.

Just as they were doing now.

PART ONE

Chapter One

Bernard Roberts never thought about anything else when he was locked in a steamy embrace with Carol Emrich. There was no reason to. He had his work—which was his life—and then he had his sex life, which consisted of his physical intimacy with Carol Emrich.

They were in his office on the fourth floor of the sprawling building that consisted of the national headquarters of Free State Insurance Corporation. The double glass doors that led to the executive suite were closed and locked, and the suite itself was empty and darkened; after all, it was almost eight-thirty p.m. Even the light to his own office was dark; the only light in the room came from the crescent moon that hung in the clear, June sky seen clearly through the plate glass windows of his suite. That was all the light he needed to engage in the flesh.

They were locked in a sweaty, steaming embrace on the cream-colored couch that flanked the south wall of Bernard's office. Their clothes were strewn over the floor, as if a hurricane had blown them off. Bernard was moving on top of her, over her, inside her, as they screwed with lustful abandon on the couch. Most of their workday romps usually took place in Bernard's office, hours after the day shift employees had gone home. Like tonight.

Carol's nails dug into his ass as Bernard rocked inside her. He could feel the pressure building and he immersed himself in it, fueling himself on and on, ignoring her own cries and moans of passion as he rushed on and released himself with a shudder. He barely felt her nails, or her teeth, as she clamped them down on his shoulder to stifle her screams of ecstasy. Her needs were the farthest thing from his mind; it was his he was concerned with.

They remained that way for a moment, Bernard still buried in her warm wetness as they both caught their breath. Finally Bernard eased himself out and stood up on rubbery legs. For a moment he paused in the moonlight, his attention momentarily distracted by the lights of Costa Mesa and the South Coast Plaza as they twinkled in the dark. It was a beautiful night, without a cloud in the sky and a big, white full moon hanging overhead. A perfect night for a little play in the office.

Bernard looked down at Carol, who was still lying on her back on the couch. She sat up slightly, now recovered from their romp. Bernard bent down and kissed her. "God, you are so good, baby."

Carol smiled. She looked up at him with those bedroom blue eyes of hers. "I could say the same thing about you."

Bernard stood up and stretched, feeling his joints crack. Carol sat up, her fingers tracing across her belly and breasts. Bernard hardly noticed her as he picked up his clothes from the lush, carpeted floor, then turned and made his way to his private bathroom and closed the door.

Once inside, the Bernard Roberts that he shielded during the day came to light in the washroom mirror when he noticed how red his eyes were. Signs of fatigue. The result of too many hours put in at the office. Unfortunately, it was the only way he knew how to combat the situation that had recently arisen, which was rapidly turning into a dilemma that was stealing his every waking moment, driving him to endless amounts of worry and paranoia.

The shell that was Bernard Roberts stared back at him with a hollow-eyed sense of weariness. Stress on the job was taking its toll. In the office by seven-thirty, not leaving until six, most often seven, sometimes eight or nine. Today was a typical day, leaving at five for dinner only to return at seven or so and put in another few hours. At least this time Carol had been willing to stay overtime to provide a much needed outlet for his frustrations. He worked these hours every day of the week. Over and over for the past three months. The amount of sweat, work, and stress was beginning to leave its evidence on Bernard's weary face.

Had it always been this evident?

Bernard turned the faucet on and splashed water on his face, washing away the sweat brought on by the toils of the day and the exertion of his romp with Carol. The cold water from the tap provided an instant relief and seemed to lift much of the weariness that permeated his bones. But the layers of weariness that had seeped into his soul over the weeks of backbreaking hours had settled in and laid themselves down to sleep. And they weren't leaving any time soon. It would take more than a two-week vacation to rid his body of those demons.

The stress would just keep him there. In eternal slumber.

Bernard turned the faucet off and reached for a towel. He dried his face and neck, trying to avoid looking at the circles under his eyes that were still present. No matter what he did, his problems would never go away. When they were coming at you from a source other than yourself and were controlled by forces beyond your reach, there wasn't much you could do but become stressed.

"Bernard!" Carol called out from the main office. She was probably still naked.

"Coming out in a minute, babe." Bernard toweled his body dry, surveyed himself once more in the mirror, and strode out of the washroom.

Carol was partially clothed when he emerged. She glanced at him, smiled, and resumed the task of pulling her skirt on. Bernard crossed the room to the couch where his slacks and shirt lay crumpled on the floor. He pulled his underwear on as Carol smoothed out her blouse with one hand, surveying herself in the mirror that bordered the wet bar. "Still need me to work on the Williamson account this weekend?"

Bernard nodded. "If you can. The board is meeting with the VP and director of Marketing on Monday morning, and I'll need all the paperwork for my presentation."

"No problem." Carol slipped into her heels, reached for her purse and coat and turned to Bernard as he sat on the couch, pulling his slacks on. "I'll be home all weekend if you need me."

He looked into her flushed, yet gorgeous, features. "I just might. These long hours at the office are beginning to take their toll. I think a weekend in Acapulco might be just the thing to alleviate it. What do you think?"

"I think that holds some very interesting possibilities." Carol smiled coyly at him. Her full, pink lips glistened in invitation as they parted in a smile. "Especially when the previous trip to Maui is taken into consideration. Or the one preceding that. The lost week."

"Ah, yes." His eyebrows rose in recognition. "Paris, France. A week that was destined to be the first of many."

"Mmm. The first, but definitely not the last." She bent down and kissed him softly. "I've gotta go." She stood, hoisting her purse over her shoulder. "Next weekend is on for me. As for this weekend . . ." She shrugged. "I guess it's work for me."

"I promise you next weekend will be well worth the wait." Bernard rose, pulled his shirt on and walked her to the double glass doors that opened into the executive suite. He opened the door for her. "I'll call you Sunday to find out how you're doing."

"Okay." They kissed once more and then she was gone, walking down the corridor to the elevators at the center of the building. Bernard watched her departure, noting the way her ass swung provocatively from side to side in the smooth confines of her short skirt. He stood there for awhile watching her go. She had near waist-length blonde hair and long, perfect legs that ended in a perfect ass. Her body was to die for, even if she did wear more makeup than he was used to. She was certainly the most sought-after woman in the building, was definitely the most attractive, and he could honestly say that he had laid his hands on the secret places of her body most men would only dream of.

But nobody would ever know of their affair. Neither of them had told anyone, nor had they made the relationship obvious. At work she was his secretary, he her boss, and they played their roles accordingly and professionally. As far as they both could tell, nobody suspected a thing. It would be career suicide if anyone found out. People in his position in a company as prestigious as Free State Insurance Corporation just didn't go around boffing their secretaries, all the while helping them up the corporate ladder, bypassing employees who had worked harder and longer for similar positions. Unfortunately, there were bullshit policies like "equal opportunity" and "sexual harassment" issues that would get him into a load of legal trouble should word leak out about the affair to the wrong people. It could very well bounce him right out of his position as president and CEO of the company and onto the street.

Well, maybe. Actually, there were other things that would probably kick him out faster. But he didn't want to think about those now.

Bernard sighed as he moved back into his suite

and resumed dressing. Why worry? With the way things were moving, his job was pretty much history anyway.

Three months ago, almost to the day, Bernard attended a board meeting where he, as well as the others on the executive staff, were informed of a very decisive and jeopardizing decision. The Board of Directors of Free State Insurance Corporation had decided to merge with a larger company, Eastside Insurance Brokerage. The move would consolidate most of the positions and job functions within the corporate structure, as well as several key departments in the company. Among them, the executive staff.

Bad news.

The merging would consolidate most of the company, squeezing Bernard and his position out the back door without so much as a sayonara or a fuck you. Not to mention emasculating his livelihood, as well as his too-healthy paycheck.

The last three months had been spent doing everything he could think of to save his position. He worked on special projects nonstop, initiated several money-saving executions and curbed spending on unnecessary transactions. All told, he probably saved the company hundreds of thousands of dollars in the past three months alone. All in places where money was being wasted endlessly, and had been for God knew how long. Long term, he had probably saved millions of dollars in unnecessary spending. He had initiated several support groups for employees, among them an African American association, and a gay and lesbian association. He had extended benefits to domestic partners, which had gone over very well with the local community. His action in forming these groups had affected the company drastically: work morale had risen, boosting production with fewer errors. Employees were beginning to take pride for the first time in what they did, and it showed in the way they handled themselves. A good work morale always resulted in improvement in the professional world.

Despite all his actions and initiatives in drawing attention to his work, those above him weren't responding. In fact, the word he got Tuesday morning was that the merger would be officially taking place in six months. With the executive positions to be relieved first thing.

Nothing he did to help the company, to improve the future of the company and its employees, mattered.

What mattered was that the company was slightly better off fiscally and employee-wise, with a secure future in the form of the merger. All Bernard had done was help push it to that financially secure horizon.

Leaving him in the dust.

These were the thoughts that settled in Bernard's mind as he resumed dressing and gathered his paperwork in his briefcase to close the day.

Chapter Two

This is all mine. That was the central thought in Bernard's mind as he strolled the first floor of the building, briefcase in hand. Exiting the elevators on the ground floor, Bernard usually did a double circle through the maze of corridors and departments that made up the ground floor of the building. The darkened offices and cubicles were empty and silent. Without the droning sound of people mulling at their tasks behind desks, typewriters clacking and telephones ringing, Bernard was able to take in everything much more clearly. Walking the grounds of the building gave him a strong feeling of ownership and superiority. To know that he was in charge of all of this propelled him to new heights of positive energy. The walks helped fuel his work energy, thus propelling him to overtime hours. He had so much to give, had given so much, been in charge of everything, and now it was all being taken away.

Out of his grasp.

Bernard sighed, rounded the corner by Data Processing and down the hall to the Security Booth. Just beyond Security and outside the side door was the executive parking lot. Bernard approached the Security Booth as a wide figure emerged in the window of the booth.

"Still at these bonehead hours, Mr. Roberts?" Clyde Alans was a short, wide man with a crown of bushy hair and a thick mustache. He leaned on the sill of the window on his side of the security booth as Bernard scribbled his name in the exit log.

"These bonehead hours are what helps you in getting your raise, Clyde." Bernard smiled, regarding the man in the booth. Clyde shrugged, a wide grin cracking his face.

"It's been three years since my last raise. You've been working these hours for the past three months. That means my next one will be soon?"

Bernard laughed. "I have no power over that. Talk to your supervisor."

Clyde chuckled. It was an inside joke between them, which they routinely went through. Clyde ribbed Bernard for his presidency status, asking him for a raise, if he could have stock options, if he would allow everybody on the night shift to pass the hours by playing video games. Bernard always laughed and took it in good stride. For the most part, the two men liked to shoot the breeze for ten minutes or so every evening before Bernard left for the evening, usually about cars.

Clyde motioned for Bernard to come in through the side door. Bernard stepped around the corner and opened the door at the sound of the buzzer that unlocked the door. Clyde met him at the outer perimeter of the bank of security screens that flanked half the room in a U structure. "Ever see a Lamborghini LP400 Countach?" He picked up the latest issue of *Exotic Car* magazine and began flipping through it. Bernard stepped up beside him, peering over his shoulders. "It's truly a one-of-a-kind, beautiful machine. Five speed transmission, twelve cylinders—"

"Let me see." Bernard took the magazine, gazing at the photo spread of the automobile, verifying its vital statistics. Clyde read over his shoulder for a moment as Bernard drew in a sharp breath. Beautiful car, at a price that he could finance easily, but who knew what the future held?

"Listen, I got to take a piss," Clyde said. "I'll be right back."

"I'll be here."

Clyde exited the side door, leaving Bernard to flip through *Exotic Car*. He grew bored as he sifted through page after page of technical jumbo and photographs of the same automobiles shot from different angles. He sighed, put the magazine back on the counter and turned his attention to the rows of screens reflecting black-and-white images of strategic parts of the building where surveillance cameras were positioned. Another source of amusement, not to mention major ego boosting. Viewing the Corporate Headquarters from different angles gave an added kick to his nightly walk through the building.

The first-level screens focused on the building exterior; six different angles on the parking lot with one panoramic view; the remaining five focused on the main points of entry. The bottom row of screens was made up of cameras placed within secured areas within the company: the Computer Room, the Computer Tape Library, the Telecommunications Systems Room, the Computer Processing Systems Room, and the Office Machines room. The purpose of the camera in two of the five areas was purely for security. Not all employees were admitted to the areas, and while nobody could access them without a security-coded badge, the surveillance cameras were just an added measure. The other three areas were secured because twenty-four-hour shifts were implemented in those particular workstations; the camera's main role was that of the watchful eye. There would be lawsuits aplenty should the graveyard-shift computer operator keel over with a heart attack and nobody see it in order to call 911.

Bernard surveyed the bank of screens, noting the dark quality of the night from the exterior cameras, and the equally white contrast of the Computer Room and the tape library room. He leaned closer, squinting at the screens depicting the computer room and the tape library. Both rooms were occupied with swing-shift operators performing their nightly duties. Nothing out of the ordinary here. But it was the lone worker in the tape library that caught Bernard's attention. He blinked hard, clearing spots in his vision, and stared down into the screen. His mind refused to believe what his eyes were telling him.

The figure on the screen was hunched in on himself, his hands covering his face. He was sitting in a chair in front of a desk set in the center of the room, the vast tape machines whirring away against the wall. The camera was set at the halfway point of the room, up near the ceiling, focused down over three-quarters of the center of the room. Directly below the camera was a desk, a filing cabinet, and a PC. Additional computer equipment flanked the left and right respectively. The man in the room lurched forward, still hunched over, then suddenly jerked upright. He was dressed in a clean pair of jeans and a cotton shirt. His brown hair was long, shoulder length, but clean looking. His hands flew away from his face as if to grasp at the air in front of him. Bernard flinched as if a 3-D image had exploded across the screen. The figure seemed to grimace, then lurched to the side of the screen. Bernard stepped back from the screen, mouth agape, still amazed at the spectacle of what he was seeing.

The man's face pulsated, the flesh elongated and hair sprouted from his cheeks. His face was tipped back with his mouth open in a snarl, showing rows of sharp teeth. The man's hands were turning into claws, hairy, with long fingers that ended in razor-sharp looking nails. His shoulders were bunching up, as if the muscles were growing right before his eyes. Bernard watched the spectacle, his mouth agape. He couldn't believe what he was watching.

The swing-shift tape librarian was turning into a werewolf.

Chapter Three

The change hit unexpectedly.

Mark Wiseman had felt the signs since midafternoon when he was down at the Student Union at Orange Coast College, studying for Psych 101. He had felt feverish through the lectures and when class had been dismissed he'd wandered out for a breath of fresh air. The feeling hadn't dissipated and seemed to grow worse as he went to the Union. He tried to squelch the feeling during his studying. While it ebbed slightly, he couldn't shake the feeling that something was going to happen. No matter how weak the feeling was, it was present, which was all that was needed for the possibility of change.

It vanished entirely when he pulled in to work that evening. He clocked in, mumbled an amiable greeting to Bob Davis, the day-shift supervisor who was the person he reported to directly. Mark liked this setup. His hours were four-thirty p.m. to twelve a.m. and Bob left the office at five o'clock sharp, no later.

Mark saw Bob for a maximum of thirty minutes a week, which suited him just fine. The minimal supervision fueled him to perform his job at a basic level and to complete his nightly tasks on time. Without the watchful eye of the boss looming over his shoulder, Mark found that he could work quickly, with less inhibition and stress, which resulted in a good performance review and a decent raise.

With the shaky feeling behind him, Mark had dived into the evening's work, not giving it a second thought until the change slammed into him at precisely eight-thirty. He had just loaded a tape onto the drive for copying when it hit him without warning. He screamed, clutching his face, trying to pull the change back. Sometimes he had control over the change, but he could tell immediately tonight that wasn't going to be the case.

He moaned, staggering slightly, trying to regain his equilibrium. Another wave of *change* slammed through him and this time Mark screamed. He threw his head back and closed his eyes to block out the pain. The muscles along the back of his neck rippled, grew taut, then tight as his whole body grew hot from the heat of the change coursing through him.

He was able to take a breath before the next wave hit. When it did, he was prepared for it. He fought it, forcing his entire will inward, pushing the change back. Sweat dotted his forehead, his face was strained as he tried to fight the change.

When it ebbed, he took advantage of it in a more combative stance. He gasped for air, lunged for the door, and made his way to the Men's Room.

* * *

Clyde returned to the security booth just as Bernard was exiting. "What, leaving already?"

Bernard nodded curtly. He tried to keep the excitement out of his voice, but couldn't seem to control the slight crack that emanated from his vocal cords. "I just remembered that I forgot something up in my office. I'll be right back."

"Hokay." Clyde plopped his girth into the chair in front of the screens as Bernard picked up his briefcase and exited the security booth. He didn't look back as he made his way down the hall to the elevators in the atrium that led to the fourth floor.

The only thing he could think of as he walked back to the elevators was that he couldn't believe what he had seen. He had to investigate. To simply dismiss it as a hallucination wouldn't cut it. He had to find out what was wrong with the man who worked the swing shift in the tape library. Most likely he was on drugs and having a bad trip. That was the most practical reasoning behind the sudden violent behavior depicted on the security screen. Still, there was that tiny voice that whispered in his mind that it could be something else. Just exactly what, was his responsibility to look into. Nobody worked a security-level job in this company under the influence of drugs as long as he was around. And if there was the slight chance that it could be something entirely different, something he could use to his advantage—

And even if it is something else, what are you gonna do? What the hell can you do?

He didn't know. But he had to find out, and that was what his mind and gut spoke to him. Catching an employee doing drugs during working hours might help him in some ways; at the very least it could illustrate to the board that he was loyal to the company. If it was something else . . . well, his mother had told him never to pass up an opportunity, nor let a lead go uninvestigated. He was curious about what he had seen in the security booth and he had to satisfy his curiosity. If it was nothing, no harm done.

And if it *was* something?

He reached the elevators and pressed the UP button. The elevator doors opened silently and Bernard stepped inside, his heart racing wildly in anticipation of what he was going to find when he reached the tape library.

I will not change, I will not change, I will not, will not, I WILL NOT—

Mark muttered this under his breath as he leaned over the bathroom sink. His head was tilted back to the ceiling, eyes closed in concentration, as he willed the change back. He could already feel some of it taking place. His hands had grown longer, the fingers slimming into needle-sharp claws with hair sprouting along the backs of them. His feet, likewise, had undergone a similar metamorphosis, splitting the seams of his Nikes. His clothes were barely holding his bulging muscles within their confines as muscle and tissue contorted and grew, only to recede, then bulge outward again. His snout elongated slightly, bringing agony to his nose and jaw. It was all he could do to block the pain out of his consciousness. The changing, shifting bones of his face and skull were always the most excruciating, if not the most dreaded part of the metamorphosis.

He clutched the counter in concentration, centering all of his will and energy to a single thought that he forced through his mind. The more the change pulsed and tried to blast past his willpower, the more he gritted his teeth and pushed back with all the force he had. He wasn't even aware of the rhythm of his breathing. He barely paused to take a breath during the change's brief interludes.

After a moment, the blackness that had swooped over his mind began to retreat, which brought a voluntary gasp of breath from him as he mustered more of his willpower and strength and continued to push the change back. It receded a little more and he felt the familiar tickle of sensation in his brain as he felt his fingers and toes shorten themselves. The feathery sensations of their receding registered more firmly as the feeling retreated further and further, feeding his strength and mind power. Any minute now and he could push it back and overpower it, hopefully keeping it at bay until he left for home.

The pain in his face diminished as it changed back to normal. The feathery feelings in his hands and feet accelerated as they became normal again, all this occurring while the blackness in his mind retreated, giving him more foothold. When it finally reached the point where it stopped, Mark released a breath of air, took a deep breath, and pushed with every ounce of mental power he had.

There was a sudden mental explosion, as if a headache had suddenly detonated in his cranium, and then he was normal again. Normal, staring at himself in the mirror with a tingling numbness echoing over his body. His mirror image stared back at itself, tousled hair in a lightly bearded face, wide-eyed and gasping for breath.

It was another moment before he regained his composure and caught his breath. He leaned forward, head bowed for a minute, letting his breathing return to normal as his body slowly recuperated from the minor attack. After a minute or two with no signs of the feeling arising for a second round, he looked at himself in the mirror and managed a slight smile. He had beaten it. For the first time in his life he had actually beaten it.

That thought set him back in motion. He grinned as he splashed the sweat from his face and washed his hands. He could feel his spirits soar as he toweled himself dry. This marked a turn. He had never been able to control the change. It had pretty much controlled him for the better part of a decade. Now that he knew that he could maintain some control over it, he felt more confident that the more he played with it, the more he learned to manipulate it, there would come a day when he would be free from it. Forever.

With this in mind, his spirits soared. He grinned at his reflection, tossed the damp paper towels in the wastebasket and exited the Men's Room.

Where he nearly walked right into Mr. Big himself.

Bernard nearly dropped his briefcase when the door to the Men's Room opened, spilling out the unknown tape librarian. The librarian nearly jumped out of his shoes, retreating slightly toward the already-closed door to the lavatory. Bernard managed a smile despite his flush of surprise. The young man stood before him, his face also reddened.

"Excuse me," Bernard said, switching his briefcase to his left hand. He extended his right hand in a friendly gesture. "I didn't mean to sneak up on you like that."

"Yeah, don't worry about it." The young man was wild-eyed, still panting. Exertion? Or the sudden shock of being startled? Bernard tried to divert his attention to this miniscule detail and concentrated on the superficial.

"Um, look, I'm sorry I startled you." Concern melted into his voice as easily as when he assumed his nice-guy persona. His charming mode. "I didn't realize I had scared you so badly."

The younger man blinked, then shrugged. "Don't worry about it." He looked into Bernard's face with a flushed and slightly guilty-looking countenance. "You just surprised me. Guess I should have been paying attention to what I was doing."

Bernard chuckled. "I guess I should have been doing the same thing. Sometimes it's hard to take my mind off of my work."

The kid nodded, heading forward, making to dart around Bernard. "I know exactly what you mean. Um, if you'll excuse me—"

"Oh, by all means," Bernard said, stepping aside, allowing the kid to pass. He managed a smile and nod. Just as the kid breasted him Bernard called out, "Excuse me. Sir?"

The kid stopped, features frozen in that telltale look of *what now*? Bernard smiled and stepped forward. "I know it doesn't seem right for the president of the company to do this, but I'd like to introduce myself." He held out his hand again, finding the ability to push away the curiosity and concentrate on the outer image. The corporate image. "Bernard Roberts."

The kid shook his hand, looking at Bernard as if he had lost his mind. His hand felt limp in Bernard's grasp. "Uh, Mark. Mark Wiseman." He looked jumpy, as if he expected Bernard to bite.

"Nice to meet you, Mark. You're in Computer Operations, right?"

Mark nodded. "Yeah." He wiped the hand that had shaken Bernard's against his jeans. "Tape library."

"Great department. I started there myself when I was in college. You a student?"

"Yeah, I am."

"Where are you going?"

"Orange Coast College."

"I went to USC myself. Worked swing shift at headquarters downtown and was a student by day." Eight years before, in 1982, Free State outgrew the building in downtown Los Angeles it had been housed in since 1898 and moved to a newer, more spacious building in Costa Mesa. "What are you majoring in?"

"Liberal Arts. I'm going for my AA degree. I can only afford to take three or four classes a semester and I should have enough credits to transfer to a state university next year." Mark's jumpiness was not as evident, although Bernard could tell he was itching to leave. "Once I do that I might major in computer science."

"Good job market in that field."

Mark shrugged. "I guess so." Awkward pause.

"Listen, it's great talking to you Mr. Roberts, but I've got to get back to work."

Bernard chuckled. "By all means, Mark. Don't let me keep you from doing your job. It was great meeting you."

"You too. Take care."

Bernard gave Mark a farewell wink and strode toward his office. Behind him, he heard Mark move toward the double doors that bordered Computer Operations' maze of cubicles. Mark inserted his security-coded badge in the slot and the lock disengaged with a click. He opened the door and stepped inside. Bernard continued on until he was sure that the door to the hallway was closed and Mark was making his way down the hall to the tape library. Then he turned and walked back the way he had come.

His features remained immobile as he rode the elevator to the first floor and made his way to the rear entrance. He barely looked up as he signed out again at the security booth. Another guard was there, a new guy whom Bernard didn't recognize and didn't care about. The guard acknowledged him with a slight wave and Bernard returned it, pushing his way through the glass door as the guard buzzed him out. Into the night.

His central thoughts as he piloted his Mercedes home was that Mark Wiseman was acting way too jumpy for someone who had just been startled. The way he'd hedged around the questions Bernard had shot at him, the nervous shifting from foot to foot as if he was antsy, waiting for Bernard to spring something on him. His features had held that weak mask of guilt that Bernard had seen a million times on former employees. The guilt of lying, truancy, or stealing from the company. Whatever it was the party was trying to cover up, Bernard could always find a way to the truth. Mark had displayed the blatant signs of a man who had something to hide. He hadn't been downright lying to Bernard as they talked, but he had been trying to break away so that Bernard wouldn't catch a glimpse of whatever secret he was trying to hide.

Bernard grinned. He had played along with the little game perfectly. He knew that the guy was hiding something, but he didn't press the issue. He played calm, casual, normal, and when the guy had excused himself he had played along with it. The better to avoid suspicion. And suspicion he had.

Now it was a point of confronting that suspicion. With hard truth. And Bernard knew just how to do it. As an executive of the firm he had a lot of pulling power. The pull of the right strings with some of the right people would help him perfectly. He'd get started tomorrow morning by talking to Paul Rogers, director of Security. Paul would be sure that everything Bernard asked him for would be kept in the strictest of confidence.

And then the 42-inch color big screen TV in his office. The VCR . . .

Bernard smiled. The plan was already forming in his mind before he could even confirm his suspicions.

Chapter Four

Mark Wiseman was nervous throughout the rest of his shift that night.

The minute he got back to his work area—a secure, thirty-by-fifteen-foot room with bare white walls and a clean white floor—he headed toward the computer and sat in front of it, his back turned to the security camera that was trained on the main section of his work area. He didn't want to arouse the suspicions of anybody in Security—Christ, he was surprised nobody from Security had come bursting in during the change—because if they saw him shaking now, they might come knocking.

Mark drew his arms close together and hugged himself, trying to control the shaking of his limbs. His mind kept tracking on the way Mr. Roberts had been looking at him when he was talking to him. The look in the CEO's eyes told Mark that he knew something . . . that he had one up on Mark, and that he was determined to find out exactly what was brewing in his head.

With nerves on edge, Mark remained in a near fetal position for nearly twenty minutes, the only sound that of the tape machines as they spit out data. A Queensryche CD had long since finished playing in the portable CD player, and at this time of the night Mark would normally have been working away with the music blasting. Now all that was changed. Now that the change had come upon him so suddenly, everything in his life had changed.

When twenty minutes passed with no invasion of Security, Mark began to relax a little. At the time of the attack he had been parked right in front of the tape machine, in direct line of the security camera. If the night-shift guard had been alert, he would have seen the near transformation take place. As it was, he was probably just doing what all security guards do on the late-night shift—either watching TV, or flipping through a skin magazine.

Or shooting the shit with the head honcho of the company.

Mark's stomach did a slow flip as the grim realization of what had just happened set in. He had worked a summer job at Free State Insurance Corporation two years ago and had become acquainted with the corporate structure during those two months. From that, he learned that Bernard Roberts had a plush office on the fourth floor, in the penthouse suite on the opposite side of Computer Operations. To exit the building after six-thirty p.m., he would have to walk to the Computer Operations side of the building and take the back elevator to the first floor, which let off right outside of Security. What Bernard Roberts was doing at the office at this late an hour Mark didn't want to guess, but if he was here doing-late night CEO work, he would have had to leave by the back exit. Which meant he would have had to sign out at Security. The security screens mounted in the booth the guards worked in were easily visible to those exiting the building. If Mr. Big-Shot CEO had paused to shoot the shit with one of the guards, he could have very well witnessed either part, or all, of his near transformation.

Shit.

Mark hoped that wasn't the case. Part of him whispered *and even if he did happen to see it on the security screen, why worry about it? All you'd have to do is change and stalk the sonofabitch and silence him forever. Big deal.* But the human part of him, the part of him that refused to give in to this primal animal nature of himself that he despised so much, refused to see things that way. It was this part of himself that was coming up with a plan, an excuse, some bullshit story to tell if he were confronted with what happened.

Yeah and what if Bernard or somebody in Security comes down and asks what the hell was wrong with you and you say nothing, and they pull out a tape of tonight's spectacle? I'm sure that'll go over quite well. Then what'll you do?

Killing Bernard and whatever security guard might be on duty wasn't the answer. The answer was lying low and waiting to see if the storm blew over. For all he knew he could have been over-reacting.

He had been so agitated after he had fought the change back that he could have simply imagined Bernard's reaction as he ran into the executive. His paranoid mind had most likely been running on overdrive, backtracking through the past fifteen minutes, trying to cover all avenues of possible witnesses.

Mark Wiseman was becoming more relaxed now, but he was still tense. Even so, he felt well enough to rise from his chair and move over to the terminal that was his main workstation. He looked down at the screen at the jobs coming across and saw that he had four in the queue ready for processing. He sat down in a second chair and began to work mechanically, going about the motions of his job with a blind routine that he had mastered over the past two years. All the while his mind was working, backtracking through the past ten years, fighting down the self-loathing he sometimes felt for himself.

He'd had the curse under control for the past four years now. When it first reared its ugly head nine years ago, when he was seventeen, it had come suddenly and without warning. Luckily for him it had come at a time when it was just himself and Buddy Vance, a kid two years older than he who had been stomping the crap out of him since the seventh grade. As fate would have it, Buddy had cornered him in an alley that afternoon on his way home from school. There hadn't been anybody around. It was just him and Buddy and the graffiti splattered walls of the alley. . . .

Buddy tackled him from behind, driving him to the ground hard. The fall knocked the breath out of Mark, and Buddy was up in an instant, swinging his booted foot and kicking him in the ribs. Something sprang in Mark's chest and pain blossomed. Buddy's voice rang high and merrily in the late spring afternoon: *"Haha-hahahaha . . . you fucking pussy! I'm gonna kick your ass again! Hahahahaha!"*

Mark had lost count of how many times he had been beaten up by Buddy Vance, but he knew this beating would result in serious bodily injury. He could tell by the ferocity of the attack, the proximity to home, and the location. All three conspired to give Buddy ample time to stomp, break, pulverize, and then perhaps spit at him, maybe pull out his wanker and finish him off with a hot golden shower before leaving him in a bloodied heap on the ground. Buddy would walk away with smug confidence; the last four serious beatings, which had resulted in a concussion, a broken nose, several broken teeth and numerous stitches, hadn't brought any legal repercussions down on Buddy Vance's head. Mark Wiseman had stopped telling his parents about Buddy Vance's various poundings on *him* because all they ever did was pound on him and beat him some *more* for disrupting *their* lives. The one time Mark had actually called the cops himself had resulted in his dad beating him to within an inch of his life. "I'm not only gonna have *faggots* in this house; I'm not gonna have any *snitches* under my roof either," his old man had thundered. "You either fight your own fights or suffer the consequences. Bring the cops into this next time, bring the cops into *my* house and I will fucking kill you, boy."

Mark had long stopped reporting Buddy's assaults, both at the school level or at the local law enforcement level. Instead he had done everything he could to avoid a beating, but every time Buddy had caught him he had been beaten to a pulp, with Mark reduced to a crying, whimpering baby in the street, pleading like a blubbermouth to *stop, just please stop.* And then later, in the humming black of the night as he would lie awake in his room, the dull throb of his injuries chasing his sleep away, the hopelessness of his situation would slowly turn to pity and rage. And he would lie in his bed, the pain and rage roiling and churning in his gut, many times his injuries left untreated by a doctor because his father was out of a job and out of medical insurance. He would lie in bed and try to sleep but the sandman never came, leaving him awake to wonder why he had been born into such a horrible home as the dawn bled away the night.

And as the years passed the rage and hate grew.

Mark was expecting a similar outcome in this beating as Buddy danced around him, kicking him in the upper thigh, the stomach, the right arm. Each kick sent a stab of pain through his body and he felt the rage blossom, exploding out of him like the eruption of a volcano. The past four years flashed by in a millisecond—the neglect at home, the physical and emotional abuse, the constant attacks from Buddy Vance, the cruel, vicious cycle of it all—and then something *exploded* in Mark and he was up on his feet.

It all happened so fast that Mark still barely remembered it. What he *did* remember came in snatches, brief images that remained imprinted in his memory banks. He remembered the look of surprise on Buddy's face as he stood up. He remembered the smile on Buddy's face as he recognized the challenge. He remembered the blinding speed of Buddy's blood as it splattered against the graffiti-stained wall. He remembered how easily his fingers slid into Buddy's throat and ripped out his trachea. There was a brief image of a whirlwind of violence and blood, all accompanied by a near silent fury, which later reminded him of the way a pit bull never makes a sound when it tears into another dog and begins the kill. There was a brief image of something flying through the air, something long—Buddy's arm pulled out of the socket—and the next thing he knew, he was walking out of the alley with Buddy's blood and scraps of flesh all over him, staining his shirt and hair. The taste of it was in his mouth. He cut through another alley, his body warm as he threaded his way home through alleys, his sense fine-tuned to cars and people blocks away, and then he was home.

Mom and Dad weren't home when he let himself in through the back door, hopping the fence from the alley behind the house to gain entrance into the backyard. He headed straight to his room, peeled his clothes off, and scrubbed Buddy's hair and blood off of him. After he was finished with his shower and all the blood had been washed down the drain, he took his bloody clothes, put them in a plastic garbage bag, which he tied securely, and placed them at the bottom of one of the garbage cans in the backyard. Since the following day was trash pick-up day, he dragged both cans outside to the curb and went back into the house.

Mark still found it hard to believe. The police had come around that evening to question him about Buddy Vance's murder; his body had been found a few hours earlier by a homeless person, and they were just making the rounds of known acquaintances and enemies. Buddy had a juvenile record a mile long. Any kid with a grudge—many of them of the same mold as Buddy—were better suspects for murder. For the first time in his life, Mark's father hadn't beaten him for "bringing the police home." In fact, Mark's father had been rather stunned at the ferocity of the attack on Buddy.

"Had to have been an animal," he'd said the following morning at breakfast. He'd been reading the write-up of the incident in the morning edition of the *Los Angeles Times*, and Mark had pretended to be interested. His dad had looked at him with unease. "A wild dog or something. You would think we wouldn't have that kind of problem in L.A., but you never know the way people just dump animals nowadays. You see any packs of wild dogs in the area, skipper?"

Mark had nodded. "Yeah, maybe." He had beaten a hasty retreat, just as his mother was rising from the prior evening's drunk. He'd spent the rest of the day at school and at the Gardena Public Library where he had done some research.

It had taken him a long time to get a firm grasp on what he was. Most of the books he had read at the library that first time were bullshit. It wasn't until he'd awakened one morning a month or so later, his clothes stained with blood and the taste of it in his mouth, that he realized he had done it again.

This time it had been a young couple out on a date. It had happened at Alondra Park, a quarter of a mile from where he lived. He remembered everything about it; the transformation in his bedroom while his parents were out at the neighborhood bar; hearing his wolflike howl of pain as the metamorphosis took place; his human-side going into shock as he watched his body shape-change; the sense of his animal-self taking over as instinct eclipsed his human side; then, slipping out of the house quietly, letting his senses carry him on. And then the attack. Their bodies had been found along the man-made pond in the center of the park, and along the park itself. There had been no witnesses.

That was the only time Mark had considered suicide. Two days after the attack he had stood in the bathroom, a bottle of his mother's sleeping pills in his hand, contemplation weighing heavily on his mind. A haunted, troubled soul encased in the body of a skinny, gawky teenager had looked back at him from the mirror. He had closed his eyes and struggled against the feelings for perhaps twenty minutes before he'd finally flushed the pills down the toilet.

He had been sixteen going on seventeen. He'd conducted more research at the library and had found more information. Roman and Greek myths, European legends, Native American stories of shape-changers abounded. Early writers of literature documented tales of werewolves that fed on human flesh, raided villages, stole babies in the dead of night. Medieval legends exploded with the myths; wolves were the Devil's agents, along with cats and other animals. Thousands of people were accused, convicted, and burned at the stake for lycanthropy on mere speculation. He had turned from the legends to books that supposedly contained true accounts of lycanthropy. He had never been bitten by a werewolf or cursed by a witch, nor had he been inadvertently placed in the hands of an evil or incompetent experimenter with youth-giving elixirs and potions. All three were grounds for one becoming a werewolf involuntarily. As involuntary werewolves, they had little control over their changes from man to wolf and back again, and their changes were subject to the phases of the moon.

The moon had been full on the afternoon he had killed Buddy Vance. And he was certain it had been full when he'd slaughtered that couple in Alondra Park.

Those who wished to become a werewolf for pleasure were said to obtain a salve from a witch, which they then rubbed into the skin. Mark remembered shaking his head at that when he'd read it. Nope, he surely hadn't rubbed salve over his body in the hope of becoming a werewolf. What bullshit.

The closest explanation he'd ever found of his condition was a book he had found in the occult section of a run-down bookstore on Crenshaw Boulevard, next to Perry's Pizza, across the street from El Camino College. He had grown tired of all the Hollywood bullshit, had grown jaded by most of the books he'd come across. But that book had been dif-

ferent. It had contained a large section on lycanthropy, which, he'd learned, came from the Greek
words *lykoi* and *anthropos*: "Wolfman." Lycanthropy
had been described as a psychiatric state in which
the patient believes he or she is a wolf, or some other
non-human animal. Undoubtedly stimulated by the
once widespread superstition that lycanthropy was
a supernatural condition in which men actually assumed the physical form of animals, the delusion
was most likely to occur among people who believed
in reincarnation and the transmigration of souls. It
was a rare condition. Examples were often linked to
schizophrenia, and the rare state of the condition
made clinical studies difficult.

Upon reading the part about schizophrenia Mark
had panicked, though he'd quickly gained control of
himself. He wasn't schizophrenic; he had seen himself change *physically*. He had looked down upon
himself covered with thick, black fur, had seen his
feet and hands change into twisted claws with razor-
sharp nails. He had felt his senses grow more acute
and sharpened. It wasn't the result of some hallucination wrought by a psychiatric disorder. Mark had
seen something more malignant and supernatural.

And then he'd found it. Buried halfway down a
paragraph on page 345, he'd found a reference to a
term called "theriomorph": a shapeshifter. A theriomorph was a being who could assume an animal
as well as a human form. A spiritual theriomorph
was someone who saw aspects of animals in his or
her personality and actions, and those aspects
shaped who he or she was.

Mark had been stunned by this revelation. For as

far back as he could remember, wolves had always interested him. In childhood he had had a fascination with wolves, so much so that he'd had books that contained hundreds of pictures of them. Whenever there was a *National Geographic* special on wolves he always watched it. Wolves fascinated him the way eagles or snakes fascinated other people. He had never expressed the desire to own a wolf, or a wolf-hybrid, but the fascination was there. After reading about theriomorphs, he supposed that the spiritual side of himself, the part that felt the wolf fascination, had tapped into that part of himself. It had been building and building in him over a long period—years, perhaps. And then it had exploded when Buddy Vance had begun his last assault on him. It had tapped into his wolf-side and allowed it to take control, changing him physically.

Somehow he'd managed to gain some control of the curse—which is what he had come to call it. As the months passed he'd become more attuned to it. He would find himself growing restless a few nights before the full moon, and he knew now that this was the curse, struggling to burst to the surface. His entire being was integrated, both human and wolf working together, until the wolf side took over, blending in to assume control. At first it had been hard to harness it, but after a few months he'd managed to gain a bit of mastery over it. He had kept it under wraps for the next year.

Six months after he graduated from high school it had come again, full-blown. He had been with his parents in a rented cabin in Big Bear, hoping to salvage something of their strained relationship. The volatile relationship had triggered the change immediately; Mark hadn't been able to control it. After it had sprung up that cold winter night it had taken him the better part of two years to get it back under control.

And now this, the first time in six years that it had burst out of him uncontrollably.

Of course he couldn't keep it bottled up. To do so would be to invite trouble. He'd eventually learned to trigger the shifting by pure will. He had it under control to a degree, but he still had to let the beast out. To not let it out would be to allow it to get the upper hand, to let it get wild. The urge followed the lunar cycles. When the moon was full, he allowed the change to take place and he roamed the night to hunt.

Because he had some sort of control over the curse, he was able to control himself when he was in the change. Most of the time he headed into the Saddleback mountain region of Orange County, where he would roam the woods. There, he would satiate himself on some animal—a dog, a deer, anything but a human. Sometimes he wasn't so lucky, though, and a human had to suffice. When that happened he at least tried to avoid witnesses. If at all possible, he tried to drive far away from the city to avoid detection. As far as he could tell, it had worked. The few times he had read of the attacks in newspapers they were always attributed to a wild animal, usually a coyote or a mountain lion. After all, the victims had been in a natural park where wild animals lived. After such incidents, the Department of Fish and Game had gone into the woods to try to flush out the beast, and sometimes they'd managed to bag a big cat or two. But they never did get the real culprit.

Mark worked mindlessly, his mind spinning through the years. There had been some close calls, especially earlier when the curse was still very much out of control and he had had to live for a time in Northern California, in the cabin of a survivalist he had killed. It was there that he had first learned to harness the curse, where he had learned to cultivate it for his own use. And it was there where he had made peace with himself and come home, back to the city.

Only now the city was Orange County; Fountain Valley, California to be exact. He hadn't lived in Gardena since that fateful night six months or so after graduating high school when—

But no. Now was not the time to dwell on that. There were more pressing matters at hand.

He only wished he knew where it had come from. Despite his own theory of the spiritual theriomorphs, he had no plausible explanation for his condition. He had gone over everything a million times: he had never been bitten by a werewolf, never touched wolfsbane, never—

Enough. Let's get through this. I'll feel sorry for myself later.

Mark Wiseman spent the rest of the evening working, his CD player churning out tunes by INXS, Guns N' Roses, Mötley Crüe, and Tesla. He dwelt on his predicament, wondering for the rest of the evening what Bernard Roberts might have seen.

Chapter Five

Luckily, Carol Emrich was a rarity, even if she did fit the physical description of an airheaded blonde bimbo. Despite her physical attributes—her bleached-blonde hair, her perfect figure, and her mile-long legs—Carol actually possessed a sharp mind. Bernard was glad he could hand Carol some work that needed to be done so he could run some errands.

His main errand the following day after his run-in with Mark Wiseman was the Huntington Beach Public Library.

Bernard pulled his coal black Mercedes into a parking spot at the library and killed the engine. The library was the farthest one from the office, but it was the better of the half dozen or so in the area. When Bernard had been married to Olivia Farrell four years ago they had lived in Huntington Beach, and this library had been within walking distance. In addition to being on a lovely piece of land, the library itself was large: four stories of books, magazines, and microfilm of newspapers and periodicals from all over the world.

Bernard wasn't sure how to approach this particular research project, so he explained it as best as he could to the librarian when he approached the counter. "I'm doing research for a paper I'm writing for a journalism class I'm taking," he explained, putting on all the charm. "It's a rather strange one. I'd like to know how I can find out if there have been deaths in the Southern California area involving wild animals—bears, mountain lions, dogs, that sort of thing."

"Our research department can help you with that," the librarian said. She was young, blonde, her body slightly chunky, her face pretty. She was chewing gum and wearing wire-rimmed glasses. She motioned upstairs. "They're located on the second floor. It usually takes them a day or two, depending on the scope of the project, and they'll explain the fees and everything to you."

"Thank you."

It was easier than Bernard thought it would be. Fifteen minutes later he was heading back to the office, a smug smile on his face, hoping that the information he'd paid the research people to come up with would be useful.

He didn't hear anything back until the following Monday morning. Carol Emrich delivered the first of the reports he would need for the morning board meeting. She looked beat. "I worked on these all weekend. Hope it turns out."

"I'm sure it will," Bernard said, tucking the reports in his briefcase. "Thank you."

There was a message on his voice mail when he returned from the meeting. The research project was finished. He drove to the library with nervous anticipation. The meeting hadn't gone over well. The board was moving quicker than anticipated with the merger. His job, his position, was hanging by a thread.

And if it was eliminated . . . if he was found out . . .

He waited until he got back to the car to open up the plain manila envelope. He flipped through the papers, heart beating wildly, and then a grin appeared on his face.

Twenty-four people over a period of five years, from San Diego to Oak Run, California. Killed by wild animals that were later attributed to one of the state's natural predators—the black bear, the mountain lion. One death was even attributed to coyotes. In every case the victims had been partially devoured.

In one instance the victim had been clutching a piece of clothing, not his own. Despite the strange circumstances—which led them to believe it was a homicide—forensic evidence clearly pointed to the killer being a large animal, probably a mountain lion or a wolf.

Many of the cases were too scattered to be connected: two in the Saddleback mountain region, one in the Angeles National Crest Forest, one in the Big Bear region, two in the Sierras, and three in Ventura County. Five cases, however, were within city limits; two in Gardena, California in 1981, and two in an unincorporated area of Los Angeles County bordering Gardena and Torrance in 1982. Two other cases were reported in Santa Ana in 1985, and Westminster in 1986, but both of those were in relatively remote areas of the city, in sections still being developed. In the urban areas it was assumed that the culprits were dogs, probably pit bull terriers due to their unsavory reputation with the public. As a result, Animal Control officers went out each time and wound up catching stray dogs in the areas of the killings almost immediately. In only one case was the dog in question a pit bull. In all cases, the animal caught was presumed guilty and exterminated.

The two most interesting cases were those that involved Jim and Mary Ann Wiseman, of Gardena, California. They had been found mauled in a Big Bear cabin on December 17, 1982.

Bernard smiled as he shuffled through the papers. His next step was a simple one. He had a good relationship with the director of Security at Free State Insurance Corporation and he had set up an appointment to see him this afternoon for some legitimate business. On the sly he was going to ask Clark if he could view a tape for review of the security budget—maybe he could spot ways in which the budget could be trimmed. Clark would be more than happy to provide him with a tape. Bernard would "randomly select" the evening of June 7, picking the footage of the tape library. He would quickly duplicate the tape in his office and have it back to Clark by the end of the day. This evening he would view the tape at his leisure and map out his plan.

Bernard started the car and drove out of the library parking lot. His nerves were tingling with anticipation. If what he thought he had seen was the real thing, he just might be able to get his way out of the mess he would surely face if the corporate take-over came.

Chapter Six

The message was on Mark's voice mail a week later when he arrived at work at his customary time of four-thirty p.m. It was from Bernard Roberts, CEO of Free State Insurance Corporation. He wanted to see him today before he started work. In his office.

He knows something, Mark thought as he took off his black leather jacket and draped it across his favorite chair. His rational side said *how can he know something? Maybe somebody nominated you for some performance award or something, and Bernard is doing the honors of congratulating you personally. That could be the reason why he had that funny look on his face last week.* The notion wasn't unbelievable; Free State currently had an employee recognition program, which recently included having the CEO of the company present the award and a gift certificate to the recipient at a surprise meeting in his office. It could explain why Mark hadn't seen Bob Davis, his supervisor, in his cubicle office when he'd arrived this afternoon. Bob was probably already upstairs.

Feeling a little better, but still apprehensive, Mark exited the tape library, went through the Computer Room, and made his way toward the executive suite, trying to calm himself down.

Mark had never been to the executive suite before and he opened the heavy glass door with trepidation. An attractive blonde woman with a nicely pressed, tailored suit was seated behind a large oak executive desk. She was typing in the computer and she looked up as Mark entered the lobby of the suite. "Can I help you?"

Mark glanced at the nameplate on her desk: Carol Emrich. "Yeah, I just got a message from Mr. Roberts. He said he wants to see me."

Carol ran her finger down an appointment book that was open on her desk and glanced at the identification badge pinned to his shirt pocket. "Yes, you're his four-thirty appointment. Go right in." She motioned toward a set of large, double oak doors behind her and flashed him a smile. Mark smiled back. Carol's friendliness put him at ease, but the palm of his hand slipped on the doorknob as he grasped it and opened the door.

Bernard Roberts was seated behind a large mahogany desk, working at a desktop computer. He glanced up briefly as Mark opened the door and smiled. "Mr. Wiseman, come right in and make yourself comfortable."

Mark stepped inside the plush office, noting the rich, wine-colored carpet, the dark oak bookcases that decorated the wall behind Mr. Roberts, the various plaques and framed photographs resting on them. To his far right was a large, plush sofa and a coffee table. There was also what appeared to be a wet bar in the far right corner. Also to his right, opposite the wet bar, was the doorway that led to the restroom (which most likely had a shower as well). It was an impressive office; the view from Mr. Bernard's windows gave him a stunning view of south Orange County. On a clear day he could probably see the Pacific Ocean.

"You wanted to see me?" Mark asked, hating himself the minute the question blurted out. He was nervous and it showed in his shaky voice.

"I did." Bernard motioned for him to have a seat in one of the two, large leather upholstered chairs in front of his desk. "Please."

Mark sat down in one of the chairs and crossed his arms in front of his chest.

Bernard rose from his chair and approached the door to his office, then closed it. For the first time Mark noticed how tall the executive was; he was over six feet tall. Bernard returned to his chair and picked up a remote control device from his desk. He smiled at Mark as he opened a drawer and turned on a large screen television that flanked the left wall. "I asked you up here because I thought you would be interested in seeing something." He pushed another button, activating a VCR and the tape already inserted inside it. The picture came through suddenly and for a moment Mark was puzzled at the black-and-white graininess of it. Then recognition set in.

It was a shot of the tape library from the upper corner security cam. The angle picked out his main work area, with the date and time in the lower left-hand corner. Mark stared at the scene, transfixed.

He watched himself on the screen as he doubled over. He watched as his celluloid version wrenched back from the workstation and struggled to keep the scream from unleashing from his jaws. His hands were quivering and he could see that they had elongated with thick, bristly hairs sprouting from them, the nails long and hooked. Even though the footage was grainy, he could see his facial muscles straining and expanding as the change fought to take control.

Mark watched dumbfounded as Bernard sat smugly in his executive chair. "Pretty impressive piece of footage, don't you think? I especially like the part when you howl in pain." He turned back to the camera, as if waiting to point out the moment. It came: Mark's video-self opened his jaws and appeared to scream; the lower portion of his face was pushing out, forming into a wolflike snout with long, razor-sharp teeth. "There!" Bernard exclaimed. "And then the part that comes up next, where it looks like you're actually beginning to lose it—"

Mark thought he would be too stunned to speak, but he did. "What is this?"

Bernard turned to him. "Why, it's you Mark. You in the flesh, caught by our surveillance cameras last week. Now I've combed through the policy and procedure manuals but I couldn't find any rule specifically making it against company policy to change into a werewolf on company hours." He shrugged.

"And for now, I don't plan to make it a policy either. In fact, I think I have a better solution."

Mark was stunned. His heart was hammering hard in his chest; he felt light-headed, as if he was going to faint. When he spoke, his voice sounded distant. "And what's that?"

Bernard Roberts turned the tape off, set the remote control down on the desk and leaned forward. He folded his hands in front of him, looking very corporate-like and official in his plush office. "An understanding. That's all."

Mark didn't know how to react. He felt suddenly warm. "An understanding?"

"Correct." Bernard smiled. "Understand this: After today, you will not speak of this conversation to anybody. If you do, I take this," He held a manila file folder and handed it over to Mark, who opened it and began leafing through it. "And that," he motioned to the videotape. "And I go to the authorities. They may scoff at what's on the tape, but I'm sure they will be very interested in the trail of bodies you've left behind the last ten years. Especially those of your parents."

Mark's stomach turned queasily in his stomach at the mention of his parents. His hands were shaking as he leafed through the papers. He had been cleared of any wrongdoing in his parents' death. There was no evidence that he had even been at the cabin that weekend and all evidence pointed to a wolf that had been the culprit. In fact, a gray wolf had been killed a few days after his parents' bodies were discovered. There would be no way charges could be filed against him for his parents' death.

"If you're thinking that you couldn't be charged in the death of your parents," Bernard began, "you are mistaken. Take a look at these." He slid a manila file folder across the desk. Mark opened it. Some were newspaper clippings, others were police reports covering his human victims over the last ten years of the curse. Bernard had them all, from Buddy Vance in January of 1981, to the last one, a homeless man in Santiago Canyon nine months ago, a man Mark had surprised as he had tried to huddle in from the cold. Mark remembered how the man's eyes had grown wide as he loomed in front of him and ripped his throat open. Mark dropped the papers on the desk, his hands shaking so badly it was hard to control them. His mind was running with a thousand thoughts. His throat was dry. "I don't understand . . ."

"We have an understanding, is that correct?" Bernard looked at him seriously.

". . . what's going on, why are you . . . why are you doing this?"

Bernard reached across the desk and grabbed Mark's arm, snapping him to attention. Mark gazed into Bernard's sharp eyes. "Your secret is safe with me," he murmured. "I won't tell anybody as long as you stay with me. Do you understand?"

Mark nodded, stammering and confused. His heart was beating so hard that it felt like it was going to burst out of his chest. "Y-yes, but—"

"No buts. I'll explain." Bernard released Mark and leaned back in his chair, appraising Mark for a minute. "I know everything about you," he said finally, speaking low and smooth. "I did a lot of checking up on you, Mark, and you weren't very truthful to us on your employment application. You never indicated you were a werewolf."

Mark felt terrified, but he was also beginning to feel a sense of anger rise in him. This was the first time he had ever been found out, the first time he had ever been challenged, and it scared the hell out of him. He sat quietly across the big desk from Bernard and regarded him as the older man smiled and continued: "But your secret is safe with me, Mark. I will not go to the authorities. I wouldn't dream of it. I don't want to hurt you. I want to help you."

"Why?" It was the only thing Mark could think of to ask.

"Very simple. I need your help. You have what I need that will help me immensely."

"And what's that?"

Bernard smiled. "This is where it gets fun." He opened his desk drawer and pulled out another manila file folder. He handed it to Mark, who opened it. Mark blinked; it was a single sheet of paper with a list of names and addresses. "The list you are holding consists of the Board of Directors of Free State. The names with the asterisks beside them are the ones that I would like you to dispose of for me."

"What?" Mark almost dropped the piece of paper.

Bernard continued as if he hadn't heard Mark's outburst. "Of course, I don't think you should get rid of all of them immediately. That would rouse too much suspicion. Because the list is rather small— only five people, really—we can spread it out. But two of them need to be killed rather soon, I'd say within the next few months. Then—"

"You're asking me to kill innocent people?" Mark was flabbergasted. He didn't understand why this was happening. His mind was still reeling from the suddenness of it all.

"Not at all," Bernard said, leaning forward. "These people aren't innocent at all, Mark. They're traitors to the company. They want to sell our firm to a larger multiconglomerate. They want to cut it up and butcher it, eviscerate our history. Do you realize what that will mean? Half the staff will suffer job losses, and our clients will suffer a decline in service. And when that happens, the industry will take a turn for the worse. Free State has always set the standards for insurance in California. If Free State gets taken over by a large conglomerate, quality of service will go down, which in turn will set the stage across the state. Before you know it, every insurance company in the state will follow a similar path until pretty soon it will be normal for all insurance companies to be run at the same shoddy standards. It will be disastrous."

Mark was listening to Bernard's half-assed explanation, but he didn't believe him. He found it hard to believe that Bernard was asking him to do this out of altruism for the common worker and the consumer. There had to be some hidden agenda. "Jobs will be lost?" he asked.

Bernard nodded. "Your job, my job, lots of jobs, Mark."

Mark was just about to ask *what do you care if your job gets lost? You can always go to some headhunter agency and get another high-level corporate job that will bring in $200K a year. What do you care?* But he didn't.

Bernard jumped back in. "In return, I will keep your secret. I will provide you with any, and all, the security you need. I will pay you handsomely. You will benefit greatly from this, Mark."

"What if I decide not to?" Mark asked, looking up at Bernard and dreading the answer.

Bernard frowned. He reached back into the desk drawer again and pulled out a pistol. He held it up in front of Mark, his features impassive. "I don't know if all the Hollywood bullshit on you guys is real, but just to be on the safe side, I had my jeweler melt down some silver of mine. He made 9mm bullets for me. I figure that even if the bullshit is wrong, being shot should do the trick anyway. Don't you think?"

Mark tried not to let Bernard know that he was terrified beyond imagination. It took all his control to keep his hands from shaking.

"So . . . do we have an understanding?" Bernard leveled a serious gaze at Mark, holding the gun casually.

Mark felt warm. He nodded. "Yeah."

"Let's have another understanding, just between us, okay?"

"Sure." Mark licked his lips. He was very thirsty.

"If you tell one person about what happened between us today . . . if you tell anybody about this conversation, I will kill you." Bernard looked vastly different from the corporate suit he was used to seeing. Now he simply looked evil and cunning. "Let me tell you what will happen if you say anything. First, the authorities will come and question me, which is the natural thing to do. I will deny it. I will have your personnel file pulled and once the authorities see it, they will notice that your file is full of reprimands, that you are on the verge of being terminated due to your inability to get along with your co-workers and to perform the functions of your job. It will be noted that you have threatened your co-workers recently, that it was suggested by your supervisor that you receive counseling." He leaned forward. "Do you understand me?"

Mark nodded. His mouth was so dry now he could barely stand it.

"Once they see that, they will dismiss your call to them," Bernard continued. "They will not make any further attempt to contact you. I will assure them that I will have our guidance counselors talk to you, try to get you some professional help. That will be a ploy just to get them out of the picture. Then, I visit you at your apartment on Bushard with this." He held up the pistol. "I have a silencer for it. I will kill you and then I will carefully wrap your body in a trash bag and place it in the trunk of my car. I will drive your body to my house, after which I will make a few phone calls." A faint smile played along his lips. "Don't think that I don't know people who will know how to dispose of a human body so that it leaves no trace. Men like me, with my kind of money, can buy almost anything."

Mark's heart was beating hard in his chest. He felt his fists clench. His body trembled with anger.

Bernard smiled pensively. "So . . . do we understand each other?"

Mark nodded. "Yes."

"Then you agree?"

Mark answered without thinking. "Yes."

"Good." Bernard hefted the gun. "I'm glad I made my point." He replaced the pistol in his desk drawer, closed it, and leaned forward over the desk. "Of course, the consequences apply if you reveal to anybody what we discussed."

"Of course." Mark was simply answering to be saying something; inside he was trembling with rage and fear.

"Take the list. I made you a copy. If possible, commit the names and addresses to memory and then burn the list. I will call you tomorrow with more information, but before I do I just have one question for you."

Mark waited for Bernard to pop the question. Bernard folded his hands in front of him. "When you . . . change . . . is it like the movies where you change on the night of the full moon?"

Mark nodded, his stomach an icy pit of fear and dread. He felt the way a small child would feel if they had been caught doing something they weren't supposed to by a teacher or a parent. "Yes."

"But you are able to control it," Bernard said. His index finger tapped the manila folder of newspaper articles. "Otherwise the stories contained in these articles I copied would be much more sensational."

"Yes, I can control it."

Bernard seemed to think about this. He sat across from Mark, appraising him, his hand stroking his chin. "When you are under the power of your . . . curse, you are able to control your urges in the sense that you can pick and choose your victims, correct?"

Mark nodded. For the first time he felt shame over what he was. "Yes."

Bernard smiled. "Just like I thought." His finger continued tapping the mahogany desk. "I may be just another corporate drone to you, Mark, but I do have a rather active imagination. I suppose you can chalk that up to all the books I read as a kid. I read everything—science fiction, fantasy, adventure, horror—whatever I could get my hands on. I know many variations of the werewolf myth and had only thought of it as simply that—a myth. Therefore I recognized you for what you are the minute I saw this tape. Naturally, I couldn't believe what I was seeing, so I went upstairs. And sure enough, we bumped into each other in the hall. What happened? Lose control of yourself that time?"

"No." He looked away from Bernard, unable to meet the other man's eyes.

"Are you sure? Looked like it to me. In fact, from subsequent viewings of the tape it appears that the curse, or whatever you call it, took hold of you very suddenly and without warning that night."

Mark didn't say anything. He felt a warm flush creep through his skin.

"Thanks to my inquisitive nature, I not only viewed the tape numerous times, I also did some research." Bernard regarded him from across the desk. "I went to the library and asked the research department if they could find newspaper articles about people who had been killed by wild animals in the state of California. Not surprisingly, I found several hundred. However, I was able to focus on a dozen that particularly intrigued me. These all involved victims who had been partially devoured by what Animal Control experts believed to be wild dogs or coyotes of some sort. Once I learned this, I hired a private detective to do some further investigating. He did some background checking on you; he found out about your troubled childhood, the brutal murders that occurred in Gardena and Torrance where you lived . . . the murder of your parents."

At the mention of his parents Mark started. Bernard noted the reaction and smiled. "Your parents, Mark? Please, tell me you didn't."

"I didn't," Mark said, shaking.

"Are you sure? They were both found pretty horribly mangled. More so than the other victims—"

"I'm *sure*!" A hint of anger sprang to Mark's voice and he instantly regretted it.

"You know, the authorities may not believe the werewolf angle, but they *will* believe hard evidence. If my investigator turns the information he has found over to the police, they will find that you were in the areas where the murders occurred. They will also find physical evidence in your apartment to tie you to at least one of the murders. That's all they'll need to cast you as a suspect in all of them— especially the murders of your parents."

Mark said nothing, trying to cope with the suddenness of it all. He didn't know what to say.

Bernard regarded him for a moment, a wistful smile on his face. "Further research indicated the other murders. Of course, my private investigator was unable to place you in some areas where partially devoured humans were discovered, but those found in the Orange County limits in the last few years . . . well, you've been living in Fountain Valley for how long now, Mark?"

"Four years."

Bernard chuckled. "Four years. And tell me, Mark, in those four years have you ever come to terms with what you are?"

Mark didn't know how to answer that. He sat in his chair, staring at the desk in front of him.

"I did a lot of research," Bernard continued. "So much that I became convinced that most of the so-called experts who wrote books on lycanthropy were blowing smoke out of their asses. I decided to play the cards that I had been dealt by calling this meeting, and here you are. It's obvious from my investigation and from the evidence I have on this tape that you are a werewolf, or something very much like one. It's also obvious from what my private investigator has found, that you are able to control your . . . curse, to some degree. You yourself admitted this to me just a few minutes ago. Is that correct?"

Mark nodded. "Yes," he whispered.

"So what is it Mark? Did you lose control the night the security cams caught you?"

"No." Mark's voice came out sounding weak and raspy.

Bernard leaned closer, scrutinizing him. "Are you sure?"

"Yes." Mark nodded, nervously.

Bernard regarded him silently for a moment. "If I find out you are lying and you *have* lost control of your curse, the same consequences apply. Is that clear?"

Mark nodded slowly. His stomach was doing back flips.

"Good." Bernard nodded. He appraised Mark silently for a moment. "You can go. I'll call you tomorrow night at your extension."

Mark felt himself rise, felt his body move across the deep plush carpet to the lobby of the executive suite, saw himself walk past the now empty desk where the secretary had been sitting, and out the double glass doors to the elevators. His body felt light, as if he were floating on clouds. He made his way back to the tape library where he pulled up a chair and sat down. He stared at the black screen of a computer terminal, his gaze directed somewhere beyond the room. His mind was a confused, jumbled mass. He was literally reeling from the suddenness of Bernard Roberts's revelation and blackmail attempt, hearing about his parents' mangled bodies found in the rented Big Bear cabin—

What am I gonna do? he thought. *What the fuck am I gonna do? He's got me. Jesus Christ, he's got me, what am I—*

Suddenly it hit him. He had some money saved, although he didn't make very much of it. It would be in his best interest to invest whatever it would cost a private detective to ferret out Bernard Roberts's address and then he could pay the CEO a visit himself on the waxing of the next full moon.

But what about the gun? What if all that crap about the silver bullets shit is right?

In Mark's experience, much of the mythology he had heard about werewolves was false. He didn't have a pentagram branded into the palm of his hand, crosses had no effect on him (which he found out a few years ago when a transient he had killed and devoured had been wearing one; he had even come into contact with it and nothing had happened), and there had even been a few occasions when he had been able to will the change on nights when the moon wasn't quite full. That surely went against the mythology popularized in countless werewolf movies and horror novels. So why would silver bullets have an effect?

Because even if they don't, being shot will affect you the way it affects every living thing. You'll die.

Bernard Roberts had most likely planned this out very methodically. He had very likely prepared some sort of backup plan in the event Mark tried to turn on him. Being armed was just one of them, but what if there were others? Surely being fired from his job wasn't that much of a deterrent, but Mark understood the subtle message that thinly veiled threat seemed to imply. *Fuck with me and I can frame you for anything. Even things that go on outside the company.*

Maybe even one of the murders in the newspaper clippings.

That decided it for him. The authorities might not believe Bernard's story of Mark being a lycanthrope, but they would believe hard evidence that Mark might be involved in murder, especially if evidence was planted. And especially if his parents' double murder was reopened. There was only one thing he could do: he would go along with Bernard Roberts's plan, whatever it was. He would wait for Bernard's call tomorrow and do what he was told. He would take this one step at a time, and he would watch his step and his back. And as soon as he found a way out, he would take it. He would work at finding whatever weak spot Bernard had, and as soon as he had it the man would be finished. Simple as that.

Mark sighed and buried his face in his hands. His stomach growled. He was nervous and tired and he still had the whole night ahead of him to brood over what had happened. It was going to be a long night.

Chapter Seven

The week following his meeting with Bernard Roberts was the longest of Mark Wiseman's life.

He got no work done the night Bernard confronted him with his revelation and subsequent blackmail attempt, and he had tossed and turned in bed for the rest of the night. He skipped his classes for a number of days after resolving to go along with Bernard's schemes. He thought of a dozen ways to thwart Bernard's plans: going to the authorities, or simply packing up and leaving town. But each time he thought of a solution, he would find a way for it not to work. At first going to the police seemed like the logical option. But as his mind ran down the possible scenarios he realized it wouldn't work. First, Bernard would most likely do what he said he was going to, and because of his prestige he would not spend a night in jail. Instead, he would come after Mark. Then there was the possibility that if Mark went to the police with the story, they wouldn't believe him. After all, Bernard Roberts was a pillar of the community. He donated regularly to charities; he sponsored job drives in the inner city. In short, he was a respected member of the community. Nobody would believe the claim that Bernard Roberts was plotting murder.

If the police *did* take Mark seriously, they would still have to investigate and that would take weeks, possibly months. They would have to tail Bernard undercover, and Mark knew that Bernard would prove to be crafty. Meanwhile, he would still be obligated to carry out his end of the bargain, which led to another scenario, one in which he informed the authorities and they secretly tape recorded Bernard's murderous plans during a phone conversation. He thought about this the following day and was almost convinced that it would work when he received his first phone call from Bernard. He instructed Mark to a public phone booth in Tustin. Once there, Bernard gave him details on the first hit he was to make. He also told Mark that he would be communicating to him through this method, which squashed all further thoughts of entrapping him.

Mark spent the next several days lying low, thinking about the hit and what Bernard had told him. He had the address, culled from the list Bernard had given him; he had read it so many times, had looked at his victim's photograph so much that he had both committed to memory. But he didn't throw away the paper containing the names, pictures and photographs. He wanted to dwell on them one at a time.

He went to work, did his job and tried not to think

too much of Bernard Roberts and the threat of blackmail. By the end of the week he began going to the library and reading the business section of the local newspaper, as well as the *Wall Street Journal.* No matter how much he delved into his research, he still couldn't figure out the real reason Bernard had set him up to kill off the board members.

Much of what he learned in the papers, Bernard had told him freely. Free State Insurance Corporation was in the midst of being merged with another, larger, national corporation. The deal was a mere three weeks from FTC approval, after which the deal would go through immediately. All it required was a majority vote from the Board of Directors, all of whom had already said on record that they were voting for the merger. As Mark read through the stories chronicling the new business deal, he realized what this meant for Bernard Roberts. When the two corporations merged, there would no longer be a need for a CEO of Free State; instead, the board of both corporations would hire a new executive staff to oversee the operations of the huge conglomerate. Which meant that Bernard Roberts would be out of a job.

So he was telling me the truth on that part, Mark thought as he leafed through an edition of the *Wall Street Journal.* He was at the Westminster Public Library and it was nearing two p.m. *Big fucking deal? Why worry about being let go with his position? With his experience and track record he could easily go to another corporation. He's a corporate headhunter's wet dream.*

Maybe it wasn't as easy as he thought it would be for a man of his professional stature to gain another similar position. After all, it wasn't like CEO positions were a dime a dozen like, say, secretaries or file clerks. They were most likely the scarcest, hardest jobs to get, and maybe this was the reason why he was so freaked out over this takeover.

He's got to make a lot of money, though, Mark thought. *So he gets laid off and it takes him a year or so to find another corporate job. Wouldn't you think with all the money he makes he'd be able to float for awhile until he found another job?*

Not necessarily. He could be living way above his means. There was that saying he had heard somewhere which opined, "the more money you make, the more you spend." With Bernard's salary, he was probably able to enjoy the good life: nice cars, a fancy home, vacations in five-star hotels, all of which cost major bucks. The elimination of his job and the high salary that went with it would surely change his lifestyle. Maybe he was addicted to the lifestyle and didn't want to give it up.

Whatever it was, he was gunning to remain in his position. And sitting here thinking about what motivated Bernard wasn't going to do much in solving Mark's own problem. He didn't want to kill anybody, but he didn't want to be on Bernard's hit list, either. And as the week wore on he realized that Bernard was playing this game smarter than he thought he was.

In the past couple of days Mark noticed that he was being followed. It was a feeling he had, a heightening of the senses. A normal person probably wouldn't have noticed, but because of Mark's extrasensory abilities he was able to pick out his pursuer. The afternoon he spent researching Free State's corporate takeover at the Westminster Public Library, he had finally gotten a good look at the guy tailing him. He was in his early forties, dressed casually in jeans and a green polo shirt, with slightly balding blond hair. He was sitting at a table directly above the lounge area of the library, perusing a book. When Mark got in his car and backed it out of the parking space he noticed the man get into a blue sedan. As he pulled out onto Talbert, heading east toward Fountain Valley, he saw the sedan three cars behind him, not going too fast and not going too slow.

If Mark tried something the guy would call Bernard. And depending on what this guy really was and represented—a private detective? A professional hit man?—one of two things would happen. Either the guy would be ordered to kill Mark immediately, or Bernard would come over and do the job himself. Mark got the impression that even if he were to head onto the southbound 405 Freeway and make a run for Mexico, the guy would be on his tail; he would be pursued relentlessly until he was caught.

What the hell am I gonna do? Mark thought as he headed toward his apartment. *What the hell am I gonna do?*

It was the morning of the full moon.

Mark had the evening off and was expecting a phone call at a public phone booth in Huntington Beach shortly before nightfall.

He picked the phone up on the first ring. "Hello."

"There's not much time," Bernard said, his voice calm and controlled. "Are you ready?"

"Yes."

"Good. Martin John owns a home in Silverado Canyon. You have the address. He's one of the main driving forces behind getting the board to vote on making this merger go through. With him gone, we're at first base. Now listen carefully: He has a habit of sitting out on his back deck at night watching the stars. He's an amateur astronomer. Has a big telescope on the back deck. You get me?"

"Yes." Mark shivered. The sun was beginning to set and a cold breeze blew in from the ocean. Spring might be bleeding into summer, but twilight along the beach was always so goddamn cold. He wanted to get in the car and get to his destination before the change started taking effect.

"Last week there was a mountain lion sighted in the area," Bernard continued. "They never caught it. A private security company patrols the neighborhood he lives in, so you'll have to park your car in the parking lot of a large strip mall in Aliso Viejo. From there, if you head into the hills behind the Lucky Supermarket, you'll reach his home. You can't miss it. It's white with black trim, and his back deck has floodlights that he sometimes puts on a dimmer. And there's the telescope. You'll have to enter the grounds through the back hills. Do you understand?"

"Yes."

"When you are finished I don't care what you do, so long as you aren't discovered and you retain no traces of him. I will call you tomorrow night. Here's

the time, location and the number I'll call you at."
Bernard rattled them off and Mark jotted them
down on a piece of scrap paper. "Don't screw up,"
Bernard said and hung up.

Mark slowly replaced the receiver. A gust of wind
blew suddenly, lifting his hair. His mouth felt dry
and tingly and his face itched, the first signs of the
coming of the change. He had about an hour before
it started getting obvious. He got into his car, turned
around, and headed toward Aliso Viejo.

He reached his destination safely and made it behind the Lucky Supermarket without being seen. He
ducked into some bushes just as his skin started to
itch and grow warm. He quickly slid out of his
clothes and once he was naked he edged out of the
bush and looked up at the sky.

The moon was a white, glowing ball. One look
and Mark felt the change come so suddenly that
even if he had tried to rein it in he would have
failed. He bit back a scream and managed a throat-
wrenching wail as the muscles along his back rippled, contorting his spine. His face was hot and
burning as his nose and jaw began pulsing outward
into a lupine snout. His body suddenly erupted into
a fireball of pain as his body was transformed, thick
black hair sprouting over his body, his face, his arms
and legs. His fingers and toes were white-hot lances
of agony as the skin split to allow for razor-sharp
claws to erupt; likewise his gums split open, blood
staining his mouth as his teeth became razor-sharp
fangs in a drooling maw of sharp, canine teeth.

As the transformation reached its climax, Mark

tipped his head to the newly risen moon and howled.

His senses were heightened a thousandfold. He could smell rabbit droppings and the skin of a newly shed rattlesnake. Far back at the mini-mall he could hear people talking as they trudged slowly from their cars. He could taste the aroma of their sweat as they shopped and clamored and lifted squalling babies into car seats. Mark turned his face to the hills, his nostrils flaring at the vast scents that drifted through the air: tumbleweed, sycamore, gravel, rodent and lizard. There were no large carnivores in this part of South Orange County; if there had been a mountain lion in the area, it had long departed. He could barely smell it and the scent he did pick up was five days old at least. He was safe.

He knew that Martin John wasn't outside even as he began making his way through the shrubbery toward the hill that led to the house. He could sense that Martin was inside the house, but if Bernard was right he would be venturing outside any moment. Mark was feeling his memory slip as his bestial side continued to push his consciousness deep into the recesses of his mind. For the most part, he was barely aware of his experiences during the change; it was like being a passenger in a car, unable to do anything as the driver sped down the highway, taking twisting turns at deadly speed. At the height of the evening he would be virtually powerless most of the time, but he would still be able to exert some form of control—primarily over the hunt itself.

The thing he had no control of whatsoever was the

change itself and the hunger that came with it. The hunger for fresh meat.

He quickly scampered up the hill. He was now deep in Silverado Canyon, and the comfy veneers of civilization lay a quarter of a mile behind him. He was aware that sound would carry in this desolate part of South Orange County, so he had to make this quick.

He crept slowly up the embankment. When he reached the top he paused and sniffed the air. Martin John was still in the house. Slowly, he climbed to the top of the hill and crouched behind the wrought-iron fence that was the only barrier between the property and the canyon below. All was clear. With a quick, sleek leap, Mark scaled the fence and crouched silently in a corner of the deck. Now all he had to do was wait.

He didn't have to wait long. Five minutes later the sliding-glass door screeched open and Martin John stepped out onto the back deck.

He was exactly as depicted in the photograph: late forties, trim build, salt and pepper hair, dressed in a billowy white shirt open at the chest to reveal a gold necklace, wearing a pair of tan shorts that fell to his knees, his feet clad in white socks and tennis shoes. He paused for a moment at the sliding-glass door, his tan features tilted up to the sky to survey the constellations. Then he padded out toward the telescope.

Mark's nostrils had been flaring the whole time, picking up the man's scent. It was heavily masked with cologne, which grated at the back of his throat, but underneath it was the taste of old, but lean, meat. The scent overpowered him, tripping his bloodlust, and he sprang from the corner of the property where he had been lurking and lunged straight at Martin.

Martin John didn't know what hit him; Mark's lunge was precise, quiet, and quick. He slammed into Martin from his right side, his jaws moving quickly to clamp down on the older man's throat and sever his larynx. Hot blood spurted in his mouth and down his throat as he brought Martin down, and he twisted his head to snap his prey's neck.

Mark paused, Martin's throat in his jaws, his blood pooling on the concrete below him. Mark's ears twitched at the night sounds: crickets chirruping, the soft susurration of the wind whistling down the canyon, the hoot of an owl, the rustle of squirrels at the bottom of the canyon. There were no sounds coming from within the house. He was safe.

He dropped Martin's corpse where it lay and sniffed it. The aroma of fresh blood reawakened his senses. Before he could rein in his hunger he felt himself wallow in it, tearing into the body like the ravenous beast he was.

He became fully aware again seven hours later. He didn't know where he was. He was still in his lycanthropic state and he was crouched over a small stream washing his face with his large, hairy paws.

He felt his human side awaken and his body shook with the suddenness of it. His heartbeat quickened and he panted, calming himself. He knew from experience that whenever his wolf side took over that he was safe; even though his human part had lost control, the wolf side would be on guard at all times. When his human side became aware again, it was always a shock to the senses.

It was still dark out and the moon was now falling in the western sky. It was probably sometime between four and five in the morning. He dipped his head and drank greedily from the stream, washing away the taste of blood and human flesh from his mouth. When he had drunk his fill he stood up and surveyed the area he was in.

The terrain was desolate with rugged hills. Judging from the sparse shrubbery and trees, he was near the Santa Ana Mountain Range. He hadn't strayed far from the Silverado Canyon area, then. He looked for the moon, found it, and tried to mentally track where he had started out this evening. Martin John's home was on the northeast side of Aliso Viejo. Therefore if he headed west, he should be able to get a better handle on where he was and make plans to reach his car before daylight.

It took him close to an hour of trudging through the brush and brambles of the desolate area before he started getting into a thicker wooded area. He climbed a slight crest and when he reached the top he picked up a slight breeze. He sniffed the air; it was far off, but unmistakable. It was the scent of man. He wasn't far off the beaten track at all.

Twenty minutes later he reached a wooded ravine and then he knew where he was. He was a quarter of a mile from the canyon that opened up into Aliso Viejo. His ears were finely tuned to the slightest sound that might be carrying from the canyon. His eyesight and sense of smell helped him maneuver his way toward civilization. A moment later he reached the wooded area and the shrubbery where he had left his clothes. He crouched behind the brush and waited, his breathing calm and even. He could make out the empty parking lot of the mini-mall. His car was the only vehicle left amid a vast blacktop.

He felt himself slowly returning to normal and he closed his eyes and took several deep breaths. It was always like this when the change was particularly sudden and brutal; he became aware of himself when he was still in his bestial self, and over the next hour as his human awareness returned, he would slowly revert back to his natural, human state. He felt himself physically revert now. The pain involved in the physical transformation wasn't nearly as agonizing as it was when the change to the wolf side suddenly gripped him, but it was still there. He gritted his teeth and concentrated, willing the pain down as his snout and jaw receded, his muscles shrank, the thick hair along his face and body slowly retreated back into his skin. Toward the end of the change his skin erupted in a painful itching, and it was then that he knew he was nearing the completion.

Five minutes later he was standing naked in the brush, looking at the parking lot from a safe distance. He looked down at his nude form, lifted his now normal hands to his face. There were specks of blood on his palms and under his fingernails. He looked down at his chest where Martin John's blood still stained it. Stooping down quickly, he donned his clothes, his mind already racing on what he was going to do next.

Once he was dressed he casually made his way

down the embankment and headed toward the parking lot. While he had lost the heightened awareness of his senses, they were still more highly tuned than a normal human's; he could sense that the parking lot and the stores that comprised the mini-mall were devoid of human life.

He sighed in relief when he reached his car. He quickly looked around, unlocked the door and slid inside. He started the car and let the engine warm up a moment before putting it in gear and driving away.

He was northbound on Interstate 5 when the shakes hit him.

It started gradually and quickly accelerated as he drove north. He felt a sob break loose from deep inside and then he almost lost control; his limbs were shaking so badly he could barely control the steering wheel. He choked back another cry and tried to pull himself together, but it was hard. He was so overcome with emotion that the only thing he wanted to do was pull over and bawl like a baby.

Fighting to keep the tears inside, he drove home carefully, being cautious to observe all traffic laws; if a cop pulled him over now he was really finished. The fifteen-minute drive felt like it took him an hour. When he made it back to his apartment complex, the sun was beginning to rise in the east. He pulled into his parking space and slid out of the car quickly, slamming the door behind him. He raced up the steps to his apartment and let himself in, locked the door and then he finally let it out, sobbing hoarsely and uncontrollably. It was a long time before he was able to pull himself back together, but when he did he was glad that the first part of this terrible nightmare was over.

Chapter Eight

The ringing of the telephone woke him from what had been a sound sleep.

He groped for the phone, picked up the receiver. "Hello?"

"Turn on the TV," Bernard said. "You made the five o'clock news. Channel two." He hung up.

Mark lay with the receiver clutched in his hand, the hum of the dial tone ringing in his ear. He groaned, reached over to the nightstand to replace the receiver, then got out of bed and padded to the dark living room.

He picked up the remote control and turned the television on. He switched over to channel two and sank into his sofa just as the Evening News was beginning.

Bernard Roberts was right. He was on the news.

The lead story was what the newscaster was calling a "vicious animal attack in South Orange County." Mark watched with a sense of detachment. Aliso

Viejo resident Martin John had been found on the back deck of his home by his cleaning lady late this morning. Police had initially treated it as a homicide, but due to the vicious nature of the slaying, along with certain physical evidence, Animal Control officers had been called in. The slaying was now being unofficially attributed to a wild animal, possibly a mountain lion.

"Residents of this remote section of Aliso Viejo reported seeing a mountain lion last week," the newscaster recited in mote fashion. She was blonde and professionally dressed in a pair of blue slacks and a cream-colored blouse. "Animal Control officers tried tracking the cat, but have been unsuccessful so far. An autopsy will hopefully determine what kind of animal killed Mr. John."

When the segment ended, Mark glanced at the clock. He had a five-thirty rendezvous with Bernard Roberts at a public phone booth in Fountain Valley. He went to the bathroom and quickly cleaned up, then donned a pair of shorts, a T-shirt, socks and sneakers, and was out the door.

He got to the phone booth at the Chevron gas station on the corner of Brookhurst and Talbert one minute before rendezvous time. When the phone rang he picked it up.

"Mark here," he said.

"How did you like your coverage?" It sounded like Bernard was grinning.

"Not as much as you, obviously."

"I've taken the privilege of talking to one of the other board members," Bernard said. "One of the men on our list as a matter of fact. He has no idea how I feel about the takeover, since I haven't made my feelings public, but he's a good guy in a personal way. We go back a long time. He was one of the first to get the news of John's death, and I called him this morning for some details. We pulled this off without a hitch, old boy." Now Bernard did laugh, a merry laugh that sent a chill down Mark's spine. "George talked to somebody at the coroner's office thirty minutes ago. They did a bite-mark check and the official verdict is that John died from some mad dog, a coyote maybe, but they're not ruling out a domesticated animal. They'll probably blame it on some wayward pit bull or Rottweiler. George said he was told the bite marks were definitely canine." He chuckled. "Of course, I don't know how they're going to explain that John was partially devoured, but I'm sure they'll come up with something."

Mark didn't feel anything when Bernard said this; he had long grown used to not feeling ashamed of himself for feasting on the flesh of his victims. After all, what was the use of slaughtering people when you weren't going to eat them?

"How are the authorities going to explain it?" Mark asked. He wanted to hear how Bernard would explain this.

"They'll assume it was coyotes," Bernard stated. "No way will a domesticated dog eat a person. Coyotes are a different story, though."

"If you say so," Mark said. He had neither smelled nor sensed any coyotes last night, nor had he ever heard of one dining on a human. He doubted Animal Control officials would find any, but he also knew Bernard was probably right; in their haste to place blame, the authorities would probably attribute John's murder to a coyote.

"So what now?" Mark asked.

"Now we wait," Bernard said. "We lay low. You keep a low profile. You don't speak to anybody about this, nor do you bring it up in idle conversation. If I hear you do, you know what happens."

"I know," Mark said, feeling his gut churn at the notion of the threat.

"I'll call you here at this number again next week, same time. We're having an emergency meeting in three days to discuss strategy due to this latest development, and I should have an idea on where we're going with this."

"Fine." He hoped that before then Bernard Roberts was killed in a car accident.

"There are three more days left in this lunar cycle," Bernard said. "What are you going to do?"

"I have tonight off of work," Mark said. "By tomorrow night the worst of it should be over and I'll be able to control it."

Bernard appeared to be amused by Mark's condition. "What do you do when the first night of the lunar cycle falls in the middle of a work week?"

Mark sighed, but he couldn't help cracking a slight grin. Despite his predicament and the way Bernard had entrapped him, he rather liked talking about his condition to somebody. He had never told anybody about the curse before, and to do so felt therapeutic. "To tell you the truth, I don't totally lose it during the lunar cycle. I used to when this first happened to me. Before I could control it, I had to actually drive out to remote areas of the state and just let nature take its course so to speak." Bernard chuckled over that euphemism. Mark smiled, wishing he could reach across the phone lines and snap the executive's neck. "As the years have gone by I've learned how to harness and direct the curse, channel it if you will. So on nights that I do work during the lunar cycle, I'm usually able to hold it inside until I get off of work. Then I can drive home and lock myself in the apartment where I can let the change come out. I have to make sure to get out at least once during the lunar cycle, though, or I'll go bonkers."

"In other words, you have to roam," Bernard said. "You have to kill."

Mark nodded, as if he and Bernard were talking face-to-face. "I'm driven to it. I'll usually drive out to the desert or some other remote area, and just let myself loose. I'll let the curse run its course and by the time night falls I'm back in control again and I can will the change back to my human form. Last night I simply let it out and it came like a bat out of hell."

"What about the night I saw you on the security tape?" Bernard asked. Mark was silent as he thought about it. He really had no answer for that; he had been trying to reach some conclusion himself, and had been unable to. He had run with the hunt on the previous two lunar cycles, doing more to purge that killing instinct. He originally thought that maybe he had suppressed that urge during the last two or three lunar cycles, thus creating a pent-up well of emotions deep in his psyche, manifesting in a sudden, unannounced change. But that wasn't the case.

"I really don't know," Mark said.

Chapter Nine

Mark Wiseman's flight from John Wayne Airport in Irvine, California to Houston International Airport was the first time he had ever flown First Class.

Mark reclined in his seat and sipped a glass of wine. There were three other people with him in First Class: a lean, tall man with graying temples; a young business type in a black suit; and a large woman in her fifties with black curly hair dressed in a purple and blue dress wearing a lot of gaudy jewelry. For the most part, the people in First Class kept to themselves and didn't pay much attention to their fellow First Class travelers with the exception of the woman in purple. Mark had caught her a few times sneaking disapproving glances his way, as if asking herself what the hell a person looking like him was doing in First Class anyway.

It was almost one full month after the hit on Martin John in Silverado Canyon. A week after the murder, Bernard Roberts had phoned Mark at the pay phone in Fountain Valley and gave him the scoop: "We did good, but there's still a motion to push the merger through. John's successor was named last night and he backs John's position. We aren't going to worry about him because he was a fence sitter to begin with and he's only voting to go through it because of John. Instead, we're going to focus our attention on a guy named David Samuels."

Bernard had filled Mark in on Samuels and Mark filled in the blanks that evening in his apartment by looking at the photograph, which showed a man in his late fifties who obviously lived well: He had the round, fleshy features and balding head of the typical corporate executive. He sat on the board of three other corporations and was CEO of an HMO in Texas. HMO tycoons wouldn't be missed.

In the weeks that followed, Bernard had fed Mark pertinent information about Samuels. He lived in a swanky section of Houston in a large, gated home, but he vacationed every August in East Texas. One of his longtime hobbies was hunting, and he especially loved to hunt and fish in the East Texas woods where he owned a cabin. In August, Samuels liked to retreat to the cabin to fish in the lake and relax on the deck that overlooked the shimmering waters. Bernard provided Mark with both of Samuels's addresses and informed him that the executive was two days into his two-week vacation. His wife normally let him go up a week early by himself; then she joined him for the remainder of the vacation. That gave Mark four days to get to Samuels before she did. The full moon would rise on the following evening.

A week ago Mark had gone to a gazebo overlooking Newport Harbor. He had stood in the gazebo gazing out at the ocean and the boats in the harbor, feeling the cool ocean breeze on his skin. A moment later he'd heard footsteps, and he'd waited until they'd walked up the path toward the gazebo. He'd turned around to see Bernard Roberts, dressed in a pair of sweat pants and a T-shirt. His shirt had been stained from exertion. Bernard had reached into the pouch fastened on a belt around his waist and had handed him an envelope. Then, he'd exited the gazebo and resumed his jog along the Newport Beach boardwalk.

Mark had waited until he was in his car before he opened the envelope.

Ten thousand dollars in cash, in hundred dollar bills.

Two airline tickets, one departing, one returning.

A short note that read: *Payment for the first. Payment for the second will be rendered upon completion.*

He had closed the envelope and driven home.

And now he was in the first-class section of a flight to Houston, where David Samuels, the target of Bernard Roberts's petty, desperate attempt at saving his skin, resided. Mark had spent the last four weeks pondering what was driving Bernard to force him to do this. He had come to the conclusion that it couldn't simply be the money. It didn't eliminate the possibility that the man was insane, but he was convinced it wasn't solely for the money. Bernard was smart. Most of the people he had read about who committed crimes of violence for financial gain had been stupid people who had everything to gain for their crime. The few people Mark read about that had stolen millions of dollars in various white-collar crimes were usually intelligent, but they were also sociopaths.

Was Bernard Roberts a sociopath?

It was possible. It was the only logical explanation to justify attempting something so foolish. It still seemed like a stupid thing to do, even for a sociopath, but then who said that the various crimes they committed were done so with brainpower?

Mark had thought a lot about the motivations that would cause Bernard Roberts to act so desperately, but there was still something missing. No matter how hard he tried to come up with a solution, it eluded him. He spent the entire four weeks pondering the problem, turning it over and over in his head. He thought about it at night while he worked, during the day while he ran his chores. It chased him into his dreams.

He caught a cab to a hotel in the city. He checked into an old, weather-beaten hotel that advertised cheap rates and vibrating beds. Bernard had told him to check into a cheap place because it was less likely that, if the shit hit the fan, a cheap hotel would keep good records on their guests. Mark signed in under a false name, paid the thirty-dollar charge for the first night, and crashed on the lumpy queen-sized mattress.

He rented a Ford Escort the following day and he spent that afternoon going over a map of Houston and East Texas, tracing the best route. It was a two-hour drive from Houston to the section of woods in East Texas where David Samuels owned his cabin. The first night of the full moon was tomorrow, so he spent the afternoon and evening driving around Houston, making plans.

The next day was overcast and windy. He drove by David Samuels's home. Bernard had informed him that Ellen Samuels drove a silver Mercedes Benz, and that she was usually home during the days when her husband had his week off. Sure enough, Mrs. Samuels's Benz was parked in the large, circular driveway. Satisfied, Mark drove out of the neighborhood, headed for the outskirts of Houston.

The drive to the woods took him a little over two hours. He stopped for gas once, and made the county line at about four-fifteen. He drove until he found a local tourist spot, found a motel, and checked in, this time using his real name. He paid in cash rather than using his credit card, for security purposes. When he was checked in he retreated to his room, unpacked the small bag he had brought from home, and took out the map. The tourist spot he was in was on the outskirts of the woods where David Samuels vacationed, and the lake was four miles north. He would have to duck behind the motel and go through the woods in order to reach the lake's south side. David Samuels's cabin was on the east side of the lake. This was going to be a piece of cake.

Mark settled back on the bed to get some rest. The weather report called for scattered thundershowers and strong winds. No big deal. He had a big night ahead of him, one he wasn't entirely looking forward to.

Joe Tripp's left hand was massaging Kelly Baker's left breast in the front seat of his Mustang, while his right hand snaked down her back, fingers roving along the bra strap. He kissed her eagerly and passionately as he felt her own hand snake down to his crotch and rub his cock through the denim of his jeans.

They had been parked in a secluded grove in the woods near the lake for the past hour. It was the only place where they could get privacy; Joe's roommate was home hogging the place, and Kelly still lived with her parents. More importantly, Joe didn't have a credit card to get them a motel room. Therefore, the Mustang was necessary for him to spend some quality lovin' time with Kelly. Because both of them had Thursday nights off of work at their respective fast-food jobs, it was only natural that they come to this part of the lake to talk, make out, smoke a little pot, and, if they were lucky enough to be alone, screw their brains out.

Tonight they were alone.

It had rained briefly earlier in the evening, and the wind was brisk, blowing warm air against the car. He broke their kiss and gazed into her eyes. The interior of the car was warm with the smell of marijuana. Even with the windows rolled down somewhat, they were fogged up. Joe was eighteen, going on nineteen next month, and Kelly had turned nineteen a few months ago. Joe had never been with an older woman before.

Kelly smiled at him, looking sexy and so damn delicious in that skimpy halter top and those cutoff denim shorts. "I love it when you get hard for me like that, Joey," she purred.

Joe grinned at her. "I like it when you *make* me hard, Kelly."

She kissed him and he kissed her back, their tongues meeting, darting out to tease and taste each other. Joe's left hand found her nipple and his fingers rubbed it, making it hard. He felt Kelly moan through her kiss, and a moment later she broke the kiss briefly to fumble with her bra. Joe grinned, his eyes growing wide as Kelly grinned back and lifted the halter top up and over her head along with the bra, revealing the nicest pair of melons this side of East Texas. They were so nice that Kelly had once been offered a job as the head waitress at Hooters even though she didn't have waitressing experience.

Joe grinned and dipped his face down to Kelly's breasts, nuzzling them. Kelly laughed and cradled his head in her hands. "Oh, Joe!" she squealed.

"Oh Kelly," Joe moaned and took an engorged nipple in his mouth.

Kelly began to moan.

Within minutes they were stripped of their clothes and Joe had moved the passenger seat back for better maneuvering. He slid inside her and she moaned louder, her nails digging into his back. He loved screwing while stoned. It seemed to heighten the senses threefold. She was so warm, so beautiful, that he couldn't control himself. She moaned with each stroke, her lips and teeth nibbling his ear, driving him crazy.

Their rhythm was rocking the Mustang on its shock absorbers something fierce; they were rocking it so hard, it was hard to tell if it was the wind gusts rocking the car or the vigor of their lovemaking. Joe lifted himself up a bit to get a better angle and glanced through the back window briefly and what he saw made him stop in mid-stroke.

His eyes widened. "Holy shit!"

"Joey! What's wrong? Why did you stop?"

Joe clambered over her into the back seat to get a better look. "Jesus Christ, I don't believe what the fuck I'm seeing!"

"What?" Kelly sounded irritated. She grabbed her halter top and covered her breasts with it as she turned around and looked out the back window. "I don't see anything."

Joe pointed. "Through those trees at the cabin up ahead. Look."

Kelly peered through the window in the direction Joe's finger directed. She gasped and grabbed Joe. "Oh my God!"

What they were witnessing was something out of a horror movie. In fact, it looked right out of one of those old werewolf movies that his older brother and his friends had taken him to when he was little: *The Howling, An American Werewolf In London.* Only what was happening in front of them was real.

A werewolf was attacking a man on the lakeside of a large cabin.

That was the only way to describe it. It was a werewolf they were looking at, mauling what looked to be a middle-aged man. It walked upright, was covered in dark gray fur. Its arms were long, ending in long, fur-shaped claws, and its face was strangely human, yet canine; the bottom portion of the face was pushed out into a very canine-looking snout, jaws filled with large, sharp teeth, while the eyes and forehead were human-like in appearance. It was a were-wolf, and it was tearing the man on the lakeshore to pieces.

Joe didn't even know he was holding his breath until Kelly's hand clutched his throat, shaking him. *"Oh my God, Oh my God, Omigod!"*

Joe scrambled to the front seat for his clothes. He was instantly sober. He slid into his jeans hurriedly. "We gotta get outta here."

Kelly remained transfixed by the scene, still looking out the back window.

Joe dug into his pocket for his keys. "Kelly, come on, get your clothes on. We're getting the fuck out of here!"

Kelly remained were she was, immobile.

"Jesus Christ," Joe muttered. He scrambled to the back of the car and gently tried to pry Kelly away from the back window. "Come on baby, we gotta get out of here. Cops see you buck naked like that, they'll haul both of us to jail. 'Specially if they smell that weed we been smokin'."

Kelly was still looking at the scene, only now her features changed in dawning amazement. "Oh my God, look at him!"

Joe swung his head around to look. And couldn't believe his eyes.

The werewolf—or whatever the hell it was—was changing.

It was standing over the body of the man it had just killed and at first it appeared to just be sniffing at its prey. But then Joe saw that it was struggling; he could see its body shake. Then he saw that its arms were shrinking, its body was straightening out and before Joe knew it, it was becoming less wolflike and more human. It was transforming into a man right before his eyes.

"Well I'll be goddamned," Joe muttered.

They remained silent, watching the transformation one hundred yards away for a good three minutes. When it was finished, a naked man with long brown hair and a lean, muscular build stood over the body of the man he had killed. Then he looked out across the lake for a minute and scanned the entire area. When he cast his gaze in their direction Joe and Kelly instinctively ducked. Joe felt his heart pound in his ribcage as he wondered if the guy had seen them. Taking a chance, he peered back over the seat and saw that the guy had turned his gaze north of them. Finally the guy stepped toward the house and disappeared into the shadows surrounding the cabin.

All was silent.

Joe was afraid to move. Beside him Kelly held her breath, stiff and still.

Silence. Not even the sound of crickets chirruping.

"This is weird," Kelly whispered.

The sound of Kelly's voice almost scared the shit out of Joe. He gulped, tried to calm himself, and nodded. "Yeah, it is," he whispered back.

"Where did he go?"

"I don't know."

"You don't think he'll come by here, do you?"

"I didn't see him come by us before."

"Well of course not. We were both pretty goddamned occupied with other things, weren't we?"

They paused, listening for any sounds. Aside from the gusts of wind, there was nothing.

"Think he went back into the woods?" Kelly asked in that same whisper.

"I don't know," Joe replied. They were both talking in low whispers to each other. God forbid the guy hear them and come over and do to them what they had seen him do to the man by the lakeshore. "Guess he did."

"What the hell was that?"

"Your guess is as good as mine."

Kelly looked nervous. For the first time it seemed to occur to her that she was naked. She reached for the front seat of the Mustang for her jeans and panties. "Let's get the hell out of here."

"You got it, baby." Joe scrambled back in the front seat and didn't even wait for Kelly to put on her clothes. He inserted the keys in the ignition and fired up the car, peeling out of the remote area fast because now he could swear that whatever it was they had seen was watching them; it was watching them from the woods and now it was pursuing them, down the long winding road that led to their make-out spot. Joe put the pedal to the metal, and as they raced down the road toward the interstate he had no idea what he was going to say to the cops when he called them, but he didn't care. He had gotten a good look at the guy, even from far away. He could at least give them a description.

"What're we gonna do?" Kelly had slid back into her jeans and panties and had put her halter top back on, sans bra. She looked scared and worried.

"Fuck if I know, babe."

"We gonna go to the police?"

"Guess we should."

"What are we gonna tell them?"

Joe was at a loss for words. *Hey officer, I just saw a werewolf kill a guy by the lake.* He sighed. "Fuck if I know. But I guess we gotta tell them something."

Thirty minutes later a state patrol car was heading toward the cabin at precisely the same moment Mark Wiseman stepped into his hotel room for the night.

Chapter Ten

Mark Wiseman was at the appointed time at yet another public phone booth two days after the hit on David Samuels—this one on the corner of Ellis and Brookhurst—when the call came. He answered on the first ring. "Mark here."

"You were seen." Bernard's voice was low and ominous. Mark didn't know Bernard well enough to detect if there was anger in the tone, but that simple sentence—*you were seen*—was enough to set the butterflies loose in his stomach.

"What?"

"Two kids smoking dope and fucking in the woods saw you," Bernard said, and now Mark could hear the stress in his voice. He could picture the executive sitting behind his large desk chewing his fingernails down to the cuticles over this. "The boy gave a general description that loosely matched you."

Mark was at a loss for words. Part of him felt elated: *Finally, it's over. Maybe now Bernard will see that this is stupid and risky.* But another part of him felt a cold fear that washed over him suddenly, drying out his mouth and making his heart pound faster.

"Lucky for you, they were smoking dope," Bernard reiterated. "They admitted it, and the troopers attributed their pot smoking to what they saw."

"What did they say?" Mark heard himself asking.

"That they saw what looked to them to be a werewolf attacking and mauling David Samuels three nights ago at his private lakefront cabin."

Mark's heart raced and he dry swallowed. He could sense that Bernard was angry, but was drawing this out as a form of torture. Obviously this was amusing to him. "What else?"

"They said they watched you change back into a man and disappear into the woods. Then they got the hell out of there."

"And the cops don't believe them?"

Bernard chuckled dryly. "Are you kidding? They think they were stoned out of their minds. Apparently they were smoking some pretty potent stuff. I hear that the THC content of pot is higher now than when I was a teenager."

Mark wasn't listening to Bernard. His mind was racing. He could have sworn that there was nobody around that night. He hadn't smelled anybody within miles of the cabin. Of course, it had been pretty windy. They could have been on the north side of the cabin. The wind would have blown all trace of their scent north, away from Mark. An icy pit of dread settled in his stomach at the thought that he was seen; he had been intending to carry through and devour the man, but he had caught the vague sense that he was being watched. The minute he had felt it he had changed back to human form, but he couldn't get a scent on anything. For the first time in years he had actually gone against his primal instinct and had listened to his human, rational side; he had changed back and gotten the hell out of Dodge. "So what happened?"

Bernard's tone turned serious again. "You did a good job with Samuels. He was chewed to shit. The authorities think it was a wild animal, probably a bear. We got off scot-free."

Mark sighed in relief, the leaden feeling fading slightly.

"But you were seen," Bernard said, his tone serious again. "That's *not* good."

"You said yourself that the kids who saw me were high," Mark said, his mind racing to calm the executive's mind. "Obviously the police think they were hallucinating. It'll be fine."

"I agree." Bernard paused a moment, then continued. "But we can't have this again. I know that what these kids saw will get brushed under the rug; nobody believes them and I'm sure they're even questioning if what they saw that night was real or not. Either way, it still doesn't address the fact that in the future there could be other witnesses. You're going to have to be more careful about that."

"Yes, I guess I will." Mark gripped the receiver tight, the worst of his nervousness gone. "I'll be more careful."

"Good."

Mark swallowed another dry lump, then mustered up the courage to ask what he had been wanting to ask. "Hopefully this will be the last one. I mean, two dead in two months has got to fuck with their plans now, don't you think?"

"That is very far from the truth," Bernard said, his voice cold as steel. "If you're thinking of backing out now just because you think we've put a little scare into them, you can forget it. These guys are stubborn, and it looks like we're going to have to do some significant damage before we disrupt their plans."

"Oh." Mark was silent, hoping that Bernard would finish and he could go home.

"In the meantime, don't say anything to anybody. Lay low. I'll be in touch in another week or so with some updated information. Let's say . . ." The rustle of calendar pages being turned coming across the line. "Next Thursday evening?"

"I'm working that night," Mark said.

"I'll call you at work."

Mark gave it to him.

"I'll talk to you next week then," Bernard said, and hung up.

Mark hung up the phone slowly. A cool offshore breeze was blowing in from the ocean. He turned and headed toward his car.

PART TWO

Chapter Eleven

When the job came in, Allen Frey had no idea it was going to involve murder.

He had sworn off handling murder investigations two years ago when he had been hired by the widow of a wealthy man to investigate the suicide of her husband. What he had uncovered had been far worse: The husband had been killed by the woman's boyfriend to cover up her involvement in a local child molestation ring in which the couple's own children were victims. The husband had found out and was in the process of turning over evidence—which she later destroyed— to the police. The evidence Allen Frey had dug up during his investigation had been so disgusting, so brutal, that he swore he would never handle another case involving violence or death again.

Yet when the well-dressed man stepped into the office of Frey Surveillance in Costa Mesa, California, he was taken with the man. For one, the potential client was not only a sharp dresser, he was polite and courteous too. He was also extremely personable and funny, cracking jokes and showing no signs of being condescending, which was so prevalent with men of his stature. Allen pegged the potential client as a banker, a lawyer, or a doctor, a financially secure man who, because of his finances, felt he could wield the world with the snap of his fingers. The minute Allen had the man pegged old prejudices sprang up; he hated rich people for their snobbiness.

Frederick Johansen possessed no such rich snob traits.

The meeting began with Frederick asking for Allen's credentials. As Allen presented them to him, the other man made small, witty anecdotes, which Allen thought were genuine and witty. Allen relaxed in the man's company, and in no time they were making small talk about the latest baseball season. It was Frederick who steered the conversation back to the business at hand.

"I'm on the board of directors for a large, national insurance company," Frederick began, leaning back in his seat. He was a tall man, standing six foot one, with a lean build, salt and pepper hair, and a white beard. He reminded Allen a little bit of the actor Donald Sutherland, only he spoke with a slight southern accent. "You may have heard of us: Free State Insurance Corporation?"

Allen nodded, smiled in recognition. "Of course. I see your ads all over the place."

Frederick returned the smile. "We're the largest and the best. But enough of that . . ." He leaned forward. "I'm going to give it to you straight and simple, Mr. Frey. I want to make sure that if I decide to hire you, and if you decide to take on this case, that we maintain a strict sense of confidentiality. I am acting alone in this. The rest of the board and the executive staff of Free State and Eastside Insurance Brokerage, with whom we are in negotiations, are not aware of our meeting today. Should you and I decide today to forge ahead with this business arrangement, I need your word that you will speak to no one about me or your investigation." He raised his eyebrows at Allen. "Agreed?"

Allen smiled and nodded. "You have my word." He began to relax even more. With the mention of a corporate merger and all the talk of secrecy, it sounded like Mr. Johansen wanted to retain Allen for some corporate snooping.

"Good." Frederick Johansen sat forward, regarding Allen pensively with gray eyes. He leaned forward and reached into a tan leather briefcase and flipped open the locks. "I'd like you to skim through the material in the briefs I have prepared for you, Mr. Frey, and tell me what you think." He extracted a file and handed it over to Allen, who began to leaf through it wordlessly.

Most of it appeared to be photocopies of internal corporate memos and manifestos. Allen recognized Frederick's name among a dozen or so others that were unfamiliar. He shrugged, wondering what to make of it. It would take him some time to get a handle on some corporate espionage and he didn't have time to pussyfoot around if Frederick was unwilling to give him the skinny right now. Frederick motioned to the file. "Flip to the papers in the back."

Allen flipped to the back. There were newspaper

articles, the first culled from the *Orange County Register* two months ago, the second from the *Houston Tribune* last month, the third from the *Los Angeles Times* just two weeks ago. They all concerned the savage deaths of middle-aged men by wild animals: a coyote in the first, a bear in the second, a mountain lion in the third. "There is still some debate as to whether the beast that mauled William Krueger two weeks ago was a mountain lion or not," Mr. Johansen said. "That is the official verdict. Animal Control officers aren't so sure, and I seriously doubt it. Especially since wildcats haven't been spotted in the Hollywood Hills in, oh, forty or fifty years or so."

"You want me to find out what kind of animals killed these men?" Allen was confused.

"I want you to find out what these men were doing prior to their deaths," Frederick said. "I want you to retrace every waking moment of their lives. I want you to talk to the people that were close to them, people they may have come in contact with. I want to know if the people these men had come in contact with noticed anything unusual at any time."

Allen was flipping through the papers again. "You're intimating foul play?"

"I don't know," Frederick said, his expression dour. "But I *do* know that three deaths in three months, all at the hands of animals, all of the victims connected professionally to the same two firms—Free State and Eastside Insurance—is pretty goddamned weird."

Allen nodded, skimming over the newspaper articles again. "Yes, it is."

"This is important to me," Frederick said. "I realize that you may have other cases, but I would like you to direct your full attention to this case if you can. I can pay double your normal fee."

Allen felt his spirits lift. Double his normal surveillance fee was something he hadn't been expecting.

Frederick was reaching for his wallet, riffling through it. "Plus expenses, of course." He pulled out a wad of bills and slapped them down on the desk. "A deposit." He met Allen's eyes from across the desk.

Allen looked at the big wad of bills, then at Frederick, who held him with his steely gaze. He reached across the desk and picked up the cash, thumbing through the bills. The deposit amounted to ten thousand dollars. "I can start today."

Frederick beamed. "Wonderful!" He rose to his feet and Allen stood up, shaking his hand. He reached into his briefcase and handed Allen another file. "This is a complete dossier on the three men. Read it over and call me tonight at this number." He slipped Allen a business card. "It's a secure line."

Allen took the dossier and the business card and walked Frederick Johansen out. "I'll be in touch tonight," he said.

When Frederick Johansen was gone, Allen went back to his office and sat behind his desk. He looked over the newspaper articles, then at the business documents, then opened the thick manila folder that contained the dossier. Looked like this was going to be a juicy one. Allen smiled and extracted the first file from the folder, opened it up, and began to read.

Chapter Twelve

They had an eight o'clock rendezvous at the Huntington Beach Pier parking lot. Mark Wiseman waited in his beaten-up Ford Pinto, a Mötley Crüe song on the radio. The beach was practically deserted and Mark knew that in another thirty minutes the lifeguards would begin driving through the parking lots telling people they had to leave. In another week the beach would be closing a few hours earlier due to the change from summer to fall. It was already getting cooler in early September. As he sat in his car and waited he felt the wind pick up, blowing a scrap of paper along the ground.

The sound of a car pulling up flitted across his senses before he actually saw it. He looked in his rearview mirror and twin headlights appeared. A moment later a black Mercedes pulled up beside him and stopped. The driver killed the engine and turned off the headlights. Mark got out of his car, opened the passenger side door of the Mercedes and got in.

Bernard looked smug and confident behind the wheel. The interior of the car smelled like new. "I hope I'm not spoiling your night off," Bernard said and smirked. "I'm sure you'll be able to head right back to the nearest biker bar and score some pussy tonight."

"Maybe you should come with me," Mark remarked, going along with Bernard's sarcasm. "You might get lucky, too."

"Oh, I don't need to stoop that low to get laid. I got me a regular piece of ass already. Blonde hair, blue eyes, big tits, young all-American beauty. The girl can suck some mean cock and she swallows too. Every drop." He grinned.

Mark grinned back. *I feel sorry for whoever it is you're fucking, you bastard.*

"But enough of this male standard of seeing whose dick is bigger," Bernard said, waving his right hand in a dismissal of the current topic of conversation. "I wanted to talk to you face-to-face this time instead of over the phone to personally congratulate you on a job well done."

"Thank you."

"The killing of William Krueger went perfectly," Bernard continued. "No witnesses, no reports of animal sounds or screaming, and to top it off the body wasn't discovered for two whole days. Imagine what he must've smelled like." Bernard scrunched his face up in disgust. "Yuck."

Mark smiled and said nothing. Inside he was controlling the boiling anger that wanted him to leap out and annihilate Bernard. He could do it, too; he could will the change to occur now and lay Bernard's throat open with one well-placed swipe of his claws. What kept him from doing it was knowing that Bernard was armed; the minute the executive sensed something was wrong, the gun would come out. The minute Mark began the change—*blam!*

"Our plan is working, old buddy," Bernard continued, patting Mark on the shoulder. "The Board is running scared. Frankly, they're rather fucked up over these latest developments. Plus, there are other things developing for Free State Insurance." He grinned wide. "Our corporate profits rose this quarter by ten percent."

"Congratulations."

Bernard continued as if he hadn't heard Mark. "Because of the sudden rise in profits, we're starting to see things come around. For one, the Board is reconsidering its position to merge with Eastside."

Mark felt his hopes soar but tried not to let it show. "Really? That's good news."

Bernard grinned. "It is good news. Obviously they're reconsidering now because of the recent turn of events with the unfortunate, eh . . . animal accidents that have occurred with other members of the Board." He chuckled, his eyes dark, his features a caricature of shrewd cunning. "Naturally, they're all rather shaken up by the coincidences. They've managed to find replacements, and just now the consensus for merging is at a low point. Especially thanks to the latest hit."

"Why's that?"

"Krueger's replacement is adamantly against the

merger. And he won't budge. The other replacements have voted for it, mainly in respect for their predecessors, but not this new guy. He's against it all the way, and because of his opinions he's actually influenced a couple other members of the Board to rethink their positions."

"Where does that leave us?"

"It means we lay low for a little bit," Bernard said, looking out at the ocean. The minute he said that, Mark heaved a quiet sigh of relief; he was dreading the thought of having to slaughter another human being for this monster. "The Board as a whole is pretty spooked by the 'strange coincidences' regarding the sudden deaths of Krueger, Samuels, and John. And I don't know who, but somebody hired a private investigator to poke around."

Mark almost jumped in surprise. "A private investigator?"

"Yes." Bernard nodded, his features grim. "Typical private dick. He came by my office this afternoon and asked me a few questions. Wanted to know about my relationship with the Board, what my views were on the merger, what my activities had been like the last few months, whether I had seen Krueger, John, and Samuels in the days prior to their deaths. I think I did a pretty good job in snowblinding him. I gave him an overview on my background with the firm, my relationship with the Board, and I was very accommodating when I gave him my rundown on my whereabouts the last few months. He seemed satisfied and left. I'm sure it was all routine, but I think I did a pretty good job in keeping the truth from him."

Bernard may have done as good a job as he claimed, but it still made Mark nervous as hell. He ran his right hand through his hair and tried to play it cool. "He won't find anything. There's no way he could find anything. No way at all."

"Exactly," Bernard said softly, looking at Mark now. "Whoever hired this guy apparently just wants him to nose around, talk to the other Board members, some of the executive staff, that sort of thing. Whoever this person is has a hunch, and that tells me he's somebody on the Board. My guess is that it's somebody from Eastside who hired this guy."

"Whoever it is might want the merger to go through, so they're thinking somebody else, probably somebody who sits on your Board of Directors, is making preemptive strikes."

"That's what I'm guessing."

"What do you think we should do?"

"Like I said, lay low for awhile." Bernard turned to Mark and smiled as he reached into his coat pocket and pulled out an envelope. "Enjoy ourselves for awhile. Let the excitement blow over."

Mark took the envelope and glanced inside. It was filled with hundred-dollar bills, bundled in rubber bands. Payment for this latest hit, another ten grand. Mark slipped the envelope in his pocket wordlessly.

"Let's meet again two weeks from tonight," Bernard said. "The parking lot of the Westminster Public Library on Talbert. I'll fill you in on the latest developments then."

"Fine. I'll be there."

"Enjoy the money," Bernard said, flashing him a smile.

Mark opened the door and stepped out of the car. He fumbled with the door of his own car a moment, got it open and slid inside, shutting him off from the cold of the beach and Bernard's company.

Bernard started his Mercedes, popped the headlights on, and drove away.

Mark remained in his car for a moment. His mind was racing with excitement. Bernard would be smart to call the whole thing off, and then the both of them could go on as if nothing had ever happened. But somehow Mark didn't think that was going to happen. Something told him that Bernard was in this for the long haul. He was going to continue at this sick game until he got his way, or until he was caught.

Mark, on the other hand, had no intention of getting caught.

Starting with the second murder, that of David Samuels, Mark had emotionally distanced himself from the killings. He knew that if he became too emotionally involved, something would happen, something would slip. He would leave some trace of his human self at the crime scene. With the second murder, when he'd reverted to his wolf-form he'd embraced the beast within wholeheartedly. He'd marked his territory in the woods surrounding the cabin where Samuels had lived, as well as the Hollywood Hills where he had killed Krueger. He had also partially devoured two of the men. Like the first killing, he had prepared beforehand to keep a fresh change of clothes, and he'd been able to swiftly don them once he'd reverted back to his human-self. He hadn't been seen in his wolf-form, with the exception of the two witnesses in Texas, and who was going to believe them? The police obviously hadn't, and the experience itself taught Mark that he had to remain in his wolf state for the duration of the evening, that to change back after killing was dangerous. It would never happen again, that he was sure of.

Mark started the car, turned on the headlights, and headed out of the parking lot.

The time off would also give him some much needed time to relax and think. He had been nervous the last few months, always on alert. He had been keeping the cash Bernard had paid him in a large manila envelope under his mattress, and had hardly touched it. The private detective Bernard had hired to tail him had slacked off somewhat and Mark had never brought the subject up to Bernard in their phone conversations, feigning ignorance. Bernard had to know that Mark was aware of the surveillance, but if he did he didn't mention it. For his part, Mark did what he was told, never let on to Bernard or the private dick that he was being followed, and within a month the surveillance had eased off. In the last three weeks he hadn't been tailed at all and Mark surmised that Bernard was beginning to trust him. He obviously knew that he had Mark in a pretty tight bind: If he cooperated, he would live and his secret would remain safe. If he didn't, he would be killed. Simple as that.

Kill or be killed. The law of the jungle.

The next few weeks would give Mark time to ponder his dilemma and perhaps come to some solutions. He could make more trips to the library, do more research on Bernard, maybe even hire his own private detective. He was hesitant about committing to something like that, though; he was afraid that Bernard would find out.

Mark drove home, humming along with the radio. He was in such a fine mood that he did stop in at a local bar that evening and got lucky.

Chapter Thirteen

It wasn't until he got to a little town about two hours east of Houston, Texas that the case began to take a turn for the interesting.

Allen Frey had already read the newspaper reports and was familiar with the circumstances surrounding David Samuels's death. Texas Animal Control officers had killed a black bear matching the rough description given to them by various campers that had been in the area around the time of the attack. Unfortunately, a necropsy on the animal failed to prove that it had been the animal responsible for Samuels's death, as no traces of human remains were found in its digestive tract. In the next few weeks, twelve other bears were killed and autopsied with similar results. Of course within a week's time the animal could have passed the matter, but Allen didn't think that was the case. By the time he left Houston, he was convinced that a bear hadn't been responsible for Samuels's death. Nor any other wild animal for that matter.

Allen started his investigation by talking to members of David Samuels's family, where he learned some very humdrum stuff. His wife told him that David had been in good spirits, that he had been looking forward to his trip. His colleagues at the country club revealed nothing remarkable, nor did his fellow executives at the HMO he presided over, as did his fellow board members of the three corporations he served on. It was through a board member of one of these companies—a textile firm—that Allen learned something the police never discovered: that David kept a mistress on the side. The mistress turned out to be a forty-one-year-old former call girl with waist-length blonde hair and a fabulous hourglass figure, who told Allen that she had been devastated to hear of Samuels's death. She had been planning on spending a few days with David at his cabin before his wife came up. Allen had grilled her and found nothing unusual about her story. He had made a note to check into her background further when he interviewed Joe Tripp and Kelly Baker, the two lovers who had claimed to the police that they had seen a werewolf.

Allen got their addresses and found Joe on the afternoon after talking to Samuels's mistress. Joe was at his apartment with Kelly, relaxing on the back deck cooking hamburgers on a charcoal grill. Allen knocked on the screen door and flashed his identification when Joe came to the door. "I was wondering if I could talk to you about your statement to the Texas State Police about what you saw the night David Samuels was killed."

"You another cop?" Joe stood behind the screen door, arms crossed in front of his skinny chest. He looked to be about nineteen or twenty, with wiry blond hair that fell about his face and a faint mustache and goatee.

"I'm a private detective."

Joe appeared to scrutinize him, then shrugged. "Might as well. What have I got to lose by telling you something you ain't gonna believe anyway?" He let Allen in and introduced him to Kelly, who had come in from the back deck. Kelly appeared to be around Joe's age and sported long, frizzy brown hair and long, tanned legs. Allen nodded at her and shook her hand, trying not to stare at her cleavage; *Christ, but when they said that things are bigger in Texas, they weren't kidding.*

"We were just grilling some burgers on the grill," Joe said, heading to the refrigerator. "Want one?"

"No thanks."

"You want something to drink?" Kelly asked, heading to the kitchen and opening the refrigerator. "We got beer and soda."

"I'll take a soda if you don't mind."

"RC okay?"

"Sure."

Kelly pulled out a can of RC Cola and handed it to Allen. He opened it and took a sip, smiling in thanks.

Joe picked up a plate with two large mounds of seasoned ground beef and two hamburger buns and motioned toward the back. "Let's sit on the deck. We'll talk there."

Allen followed them to the back deck and was surprised to see that it was bigger than he had expected. It was big enough to accommodate a small grill, a small tray that served as a table, and three chairs. Joe plopped the meat on the grill and placed the lid down while Kelly set down a second plate of condiments. She scooted around Allen and sat down, sipping a bottle of Evian water. Joe grabbed a can of Coors and took a sip, eyeing Allen suspiciously. "So what do you want to know about that night, Mr. Private Detective?"

"Everything that is and isn't on the police report," he said, squinting up at Joe.

"How'd you find out about us?"

"You were in the report."

Joe smirked. "How crazy did that police report say we were?"

"To tell you the truth, the report doesn't mention what you told the officers," Allen said. "It just says that the two of you were interviewed as potential witnesses in the Samuels killing."

"Potential witnesses . . ." Joe let the words trail into a whisper. Kelly cast a glance toward them and said nothing. "What a joke."

Allen smiled. "The report says nothing of what you reportedly told Officer Lansdale."

Joe's eyes narrowed suspiciously. "So he told you, huh?"

"Yep."

"And what do you think?"

"I want you to tell me what you saw in your own words."

"What for? You already know the story and you already know he thinks we were hallucinating or something. Why the fuck should we tell you what you already know?"

"Because I want to hear it from you myself," Allen said, taking a sip of RC. "Plus, I want you to tell me the whole story. If there was anything you left out of your statement to Officer Lansdale, I want to hear it."

"What for?" Kelly's upper lip curled back in a sneer. "So you can catch us in a lie or something?"

"Nothing of the sort," Allen said calmly. "You might remember something you had forgotten to tell Lansdale. And no, I have no intention of going to the police on anything you tell me. I'm not working for them."

"Who are you working for?" Joe asked.

"If you don't mind, that's private."

Joe appeared to regard this as he opened the lid of the grill to check the burgers. Satisfied, he closed the lid and sat down on the remaining chair. He traded a glance with Kelly, then took a sip of his beer.

"Sure you don't want anything stronger than that RC?" Joe asked. "You might need it after you hear this."

"I'm fine," Allen said, leaning forward in anticipation.

Joe and Kelly traded one more glance and then, each of them taking turns, they told him. As the story poured out they opened themselves up to him little by little. By the time they were finished, they were spilling the beans on their own little pot-growing operation they had set up in a spare bedroom at the apartment.

During the narrative, Joe checked the burgers, flipped them over, and threw buns on the grill for toasting. Ten minutes later he and Kelly were wolfing down them down, finishing the narrative between gulps of food. Allen listened patiently, interrupting only to ask for clarification on a few spots. When the story was finished Joe asked: "So what do you think? Are we full of shit, or what?"

"Not in the least," Allen said.

Joe and Kelly looked at him as if they couldn't believe what they had heard. "You shittin' me? You mean to tell me that you believed what we just told you?"

"Why not?" Allen said, shrugging. Officer Lansdale had repeated Joe and Kelly's story earlier that morning, dismissing it as the figment of "a bunch of nutty kids on dope." It was the reason Allen wanted to talk to Joe and Kelly himself. Frederick Johansen thought there was something strange about the deaths of his colleagues, and the minute he started digging around the circumstances surrounding David Samuels's death, his suspicions began to become evident. Allen was simply following his instincts.

"Because it sounds like bullshit," Joe said, picking at the remainder of his burger.

Allen looked at Kelly. "Do you think what you saw that night was bullshit, Kelly?"

Kelly looked down at her feet for a moment, then up at Allen. "No," she said.

"The two of you obviously saw something," Allen said. He took a sip of RC, then set the can down on the small tray that held the plate of condiments. "Much of what you described matched the wounds Samuels received that night."

"The cops think that we saw the bear that killed him," Joe said, flipping a lank of hair back from his face.

"But they think we were tripping when we saw it," Kelly said, looking nervous and slightly embarrassed. "We might have been smoking, but—"

"We weren't tripping," Joe said, shaking his head. "We had a little buzz going, yeah, but—"

"We weren't like, so wasted that we were seeing shit," Kelly said.

"Yeah. Plus, I ain't never heard of two people having the same trip." Joe looked at Allen. "You know what I mean?"

Allen nodded and stood up. "I know exactly what you mean. If you have the time, I was wondering if you'd take me out to the spot you were parked at and show me."

Joe and Kelly exchanged surprised glances, then turned back to Allen. "Sure," Joe said, shrugging. "Just got to clean up first."

Allen helped them clean up the barbecue, then helped Kelly in the kitchen. As they worked, Kelly asked him what he thought it was they had seen. "I don't know," he said, "but I'd really like to find out."

When the dishes had been put in the dishwasher, they left the apartment and Kelly and Joe got into the Mustang. Allen followed them in his rental car.

It was a twenty-minute drive to the side road that took them to the spot where Joe and Kelly had been parked. When they got there, Allen got out of his car and walked over to the Mustang. Joe and Kelly got out of the car and Joe pointed through a grove of trees toward the lake. Allen followed with his eyes, shielding them from the setting sun, which was casting sharp rays against the shimmering water. "See the cabin over there? That's the Samuelses' place. We were parked right here."

"You were just sitting here smoking dope and hanging out, right?"

Joe glanced at Kelly and she gave him a look that said *don't you dare*! Allen caught it and grinned. Joe looked at him sheepishly. Kelly turned away, blushing. Allen supposed that if he were Joe he would have been trying his hardest to get into her pants if he was up here alone with her, too. "We was . . . well, you know . . ."

"I was young once," Allen said, smiling. He paused to wink at Kelly, who blushed harder. "I lost my virginity in the back seat of my daddy's car in a spot overlooking L.A. that was secluded like this. There's something about ruttin' in the backseat of your car with your sweetheart that is, oh I don't know . . . primal, I guess."

Joe chuckled and even Kelly grinned. Allen laughed, hoping to break the awkwardness. "Okay, so you drove up here to get stoned, listen to some music, do the horizontal bump and grind, whatever. I'm hip. Then what?"

Joe picked up where they had left off. He motioned toward the Mustang. "We were in the car. The seat was folded back like this." He stooped inside and folded the driver's side seat back. He turned back to Allen. "And we was, you know laying here getting it on—"

"*Joey!*" Kelly cried. It looked like she was going to protest again, but she covered her mouth with her fingers, looked at Allen and giggled, her cheeks blushing again.

My, but she's a bashful one, Allen thought.

"That was when I saw it," Joe continued. "I actually heard it before I saw anything. I heard a man yell and I heard this sort of . . . like a growl."

Allen turned to Kelly. "Did you hear it too?"

Kelly shook her head. "I didn't hear anything at first."

"I heard it," Joe continued, "and I looked up and saw this . . . *thing* attacking Mr. Samuels."

"Can you describe it to me?" Allen asked.

Joe and Kelly traded a glance. They looked embarrassed again. "To tell you the truth, Mr. Frey, it looked like a werewolf."

Allen was expecting this answer and he nodded, looking out across the lake at the cabin. "A werewolf."

Kelly broke the short pause. "I saw it too, Mr. Frey. Joe was like, going all crazy in the car, going, 'Oh my God, will you look at this.' And I got up to look and saw it too." She looked at him steadily. "The only way I can describe what I saw was that . . . well, it looked like a werewolf."

"It was about six feet tall, maybe bigger," Joe said, motioning with his hands as he described it. "It had dark hair all over it. It had a snout like a wolf, and it had a strangely shaped head, half human, half animal I guess you'd say. It walked upright like a man, but it was hunched over."

"Its legs were *huge*!" Kelly said.

"Yeah, and so were its arms," Joe said. "And they were long. Its hands, paws, whatever, were big."

"What did it do after it killed Mr. Samuels?" Allen asked.

"That's when it changed back into a man," Joe said.

"You watched it change?"

Joe and Kelly nodded.

"What was it like? I mean, was it like the special effects in a movie?"

Joe and Kelly glanced at each other and shrugged. "Kinda," Joe said. "But . . ."

"It's hard to explain," Kelly said. "It was as if . . ."

"I guess it was kinda like that," Joe said. "He just started . . . changin'. He sorta hunched down and . . . you could just see him changin'. That's all there was to it."

Allen let this sink in. He didn't believe that what Joe and Kelly saw were simple hallucinations. They had seen something; exactly *what*, Allen didn't know.

"What happened after it changed? What did you see?"

"A man," Kelly said. "A naked man just standing there."

"What did he look like?"

They told him, and this time Allen actually heard more than what Officer Lansdale told him. The naked man was of medium height, perhaps five foot seven inches tall with a lean, but muscular physique. He had shoulder-length brown hair.

"What about facial features," Allen asked. "Could you tell from that far away?"

"He looked like a good-looking man," Kelly said. "He had . . . I don't know . . . fine features. He might have had a light beard."

"So he had a nice face," Allen said.

They both nodded.

Allen looked out across the lake, his mind tracking on what he had to do.

"I have a partner who is an artist. If you give me an exact description of the man you saw and I tape it and have him do up a sketch, could you ID him?"

Joe and Kelly nodded. "You bet," Joe said.

"Do any of you have access to a fax machine?"

"I do at work," Kelly said.

"Great." Allen removed a business card and a pen from his shirt pocket. "Let me have it."

Kelly gave him the number and Allen pocketed the card and pen after jotting it down. "Okay," he said. "So he changed into a man. Then what?"

"He just sort of stood there for a minute," Joe said. "It was kinda windy that night, and he just sorta stood there, looking around. Then he headed into the woods by the cabin."

"And you didn't see him after that?" Allen didn't want to venture that if it wasn't for the wind, the man—or werewolf—might have caught their scent and come after them.

"Hell no!" Kelly exclaimed. "We got the hell out of there."

Allen nodded and looked back out across the lake at the cabin. Animal Control had conducted a thorough search of the woods surrounding the cabin and had found no traces of anything suspicious. There had been a few animal tracks of indeterminate origin, but the park ranger determined that they were from a bear. "How do I get to the cabin from here?" Allen asked.

"Head back down this road, make a left and make

another left at the first road," Joe said. "It'll be a private road; should take you right up to it."

Allen nodded. "Great." He turned to Joe and Kelly to shake their hands. "Thank you for your help. I really appreciate it."

"So you believe us, then?" Joe asked. He still looked amazed that Allen believed them.

"Why shouldn't I? You're telling the truth, aren't you?"

"Well, yeah."

"Then, I believe you." Allen headed toward his rental car and opened the driver's side door. "I wouldn't want to check out the cabin if I didn't believe you."

"You gonna check the cabin out?"

"Yep." He got into the car and Joe and Kelly headed to the Mustang. "I'll call if I need anything else," he said, smiling. "Thank you for your help."

Joe and Kelly waved and Allen waved in return as he pulled away.

As he headed down the road his mind raced with a thousand questions. There had been no trace of mountain lions in Silverado Canyon when Martin John had been savagely mauled. Ditto on the Hollywood Hills case. The bears caught and autopsied in Texas showed no signs that any of them had attacked and partially consumed Mr. Samuels—hell, judging from the man's wounds, it appeared Mr. Samuels wasn't eaten by whatever had killed him anyway. He was mauled horribly, yes, but eaten? Joe and Kelly said that whatever it was that had killed him had changed into a person, then had disappeared into the woods.

Allen's mind went back to the old Hammer Horror films he had watched as a kid. Maybe the werewolf, or whatever the hell it was, had gone off into the woods to hunt out Joe and Kelly, he thought. Maybe it had sensed them and they had narrowly escaped their own deaths that night. Between the time they had left the area and the time the first patrol car arrived at the site, a full forty minutes had passed. Surely that was enough time for whatever it was that had killed Mr. Samuels to disappear. In fact, it could have disappeared when it heard the sirens. Didn't animals hear better than humans?

Allen made a left on the highway, his mind racing. The case at hand was dragging him in. This was some really weird shit here. Probably the weirdest he had ever been involved in, and he was determined to find out what was behind it.

Thinking of werewolves, Allen made a left at the next road, which was marked with a sign that read PRIVATE.

Chapter Fourteen

Mark never bothered to register for the fall semester at Orange Coast College. He had other thoughts on his mind.

Namely dealing with the curse of the moon, which was more ravaging to his body and soul now than it was when it had first reared its ugly head nine years ago.

Mark could feel his anger running hot in his veins. It was something that told him to lay low that nudged him into declining next semester's classes. He told his guidance counselor that a family emergency was going to keep him out of state for the rest of the year, but that he would be back in touch by December to register for spring. In reality, Mark couldn't go back to school because he knew that he would be a miserable failure this semester. He wouldn't be able to concentrate on his studies. All his thoughts would be on Bernard Roberts and whether or not his plan was working.

Goddamn him!

Luckily, a day position opened up in Computer Operations and he took it. It was the same job he was doing now, just the day shift. This left his nights free and from September through December, during the full moon, he headed off to his customary remote spots to let the curse run free. He was always able to maintain some semblance of control, although it was harder now to resist the urge to give in to his blood lust. He satiated his hunger with the natural California wildlife: He took down a fallow deer in September, a mountain lion in October, rabbits in November, and another deer in December. During those four months he kept in contact with Bernard, who provided him with updates on the developments of the investigations, which had fizzled to nothing. He also scanned the local papers, keeping his eyes peeled to anything that might give him a cause for alarm. As always, there was nothing.

When the full moon occurred on work nights Mark would run with the curse, then revert back to his human state in the early hours of the morning. He would drive home, catch two hours of sleep before waking up at seven-thirty to shower and change for work. At least he didn't have to worry about keeping the curse bottled inside. He could let it out, let it ravage and plunder.

He could feed it.

During the three months of working during the day he didn't see Bernard at all; the executive was aware of his new work schedule, but he didn't go out of his way to see Mark, which was fine. Instead they communicated once every two weeks through prearranged phone calls at various public pay phones. Each time, Bernard had nothing to report.

"Everything is going great," he told Mark in November. "The move to merge is on hold until the new fiscal year, which is January. Then the board reconvenes and will vote again. If the vote is to merge, we'll have to take down the chief board member."

Mark hoped it didn't come to that, but he kept that to himself. "Whatever you want me to do," he had said. "Just give me the word." He had grown with ease into his relationship with Bernard; he might hate the man, might want to kill him with his bare hands, but for now he had to survive. In order to survive, he had to play this game Bernard's way. That meant catering to him, making him feel that Mark was on his side, that he was doing everything he was told to do.

In the meantime, Mark was trying to think of a way to end this destructive, symbiotic relationship.

In late October he sat in his car in the vast parking lot of Free State's corporate offices waiting for Bernard to stroll out the front door. He was a good hundred yards away, but he could see the executive perfectly. He watched as Bernard strolled, briefcase in hand, to his black Mercedes, got in and closed the door, then pulled away from his parking space. Mark followed him at a very safe distance.

Bernard had no idea he was being followed.

Mark wasn't surprised when the executive headed into Newport Beach. Free State's offices were in Costa Mesa, right down the street from South Coast Plaza and Crystal Court Shopping Center, favorite shopping spots for the upper echelons of Newport. Mark stayed a safe distance from Bernard and relied mainly on scent and sight to guide him to Bernard Roberts's hum-ble abode, a nice, sprawling ranch home tucked in the hills overlooking the ocean.

Mark parked down the street and turned off the engine. He sat in his car, watching the house. He could very well come back at a very late hour—say, two a.m.—gain entry into the home and end it all by slashing the executive's throat while he slept, but there were things to think about. Was his house rigged with a silent alarm, or even worse, guard dogs?

Shortly after the third hit, Mark realized that he couldn't will the change to come over him like he normally could during nights that the moon wasn't waxing. If he still had that ability, it would be simple to just change, head into the house, and kill Bernard. He was fairly confident that being shot by silver bullets would have the same effect on him as being shot by regular bullets—he had actually touched a piece of silver over the summer to see what the reaction would be, and was relieved to find that there was none. Which meant the silver bullet theory was simply that—a theory based on myth. That still didn't put his mind at ease regarding firearms in general. He had never had to face a gun before; he didn't want to have to face one now just to see if the old myths were correct.

So he drove home, furious with himself for his fear of crossing that line, angry with himself at giving up so easily. As the weeks went on the anger subsided; there was really nothing he could do. Best case scenario was that he would kill Bernard somehow and get away with it, but knowing Bernard, the executive had already laid some kind of incriminating evidence that would point directly at him should

Bernard meet his fate in foul play. Without knowing one hundred percent, Mark couldn't go through with it. The worst case scenario—of course—was being shot and killed by Bernard.

He began to drink more at night, especially as October bled into November and then into December. Especially when the moon waxed.

Perhaps the only positive aspect of his new work schedule was his social life. Prior to working days, his social life was severely limited. He had a nodding acquaintance with a few guys from Charlie's—a local bar and grill he frequented—and on occasion he met women with whom he would have brief flings. Working days opened him up to socializing with more people, since now he was interacting more with his co-workers than before. Within a few weeks of his new work schedule he was being invited out to after-work happy hours at various nightspots with them.

He began to accept the invitations in October.

By November he had fallen in with a group of closely-knit guys at work who hung out together at work, and on Friday nights after work. Mark enjoyed their company; they were roughly his age, most of them were single, and they liked the same music, sports, and movies. They would take breaks together, talk about the news, sports, wherever their muse took them. Friday nights they would go out to various sports bars, drink beer, and have a good time.

In early December Mark trudged along to a new sports bar with the group—Baxter's in Costa Mesa—and he knew right from the start that he shouldn't have gone. He was in a dour mood and as he sat at the bar, barely paying attention to the conversation around him, he realized he was in a funk. Next month was January, the start of the new fiscal year. He would discover his fate then, whether he would continue in the slump he was in now, or resume his killing spree.

Other people from various departments of Free State had found out about their happy-hour excursions and had invited themselves along. Mark had only been dimly aware of them, and he recognized a few as he sat at the bar. They were laughing and talking to each other as if they had known each other for years. Mark was bored, felt out of place, and was just about to leave when a woman next to him said, "They bore you, too, huh? Welcome to the club."

Mark turned to her. An attractive blonde in a business suit that clung to her curves smiled at him and lit a cigarette. A glass of wine sat within easy reach. Mark recognized her face vaguely, but couldn't place it. "Why do you think I'm bored?" he asked.

"You've been sitting there the past half hour just staring at the mirror behind the bar," she said, smiling. Mark smiled back. Her makeup was artfully applied, her lips red. The top three buttons of her blouse were unbuttoned to reveal deep cleavage. Suddenly Mark recognized her as Bernard Roberts's secretary.

Mark smiled back. *Just play it cool*, he thought. *Pretend you don't recognize her.* "Yeah, I guess I am a little bored," he said. *What the hell does she want? Did Bernard send her here to spy on me?*

"I don't blame you," she said, looking around the bar. "Sometimes these places just suck the life right out of you."

"Yeah, they do." Mark finished his beer and was just about to politely excuse himself when she reached out and lightly touched his arm.

"Let me buy you another drink," she said.

"Thanks, but really, I've—"

"It just got interesting," she said. Her blue eyes were penetrating, entrancing. Mark felt drawn to them. She smiled at him, then turned to the bartender. "One more of what he's having and another glass of wine."

That really put him on the spot. Mark remained seated and tried to think of something to say that would be polite and extract him from Baxter's pronto. Since starting his new shift, he had heard from the guys he worked with that Bernard's secretary had a reputation as a woman who had fucked her way up the corporate ladder. In the five years she had been employed with Free State, she had held six secretarial posts, and each one was a loftier position than the one before. All of the bosses she'd worked for were men, all of whom bestowed jewelry and other gifts upon her. Mark had dismissed the rumors because at the time he didn't care. Now that she was sitting here next to him trying to start a conversation, he remembered the rumors and tried to figure out what she wanted from him. For all he knew she could be sincere in wanting company.

"You work in the Computer Room, right?" she asked, lighting a cigarette.

"Yeah," Mark answered as the bartender brought their drinks. "In the tape library."

She smiled. "I'm sorry, I forgot to introduce myself." She held out her hand. "I'm Carol Emrich."

"Mark Wiseman." He shook her hand. Her skin was cool and soft.

"How long have you been with Free State?"

"Four years."

"Really!" She raised her eyebrows in surprise and took a drag. "I've never seen you before."

"I used to work the swing shift. I just started days a few months ago."

"That explains it. Do you like days better?"

"It has its advantages, but then so does working nights."

He sipped his drink and talked with her. As the conversation wound on he found that Carol wasn't at all like she had been made out to be; she was a nice, witty, warm person. She seemed interested in hearing about what he did in his job, but it didn't sound suspicious. After five minutes of talking to her he could sense that she hadn't been sent to Baxter's to spy on him. He could tell by her demeanor, by her body language, by the way she spoke and moved.

Spying on him for Bernard Roberts was obviously the furthest thing from her mind. What appeared to be first and foremost on her mind was wondering what Mark would be like in bed.

Part of the benefit that came with Mark's curse was being able to read people's emotions and needs. Like a dog that could sense fear in a person, it could also sense sexual arousal in the opposite sex of its species, relying primarily on scent. Likewise, Mark could not only sense fear in other people, he could sense a wide range of other emotions and scents in them as well, including sexual desire.

The way Carol Emrich spoke and reacted to Mark as they talked at the bar told him that she was attracted to him.

Mark's first thought was one of paranoia: Bernard had set her up to seduce him to get some kind of information from him. But the more he thought about that, the sillier it sounded. If Bernard wanted information from him, he would simply hire his private investigator goon to do some snooping. He wouldn't send his secretary in to flirt with him. Which took his mind on another track—

How much did Carol know about her boss's personal life?

Mark shifted gears; he went from bored disinterest, to interest. He asked her what she did at Free State and when she told him that she was Bernard's secretary he feigned surprise.

"Wow! So you sit up there in that nice office all day, huh? Must be nice."

"It has its benefits."

"I bet."

"But it's not all fun and glamour, either. Trust me." She took another drag off her cigarette and looked at the mirror behind the bar. Mark regarded her from his position at the bar and noted that she really was attractive. Even if she did wear too much makeup.

"What's Bernard Roberts like?" Mark asked, innocently.

Carol turned to him. "You really want to know?" Her tone of voice and expression conveyed that Bernard Roberts was a subject matter that wasn't worth discussing.

Mark shrugged. "Why not? We all work for him. I just thought it would be nice to hear what he's like."

Carol took a sip of wine. "You won't hear me say anything around this group," she said, her voice lower. "Not the way this crowd gossips."

Mark nodded. "I know what you mean."

"But enough of work," Carol said. She turned to Mark with a smile. "Tell me about you."

From there it went on. The flirting, the laughing, the drinking. They had a few more drinks and Mark bummed a couple of cigarettes from her—he had quit smoking two years ago, but whenever he drank in a bar the urge always hit. Before he knew it, he was on the dance floor with her and had forgotten all about the group of people he had come in with. He was dancing with her and her flirtations were becoming more obvious. On the dance floor she moved seductively against him, and Mark found himself reacting to her advances. His arms slipped around her waist and when the song was over they headed to a corner booth, their arms draped around each other. "I need another drink," Carol said.

Baxter's had seemingly transformed into a full-scale dance club/pick-up joint. The place was packed. Mark craned his head and tried to find his friends over the sea of people, but he couldn't find them. He glanced at his watch and saw that three hours had passed since Carol had sat down next to him at the bar and started a conversation. In that time he had become so lost in her that he had forgotten all about his friends. The only thing he had paid attention to was her.

He didn't care about the rumors he had heard about her. Or that she was Bernard's secretary. All he cared about was her reaction to him and her seeming eagerness to get better acquainted with him.

Drink orders were placed and they reclined in a corner booth, smoking cigarettes and talking. When the drinks came they relaxed a bit, holding hands, sitting close together. Mark felt a stirring of sexual energy between them and before he knew it she was talking about Bernard. "Working for him is not all that it's cracked up to be. He's been worrying me lately."

"How so?" Mark said, not really paying attention. His fingers stroked her hand.

She looked at him. Her lips were moist and inviting. "I think he's . . . I don't know how to explain it."

Mark leaned close to her, their faces inches apart. "You think he's under a lot of stress?"

Carol nodded.

"How much do you know about what he does?"

"A lot," Carol said, her eyes locked on Mark's.

They looked into each other's eyes for a moment, lost in each other.

"And what do you see?"

"Bad things."

The music throbbed loudly amid the roar of the crowd. Mark's heart raced as he gazed into Carol's eyes. *She suspects something*, he thought.

Carol leaned closer and kissed him.

The kiss didn't come as a total surprise; he could feel the energy building up to it. He kissed her back tenderly and his skin tingled as he felt her arms go around him. He pulled her closer as the kiss grew

GET UP TO 4 FREE BOOKS!

You can have the best fiction delivered to your door for less than what you'd pay in a bookstore or online—only $4.25 a book! Sign up for our book clubs today, and we'll send you **FREE* BOOKS** just for trying it out...**with no obligation to buy, ever!**

LEISURE HORROR BOOK CLUB

With more award-winning horror authors than any other publisher, it's easy to see why CNN.com says "Leisure Books has been leading the way in paperback horror novels." Your shipments will include authors such as RICHARD LAYMON, DOUGLAS CLEGG, JACK KETCHUM, MARY ANN MITCHELL, and many more.

LEISURE THRILLER BOOK CLUB

If you love fast-paced page-turners, you won't want to miss any of the books in Leisure's thriller line. Filled with gripping tension and edge-of-your-seat excitement, these titles feature everything from psychological suspense to legal thrillers to police procedurals and more!

As a book club member you also receive the following special benefits:

- **30% OFF all orders through our website & telecenter!**
- **Exclusive access to special discounts!**
- **Convenient home delivery and 10 days to return any books you don't want to keep.**

There is no minimum number of books to buy, and you may cancel membership at any time. See back to sign up!

*Please include $2.00 for shipping and handling.

YES! ☐

Sign me up for the Leisure Horror Book Club and send my TWO FREE BOOKS! If I choose to stay in the club, I will pay only $8.50* each month, a savings of $5.48!

YES! ☐

Sign me up for the Leisure Thriller Book Club and send my TWO FREE BOOKS! If I choose to stay in the club, I will pay only $8.50* each month, a savings of $5.48!

NAME: _____

ADDRESS: _____

_____

TELEPHONE: _____

E-MAIL: _____

☐ **I WANT TO PAY BY CREDIT CARD.**

☐ VISA   ☐ MasterCard   ☐ DISCOVER

ACCOUNT #: _____

EXPIRATION DATE: _____

SIGNATURE: _____

Send this card along with $2.00 shipping & handling for each club you wish to join, to:

Horror/Thriller Book Clubs
1 Mechanic Street
Norwalk, CT 06850-3431

Or fax (must include credit card information!) to: 610.995.9274.
You can also sign up online at www.dorchesterpub.com.

*Plus $2.00 for shipping. Offer open to residents of the U.S. and Canada only.
Canadian residents please call 1.800.481.9191 for pricing information.
If under 18, a parent or guardian must sign. Terms, prices and conditions subject to change. Subscription subject
to acceptance. Dorchester Publishing reserves the right to reject any order or cancel any subscription.

JOIN NOW!

and everything else was forgotten: the club, his friends, what people would say at work if they found out he had been seen making out with Carol Emrich at Baxter's. All that mattered was being in her arms, kissing her, feeling her close to him.

When the kiss broke Mark looked into her eyes, their faces close together, their lips barely touching. Part of him wanted to say something to her, tell her he knew what was going on with Bernard, but he held it in. Whatever it was she had been on the verge of telling him, it was forgotten. "I don't want to talk about work right now," she said.

"I don't either," Mark said, kissing her again.

"Let's go," Carol said. She reached down to take his hand and brushed the bulging strain of his crotch.

"Yeah, let's go," Mark said. He slid out of the seat and, leading her by the hand, they threaded their way through the smoky, thronging mob. The desire for each other was strong; it propelled them through the club and out into the chilly evening with hungry abandon. Once outside, Mark put his arm around her waist. Whatever hint of a buzz he had gotten from the alcohol was gone now.

He followed her to her condominium in Huntington Beach. The minute they crossed the threshold she was in his arms, kissing him, her fingers fumbling with his clothes. They left a trail of clothing up the carpeted stairs to her bedroom, where they spent the next three hours making love as if it was the last thing they would ever do.

Chapter Fifteen

The first weekend he had ever spent the entire weekend in bed was when he met Carol Emrich.

With the exception of a brief sojourn to his apartment for toiletries and a change of clothes; a brief stroll through the Huntington Beach Promenade early Saturday night; and dinner in a cozy restaurant, Mark and Carol spent that entire weekend in bed. When they weren't making love they were reclining against the headboard, talking, watching TV, nibbling on take-out Chinese food, or simply snuggling. The only time they weren't in bed—with the exception of Saturday night—was Saturday morning and Sunday morning, when they took a long, leisurely bath together.

Mark tried to tell himself that he wasn't falling in love with Carol that first weekend. The more they talked, the more they kissed, the more they made love, the more he had to tell himself that this was simply a weekend fling. It was a meeting of the flesh, a mutual inclination for carnal desire. He wasn't really falling in love with her, and she surely wasn't falling in love with him.

He tried to reassure himself of that fact when he finally left her place Sunday morning. "I'm going to miss you," Carol said, smiling as she walked him downstairs. She was dressed in a red satin bathrobe.

"I'm going to miss you too," Mark smiled back. "But hey, I'll see you tomorrow, right?"

"Of course."

During the course of that weekend they had decided to keep their relationship under wraps. During the Saturday morning sobering up, they discussed the possible repercussions they would be facing via the rumor mill come Monday morning, and what the long-term effects would be. Mark, for one, was petrified that Bernard would find out. And while she had tried to remain cool about it, he could tell that Carol was worried about it as well. "If anybody says anything or asks, we'll just tell them that we got drunk and danced a lot," she said. "I don't remember seeing anybody from work as we left. For all we know, they could have all split before we even hit the dance floor."

While that was a distinct possibility, Mark wanted to make sure. So when he went to his apartment to gather a few things he had called John Rizzo, one of his coworkers whom he had gone to Baxter's with. "Hey, so what happened to you guys last night?" he had asked.

"You tell me, guy," John said. "It looked like you were having a pretty intense conversation with the Big Chief's secretary. So give me the juicy details."

"What details? We were just talking."

"Just talking, huh? Yeah, and monkeys might fly out my ass."

"It's true. Besides, I tried looking for you guys and you were gone."

"That's because the place got so fucking crowded, you couldn't hear anybody you were talking to. And besides, those people from Quality Control were there and they're as annoying as shit, so we left."

"And you *left* me?"

John chuckled. "Like I said, you appeared to be having a good time. Besides, you're a big boy. I'm sure that after you fucked her, you just drove yourself on home."

It took fifteen minutes to convince John that he didn't do what he really did. The more he tried to convince him, the more he became annoyed with himself for even having to do so. What business was it of John's or any of his coworkers to know who he had done the bone dance with anyway? If it was anybody else, Mark would have admitted it freely, and might have spilled details. Because it was Carol Emrich—a woman with not only a reputation, but who was Bernard Roberts's secretary—meant that he had to keep it under wraps. Because if the guys were convinced it had happened, it would spread and get back to Bernard. Carol had already told him that she didn't want that to happen, and he had his own reasons for not wanting it to get around.

"Okay, so you hung out and talked for a really long time and got drunk," John finally admitted after Mark kept hammering that point home. "But I bet you wanted to fuck her, didn't you?"

"Who wouldn't?" Mark laughed.

He came away from the phone call feeling fairly satisfied that John was convinced nothing had happened between him and Carol.

That Monday at work proved to be the testing point. With the exception of Shawn Jackson trying to pick the details out of him, nobody asked him about what happened Friday night. As the day wore on Mark grew more relaxed; it was obvious that John believed him and the other guys had either been too inebriated themselves, or didn't care. By the end of the day he left work feeling almost one hundred percent confident that nobody had paid attention to him and Carol at the bar. If anybody in Quality Control had seen them, the story would have been all over the building and he would have heard something. The fact that that hadn't happened was nothing short of a miracle.

He met Carol that evening at Charlie's over drinks and dinner. "How did it go with you?" he asked.

"Fine." Carol smiled at him from across the table. She was dressed in a pair of blue jeans that clung to her shapely legs, and a black, long-sleeved sweater. Her hair was brushed back into a ponytail and her makeup was sparse. "Fortunately for me, the people I work with all day don't get into the night-life scene, and don't associate much with the crowd downstairs. None of them know that I sometimes tag along with some of the people in Data Processing, so nobody knew that I had been at Baxter's."

"Not even Bernard?"

"Not even Bernard."

The question had been burning in Mark's mind all

weekend and now he was bursting at the seams to ask it. "What did you mean the other night when you said that . . . you knew bad things about Bernard?"

Carol looked down at the table, then back at Mark. She looked hesitant. She gave him a weak smile. "Nothing," she said. "I guess I was just drunk."

"Really," Mark said, reaching across the table and taking her hands in his. He leaned forward. "You can tell me."

"I said it's nothing."

Mark decided to shift gears. "Okay. But you can tell me anything you want. I won't . . . I won't say anything you tell me in confidence. You can always trust me. Okay?"

Carol nodded and Mark smiled. That seemed to be the end of the subject for the evening.

He thought about it for the rest of the week, though.

Mark and Carol didn't see each other for the remainder of the week, but they kept in touch by phone, talking long into the night. Carol told Mark more about herself than he figured anybody at work ever knew about her; that she had been elected homecoming queen in high school; that she had majored in English Literature in college and actually received a BA in it from the University of Nebraska. "But what kind of job can you get with a degree in English Lit?" she said, laughing. "I surely didn't start out intending to be an executive secretary."

What she had started out doing was moving out to California when she was twenty-two, shortly after graduating from college. She took a job as a proof-reader in a print shop, but it didn't pay well. It was the following week, when they were in bed at her place, that she told Mark that she had supplemented her income for a few years as a stripper.

"Really? Who would have thought?" Mark said, his left arm draped casually around her bare shoulders. During the course of the week she told him that she had a younger brother, her father was an electrical engineer, and her mother was a high school teacher. He also learned that she was at least three years older than him.

She slapped him playfully. "I just did it for the money. Thanks to that job, I met a guy at the club who was a recruiter for Free State. He got me my first secretarial position and I was able to quit stripping. The secretarial position paid less, but it was better than that other job I had. Plus, despite all you hear, being a stripper isn't as glamorous as it seems."

"I didn't think it was."

He refrained from asking her how she moved up in her secretarial positions. She freely divulged the information. And the more she opened herself up, the more he realized that Carol Emrich was a victim of office innuendo; she had been far better as a secretary than her predecessor. She got a raise four months into the job. Another supervisor in her division liked her work, and three months later she was at a bigger desk, at a higher position, with more responsibilities and higher pay. And over the next four years she climbed up through various positions, each one better than the previous one. "I know what they say about me at work," she said. She looked up into Mark's face. "I know you probably heard all . . . all those—"

"Stop," he said, putting a finger to her lips.

She took his hand and kissed it. She sniffled, wiped her eyes with the back of her hand. "I've never fucked anybody to get a job before. Never! The guy that hired me into my second job in Quality Control fired his secretary to get me. The secretary he had was a fucking idiot. The woman couldn't type worth shit, couldn't compose a memo, didn't know how to file—she was completely worthless. She had been at that desk before he had gotten that job and he was trying to help her improve her skills, but it wasn't working. So he had her fired and he brought me in." She paused. "It turned out she was friends with Terry Stewart in Q.C. They were like this." She held up her hand, index and middle finger crossed together. "Gayle, the woman I replaced, was convinced I got the job because I was young and pretty, and she was old and fat. Old and fat had nothing to do with it. She was stupid. But that didn't matter to Terry. Her friend had been fired and she was convinced that I had something to do with it. After all, my boss—Greg Donahue—was a man, and you know how men react around women who look like me." Carol burst into tears.

Mark awkwardly tried to comfort her. He put his arms around her, feeling stupid for not knowing what to do or say. "Carol, it's okay," he said.

Carol's voice hitched as she stifled the tears. "No, it's *not* okay. I didn't ask to be born with a pretty face, a . . . a . . . good body. B-but . . . I was, and every man I've dealt with takes one look at my boobs, and then my face and they fall all over themselves trying to give me what I'm trying to work honestly at getting. And they always want something in return. I've been living with . . . with . . . *shit* like this all my life. I'm *tired* of it!"

She cried some more and all Mark could do was hold her, comforting her the best he could. After five minutes or so her crying subsided into sniffles.

"If it makes you feel any better," Mark said, brushing her hair back from her face and tilting it up to meet his. "I am not with you because of the way you look. I really like you for who you are."

"Oh, Mark," Carol said, her fingers touching his face. "That's really sweet, but—"

"No buts," Mark said. He brushed a tear away from her cheek and kissed her. "I admit I may have been swept up in your beauty last week, but as this week has gone by I've gotten to know the person inside." He tapped her chest above the swell of her breasts. "And the person I've gotten to know is the person I've fallen in love with."

Carol looked up at him, taken aback. *Christ, I've said it now*, he thought. He had been telling himself for the past week he wasn't falling in love with her, but he had to face the facts that he really was. He felt his pulse quicken.

"Are you serious?" Carol asked, gazing up at him, her eyes imploring him to tell the truth.

He nodded, swooning from the realization. "I am."

"Don't lie to me if you don't mean what you just said."

"I mean what I just said," Mark said, drawing her closer to him, holding her close.

What transpired next was best left to the expression of the physical action of love.

* * *

The Christmas season was a wonderful time to be in love.

For the next few weeks, Mark Wiseman and Carol Emrich spent as much time together as they could. They were like two kids in a candy store. Weekends were spent at either Carol's condo in Huntington Beach, or at Mark's Costa Mesa apartment. Weeknights were spent on the phone talking, or in corner booths in darkened restaurants talking over coffee. As Christmas approached, they grew closer and closer. Carol finally admitted that even though she had never slept with anybody to climb up the corporate ladder, she did admit to an affair with Bernard Roberts. "But it's over," she said one night at his place. "I haven't seen him since late November. I don't know what I saw in him in the first place."

Mark was a little surprised to hear the confession, but he hadn't been shocked. After all, Bernard had alluded to an affair that summer, although at the time Mark had no idea it was with his secretary. It was obvious then and now that he had regarded Carol as nothing more than what the rumor mill in Free State had trumped her up as: a cheap whore, a status fucker, a woman whose only worth was what lay between her legs. Carol had known about the rumors that Terry Stewart had started and was hurt by them, but she also knew herself for who she was. "It doesn't matter what others say about me," she said one night. "After all, I have my friends outside of work. They're more important to me than what people here say. I have my life, which is more important than anything I will ever accomplish in this fucking company. But I've got to admit, after hearing sick lies about yourself for four years, they eventually get to you."

For the first time in six years, Carol wasn't flying home to Nebraska for the Christmas holiday, but she was taking the week between Christmas and New Year's off. Mark had already told her weeks before that both his parents were dead, that they had been killed in an auto accident. He revealed a little of his past, but not the part about his curse. He figured that when the time came for the moon to wax, he would simply pretend to be ill and unavailable. He said nothing about the murders, or Bernard's blackmail attempt.

But they did talk about Bernard Roberts. Extensively.

He came up in conversation a few times a week, always in an unfavorable light. Carol described him as a manipulative, controlling man. "He's somebody who takes advantage of people," she said. "I saw it when I was with him, and God knows why I stayed with him."

"You stayed with him because you were enamored with his other qualities," Mark replied. They had been talking at her place. They were sitting in the living room, the stereo turned to an Enya CD. "After all, he's a good-looking man."

"Yes, he is," Carol said. "But sometimes I think he can be dangerous."

"Why is that?"

Carol wouldn't elaborate. Mark didn't press the issue. In the end, they decided it was imperative that they keep their relationship a secret. "After all, he's been calling me a lot lately," Carol said. "He just called me two nights ago. He wanted to take me to Vail for a skiing trip over the holidays. I told him I was going back to Nebraska to visit my parents."

"Have you thought about just . . . well, breaking it off with him?"

"More than once."

"Why don't you?"

"It isn't as easy as you might think. After all, he *is* my boss."

It was that notion that decided it for her: After the holidays she was going to look for another job.

But first, there were the holidays . . .

They spent them together. They flew up to San Francisco on December 22 and spent Christmas Eve in a charming cottage along the California coast, just an hour south of the city. A colleague of her father's owned it, and Carol was able to rent it for the week. They spent seven days at the cottage and had a wonderful Christmas morning together. They even bought a little tree, draping it with tinsel and decorations. They placed their carefully wrapped gifts to each other under the tree on Christmas Eve and opened them the next morning with the eagerness of young children. Mark smiled as Carol peeled the paper back on a box of perfume from Macy's; he was swept up in a hug when she opened the box containing a diamond necklace. "It's beautiful, Mark, but you shouldn't have. How could you afford—"

"It's okay," Mark said, smiling. The necklace had cost him five thousand dollars. It had been the first thing he had bought with the blood money he had earned from Bernard.

"Thank you."

But her favorite gift was one he'd found in a secondhand bookstore. She unwrapped it slowly, her mouth opening in surprise as she uncovered the book and held it up. "Oh my God! I can't believe it! Where did you *find* this?"

"Book Baron in Anaheim," Mark said, grinning.

Carol turned the book over in her hands. "Do have any idea how long I've been trying to find this?"

"I don't know, but when you said it had been your favorite book as a child . . ." Mark shrugged, letting it trail off. He smiled as she flipped open the book, paging through it. The book in question was a first edition of John Steinbeck's *Of Mice and Men*. Carol had a paperback copy of the book, but she had told Mark during one of their conversations that she had once had a first edition of the book, given to her by her grandfather. "It got lost somehow," she had said. "I was devastated. That book meant so much to me."

Carol was gushing with excitement. "I just don't believe this . . . this must have cost you a fortune!"

"It wasn't that expensive," Mark grinned, the lie slipping through effortlessly. He had paid almost two grand for the book.

"I just can't believe it," she said, sweeping Mark up in a hug. "Thank you."

Mark was equally surprised with his gifts. A brand-new sweater, a bottle of cologne, and some CD's that he had been wanting. But it was the last gift he opened that had been his favorite. He held it up, his heart swelling as he held it in his hands. It was a harmonica. Carol smiled at him. "You said you used to play a mean harmonica when you were a kid, so . . ."

"I did," Mark said, cupping the instrument in his hands. He looked across at Carol. "Thank you."

They spent the next few days at the cottage, traveling into the city for sightseeing, eating in quaint little restaurants. They spent their evenings at the cottage making love in front of a warm fire. They flew back to Irvine on December 29, and spent the rest of their holiday at Carol's condo. There were three messages on Carol's answering machine from Bernard; on the last one he said he had just called to wish her a Merry Christmas, and was spending the holidays with his brother and sister-in-law in Iowa, but would call January 3 when he came back. Maybe they could go out. "Not on your life," Carol said, pressing the rewind button.

They returned to their jobs and maintaining the illusion that they weren't a romantic item on January 4. Carol called him that night, her voice tinged with annoyance. "First thing Bernard did when he came in was ask to meet with me in his office," she said. "I go in there, he closes the door and starts trying to kiss me. I pushed away from him and told him, 'Look, I don't think we should be doing this anymore.'"

"What did he say?"

"He was confused. He just kept trying to, you know, paw at me. I finally told him that I was sending my resume out and was looking for another job. And that I wasn't interested in him romantically anymore. He wouldn't accept it until I told him I had met somebody else. Then he got the message."

"Naturally, you didn't tell him who you were seeing."

"Of course not."

"Were you ever . . . interested in him romantically?" The last few times Bernard had come up in conversation, Mark had felt a flare of jealousy.

"The truth?"

"Yeah."

"Not at all," she said. "I used him sexually as much as he used me. He meant nothing to me."

"And me?"

"You mean the world to me."

Hearing her say that warmed his heart. "You mean the world to me, too."

As good as Carol's words made him feel, Mark's heart felt heavy with dread. A rendezvous of his own with Bernard was coming up, one he couldn't back out of. For a moment, Mark thought that he should just dump it all: take Carol and flee California, retreating into the wilds with her. But part of him knew that Bernard would be close on his trail, hunting him down. And he knew that as long as he was in his human form, he would be vulnerable to law enforcement; after all, Bernard had him by the short end of the stick. Even if he did get away, Bernard would tip the police to his involvement in the murders. Then he'd be the subject of a nationwide manhunt.

It was this thought that almost made him tell Carol everything, but he held back. He would wait and see what became of this upcoming meeting. If the plans to merge Free State were scrapped, then he had nothing to worry about; Bernard would leave him alone, and that would be the end of it. But if the plans were still on the drawing board . . .

. . . if Bernard still wanted him to hunt and kill . . . God help him.

They met the following week, on a Tuesday night, at the usual location: the Huntington Beach Pier.

Mark was waiting for Bernard at the end of the pier. He approached, dressed in a long trenchcoat, a black shirt and slacks. "Hello, Mark," Bernard said.

"So what's the scoop?"

"No formalities?" Bernard asked, moving to the rail to peer out into the ocean. "What happened to, 'Hi Bernard. How are things? How were your Christmas holidays?'"

Mark sidestepped the question. "I just want to hear the latest news. Are we going through with the next one, or not?"

Bernard smiled. "Can't wait to get on with the hunt, can you?"

"You could say that." In reality he wanted to cut through the bullshit and find out what was going on.

"Good! I love it when I hear enthusiasm over a job." Bernard stepped back, hands in his trenchcoat pockets. "There is a man named George Fielding on the list. He lives in Las Vegas. He has successfully convinced those few fence sitters on the board to vote for the merger this spring. He needs to be taken out."

"Why not just take out the fence sitters?" Mark asked.

Bernard looked at him curiously. "Are you questioning me on this?"

"No. Not at all."

"It sure sounded like it."

Mark shrugged. "I just thought that if we took out the fence sitters, that would cut out the opposition. You know, strike at the marrow of this thing."

Bernard regarded Mark for a moment, as if he were some new species of insect. Then he burst out laughing. "Oh, Mark. I love it! You're really involved in this, aren't you?"

Mark shrugged. "I just want to get this over with. That's all."

"And we will, Mark. Don't worry, we will." Bernard stepped closer to him, his features menacing. "But I don't need you to question my plan. I have my reasons for wanting George taken out, not the least of which is his influence on the board. Once he's gone, I'll worry about the others."

Mark nodded. The way Bernard had said that made him think that Bernard was into this for reasons other than simply saving his hide. It had been a few months since he thought about why Bernard was using him to kill the board members, and now as he stood on the pier with Bernard it suddenly hit him: *It's not just his hide he wants to save. He's enacting some other deep, hidden vendetta. Because if he really wanted to save his hide, he'd have me go after one of the board members that were fence sitters. He wouldn't go after this George Fielding guy.* "When?" Mark asked, resigning himself to the fact that this mad game had to continue.

Bernard turned toward the ocean. "This weekend. You have the address and the dossier on George. Make it look like the last one."

Mark was silent for a moment. From what he remembered, George Fielding lived on the outskirts of Las Vegas, in a big custom-built house with a top-notch security system. Breaching the system would be difficult, but he should be able to get past it. He'd been studying security systems with the vague hope of bypassing Bernard's some day. "Any changes to his security system since last summer?"

"None," Bernard said. "In fact, he was recently divorced. He's been spending his evenings alone." Bernard reached into his coat pocket and pulled out an envelope. He handed it to Mark. "You leave Friday evening, out of John Wayne Airport at eight-fifteen. Your return flight is midnight, Sunday. I expect to talk to you Sunday at noon, at the phone booth on the corner of Ellis and Beach Boulevard at the Jack-in-the-Box. Got it?"

"Got it." Mark took the envelope, turned, and started heading back down the pier.

"Oh, and Mark?"

Mark turned around. "Yeah?"

"It won't be long now." Bernard grinned.

Mark mustered a weak smile, then turned and headed toward the parking lot where his car was. He wished he could believe Bernard.

Chapter Sixteen

Mark replayed the conversation in his mind as he reclined in his seat on Flight 798, from Irvine to Las Vegas.

"Remember the buddies from high school I told you about a few weeks ago? Doug and Paul Lewison? Well, they invited me on a trip to their cabin this weekend. They wanted it to be just us guys, give us a chance to catch up on what we've been doing the past year." This was the lie he had given Carol during idle conversation a few nights ago. He'd mentioned that sometimes he took off for a few days at a time to hang out with Doug and Paul, a ruse to provide cover on those nights when the moon affected him.

"When can I meet them? They sound like great guys."

"You will. I promise."

He sat back in his seat, a glass of bourbon in hand, his eyes set on the vast black night stretching out past his window. He hated lying to Carol, but he didn't know how else to break the news that he was going to be gone this weekend. It was the first time he'd had to deal with his lycanthropic state since they had been together. He didn't know what he was going to tell her if they were still together a month from now; or a year.

Mark smiled to himself at the thought of still being with Carol in a year. He was thinking about that a lot now. It was romantic, wishful thinking, but part of him knew that it would never be. He couldn't keep this secret from her much longer. And when she found out would she still want him?

Mark sipped his drink. Somehow, he felt that she would. Because in the last few days he had the feeling that Carol was struggling with something herself. He supposed it might have been his imagination, but he got the feeling that she sensed something was going on. She definitely knew something was up with Bernard, but to what extent, Mark wasn't sure. She told him this morning as they were getting ready for work, both of them dressing with phones in hand, that she had overheard Bernard in his office the other day trying to talk one of the board members out of something. "I think he's been pulling some shit behind their backs," Carol had said. "He kept saying, 'No it wasn't me,' and 'Look, I can prove I didn't have anything to do with it.' It kept going on and on, and I could tell it was bothering him. He was jumpy and nervous all day yesterday."

Mark had given her his opinion. "You think he might be up to something illegal? Fraud, or something?"

"I wouldn't put it past him," Carol had said. "It might explain why he's so against this merger."

"So you know about that, then?"

"Oh yeah. I've been in on that since the beginning. Bernard has always been adamantly against it."

"Why do you think that is?"

There had been a short, pregnant pause. Then Carol had said, "Between you and me? Bernard has been in charge of some of the funds at Free State. I think he's been abusing his power. I think he's been passing information on to our competitors and pocketing the profits."

"So he's committing fraud?"

"That and more than I'd even care to think about."

He had let the issue hang at that, told her he'd talk to her in a few days when he returned from his trip to Big Bear with his friends. And now he sat in his seat, turning the issue over in his mind. Carol knew something. She might even suspect that Bernard was behind the foul play regarding the murders of his colleagues. But she would never suspect Mark's involvement in it. Not unless he told her.

As the plane prepared for landing at McCarran International Airport, a white-hot feeling of hatred enveloped Mark. He clenched his fists as the plane's wheels hit the concrete, his teeth gritted as the brakes were applied to slow the big jet down. He had never felt as much hatred for another human being as he felt for Bernard Roberts. He hated Bernard more than he had hated his father. Dad had been a drunk, an abuser of his wife and only son, and he had been the type of man who picked fights with other men when he was intoxicated. But he hadn't been as downright evil as•Bernard was; he never relished control over other people the way Bernard did. He hadn't been a lying, self-righteous hypocrite the way Bernard was. When Mark thought about how Bernard had used both he and Carol—especially Carol—the urge to kill him surged stronger than ever.

As the plane cruised into the terminal Mark's mind raced. He felt like a pawn in Bernard's little game. He felt a brief flurry of anger for letting himself get caught up in it, but he dashed it aside. He was as much a victim as the three executives he had killed for Bernard. There was no way he could go through with the execution of George Fielding.

The plane finally stopped at the terminal. People began rising from their seats and extracting luggage from overhead compartments. Mark stood up and reached for his carry-on luggage, not looking at his fellow passengers as he grabbed his bag and made his way out of the plane. Tomorrow was the first night of the full moon. Already he could feel the power of the moon pulling at the curse inside him. He couldn't go through with the murder of George Fielding. But he knew that if he didn't he would be facing the consequences.

Mark Wiseman sat in his rental car—a white Ford Escort—in a housing tract in North Las Vegas, which was an upper-class area of the city where the rich retreated from the world.

It was six p.m., the evening following his arrival in Las Vegas. The curse was running strong through his veins, begging for release. Mark gripped the steering wheel, his knuckles growing white. He was feeling quite stoned from last evening and this morning; he had spent much of that time at the hotel casino drinking and playing blackjack, losing money without caring. It was money that Bernard had given him. "For pursuing whatever vice you want," he had said two nights ago when the two had met again. "In fact, if I were you, I'd buy myself one of those nice, high-priced whores. You need to let loose, my friend."

Mark had let loose all right. The minute he arrived at the Golden Nugget, a cheesy hotel at the eastern edge of the strip, he had headed straight for the casino. He had spent the rest of the evening playing slot machines, craps, and blackjack and getting completely shit-faced drunk.

Finally, at two a.m., he had retired to his room and opened the liquor cabinet. He had opened a bottle of Scotch and drank half of it before passing out in his bed.

He had awakened at ten-thirty with a splitting headache and a dry mouth. He'd drunk some water, then showered, his head pounding the entire time. When he was finished with the shower he had taken a few shots of the Scotch to calm his shaky nerves and ease his head. It had seemed to help. By the time he was dressed, he'd felt better and the Scotch was gone. He'd headed downstairs for breakfast, and had not only gotten some food into himself, but he'd gotten drunk again at the hotel bar. By three p.m. he was wasted again.

It had been years since he had used liquor to escape from his problems, and that's what he was doing now. He did not want to go through with this hit tonight. He couldn't kill another innocent person for Bernard, but he didn't know what else to do. If he didn't go through with it, Bernard would kill him. He was sure of it. And if he were to take off from Vegas, just get in the rental car and drive to points east, Bernard would find him. He would alert the authorities with the information that Mark was the culprit in the murders of the three board members. He would produce the evidence needed. They would be able to get access to Mark's information at work, and within the space of a day his mug shot—courtesy of his employee ID badge—would be plastered all over every law enforcement agency in the country.

Mark had no choice. He had to go through with it.

Mark sat in the car quietly, his mind woozy from alcohol. He had slept for a few hours before showering, changing, getting a small baggie to stow his clothes in, and some toiletries he would need to clean himself with after the job was done. He had performed these tasks in a semi-drunken state, pausing every now and then to sip from a bottle of vodka. By the time he headed out toward North Las Vegas, he was well on the way to being shit-faced again.

As he drove he kept hoping he would be pulled over by a Las Vegas Police car.

That never happened.

He found the neighborhood and drove until he found George Fielding's home. It was in an exclusive neighborhood and it sat on a small crest, surrounded by a concrete fence. The driveway was long, blocked off by a large, wrought iron gate. It was like a castle in the middle of the desert. Mark made a note of it, and drove on, cruising half a mile to the subdivision a few developments over, where he parked and waited for nightfall.

The pull of the moon had been strong since yesterday. Only now it was tugging at him fiercely. He had driven around the area, looking for a remote spot where he might stow his clothes, but there was none to be found. The land was all desert, with no cover for miles. He couldn't very well change in his car, then walk the half mile in his lupine state unless he wanted to attract attention. Therefore he would have to drive over to George Fielding's home, break in undetected, and shapeshift in the house somehow without being seen.

He could do that! Mark chuckled, started the car, and pulled away from the curb, heading toward George Fielding's spacious mansion.

Once there, he parked the car at the curb next to the large gate. The street was quiet. He got out of the car and closed the door. A cold wind blew from the north, but it didn't faze him. He sniffed the air; the inhabitants of this neighborhood were all in their homes, some were sitting down to a late supper. As for George Fielding, he was home. Mark tried to listen for sounds amid the rising wind, but couldn't get an accurate read on what was going on. Nevertheless, George Fielding was home, and he was alone and vulnerable. Time to get this show on the road.

Mark Wiseman circled the grounds and noted the signs erected by Base Security. He figured the security system was activated, but who gave a fuck? If security came all he had to do was lie in wait for them and then—wham! Reduce those amateur police officers to bloody tatters of bone and ripped flesh. No problem.

Mark Wiseman grunted, pulled himself up on a rock, then stood on a sturdy bush that rested by the north side of the wall. His fingers gripped the top of the wall and, using all his strength, he pulled himself up on the wall, swinging his legs over. For a minute his vertigo swam; he was still drunk, but fuck it. He had a job to do, and he might as well do it. What did he have to live for, anyway? Even if he successfully pulled this off, even if he managed to kill everybody on the Board of Directors for both companies, Bernard Roberts still wouldn't be satisfied. As long as he knew Mark's secret and had those photos, Mark would be under Bernard's thumb for the rest of his life.

Mark dropped to the ground on the other side of the fence. He crouched there for a moment, ears alert to the slightest sound. He didn't hear an alarm, but if there was one, it could be silent. If that was the case he had to move quickly. He sprinted across the grounds, keeping to the shadows as he traveled the side of the house to George's back deck. He climbed onto the deck, then paused to listen. All was silent. George was somewhere upstairs, that much he could tell with his sense of smell. Mark sniffed the air, catching a whiff of soap, cologne, and steam. He smiled. George Fielding was in the shower. Perfect.

Mark burped loudly, then walked to the back door. He touched the doorknob and twisted it. Locked. He looked around the back deck, noting the windows were all secure and locked. If he hadn't set the alarm off by going over the gate he would surely set it if he broke the window. But maybe George Fielding hadn't set his alarm yet. A lot of people didn't set their alarms until they went to sleep or left the premises. *I would think if he's showering he has the alarm on*, Mark thought, looking for something with which to smash the window. He found a gardening tool on a table, picked it up, and turned to the plate-glass door. *Here goes nothing*, he thought, as he swung the tool at the door.

The glass shattered in a loud explosion. Mark winced at the suddenness of the sound and tensed up, waiting for the cloying beep of the alarm system. It never came.

Mark stepped inside the house warily, his senses on full alert. He saw the keypad of the alarm system right away, positioned by the kitchen phone. It was on, but it wasn't activated. Which meant that he and George were here alone. Mark chuckled drunkenly and almost tripped as he strode across the kitchen to the dining room. His mouth was dry and his head was ringing. *Damn, but I'm thirsty*, he thought. His stomach muscles clenched in his abdomen.

He was just beginning to ascend to the second floor when a man stepped out from the second-floor hallway. He had a towel wrapped around his portly waist, and his gray hair was dripping wet. There was light from the kitchen below, and a light coming from somewhere on the second floor illuminated the second-floor landing. George Fielding took one look at Mark and almost let go of the towel he was holding around his waist. "What the—"

The man's sudden appearance on the landing took

Mark Wiseman completely by surprise. For a moment he was too stunned to react; the alcohol in his system had slowed his reflexes. His stomach lurched and Mark felt the curse struggle to the surface. He let it out, feeling it ripple over him, changing him almost instantly. Mark could dimly hear George Fielding give a startled yelp as Mark bounded up the steps after him, and then he was on him.

He launched himself at George Fielding as the older man ran down the hall to the master bedroom. Mark crashed into him, bringing him down to the plush carpeting with a bone-crunching smash. The air whooshed out of George Fielding, and the momentum created a sickening surge in Mark's stomach. His head swam. All the scents in the house: of soap and warm water, of cologne and shampoo, of steam and hair and sweat, were swimming dizzily in his head, making him sick. George screamed and tried to scramble away and Mark pushed down on his back, his claws gouging the flesh. Blood spurted. George screamed again.

Mark brought his jaws down to clamp onto the back of George's neck, but George's thrashings made him miss his mark; instead, he tore out a chunk of the man's shoulder, sending him into a frenzy. The taste of blood in his mouth simultaneously stoked the curse and his drunkenness; his stomach lurched crazily. The room swam in his vision. It felt like the time he had gone to a frat party and gotten so smashed that when he'd passed a plate of food the mere scent of it had made him sick. The smell of fear, sweat, and blood coming from George Fielding, now coupled with his mad scramble to fight, was making Mark nauseous. The more his brain tried to tell his inebriated muscles to over-power and take down his prey once and for all, the more they failed him.

Mark slashed out and raked deep cuts in George's upper arm. The force of the blow turned the man over on his back, and George yelled when he got a good look at Mark. "Oh my God, *nooooooo!*"

"*Shut up!*" Mark screamed. What came out was a snarl.

George rained blows on Mark's chest. Mark batted them aside, though a few of them met their mark. One glanced across his snout. He slapped George openhandedly. George screamed again.

Mark tried to rip George's throat out with his teeth again, but George scrunched his neck up, his arms flailing out to fight him off. Mark's teeth tore deep furrows into George's upper chest and the bottom of his chin. George screamed, his fists crashing against Mark's skull. *Goddamnit, you miserable fuck*, Mark screamed in his mind. He clamped his jaws over the top of George's head and sank his teeth in. He felt his teeth pierce skin, then bone. George screamed louder, his body thrashed harder. Mark chomped down on the man's skull and was satisfied when he heard a small crunch. George gave one final scream and swung his fist out, smashing into Mark's left eye. The blow knocked Mark back against the wall and his head slammed into it. The room swirled like a tilt-o-whirl and then the sickness surged again, overpowering him. He couldn't fight it any longer. He turned to the side and vomited.

His stomach muscles clenched and unclenched;

wave after wave of nausea washed over him and he threw up. It passed for a moment and Mark was able to catch his breath, then another wave of sickness surged and he dry heaved. Finally, after two minutes of dry heaving, the feeling passed. He fell back against the wall, breathing heavily, drool running down his chin. His vision was blurry. He looked over at George Fielding's limp form sprawled on the hallway floor.

He padded over to it and took a faint whiff. Immediately he was assaulted by nausea, and he had to close his eyes and wait for it to pass. The smell of blood and sweat swirled in his nostrils, making him sicker, and he bent over and dry heaved again, gagging on his bile. When it passed again he regarded the body with bated breath; he couldn't detect breathing and George Fielding was very still. A small pool of blood had gathered on the cream-colored rug beneath the body. Mark felt too sick to make sure that George was dead, but he was fairly confident he was. He had crushed his skull with his jaws; that should have been enough. He moved down the hall into the master bedroom, crying out with relief as fresher air came into his lungs.

He saw himself in the large wall mirror and the thing that glared back at him with haunted, sick eyes was a crude caricature; he had only changed halfway. His features were human but grossly wolfish in appearance, his lower jaw pushed out like a deformed fetus. His teeth sprouted out at crazy angles from his mouth. His body, though more sparsely covered with hair, was still hairier than normal. Only his hands had completed the change, and as he held them up to his face he saw that they were already starting to transform to normal. Sobriety set in almost instantly and within moments he was able to will the change back to human form. He looked at himself in the mirror—his clothes were torn, blood-stained, in disarray, his eyes were sunken, his face pale. Mark began to cry.

He couldn't remain in this depressed state now; he had to get the hell out of here. He exited the room and made his way down the hall, being careful to hold his breath as he came upon George Fielding's corpse. The urge to push the change back through, to lay open George's throat just to make sure he was dead popped into his mind, but he dismissed it. He was still feeling the faint tinges of nausea and to even catch a whiff of George Fielding's blood would bring the sickness back again. Just thinking about it was making him ill, so he clomped down the stairs and made his way through the house to the shattered back door. Once in George Fielding's back yard, he took deep breaths and closed his eyes, willing the sickness to pass. The wind whispered in the winter desert night and the sounds that came back told him that the violence he had wrought in the house had not disturbed the natural rhythms of the evening. He opened his eyes. His vision was no longer blurry and he didn't feel woozy anymore. Mission accomplished.

He made it over the fence and to his car without attracting any attention. He started the car and looked around cautiously; the street was deserted and silent. His nerves settled. Despite the problems he had encountered, he had pulled this off successfully, though barely. Taking a deep breath, Mark put the car in gear and pulled away from the curb. He drove back to his hotel calmly, feeling better the closer he got to the Golden Nugget.

But his hands wouldn't stop shaking.

Chapter Seventeen

The ringing of the telephone woke him up from a sound sleep.

He groaned and reached for the phone with a groping hand. His head still hurt and he was still feeling the effects of two nights of hard drinking. The plane trip home had been murder and he had tried to counterbalance the effect of the alcohol by drinking coffee. While the caffeine had helped, it had made him more wired than anything, and when he'd landed at John Wayne Airport at one-fifteen a.m. he was wide-awake. Thankfully he had been hungry, so he'd driven to a Denny's and eaten a Grand Slam breakfast with two glasses of orange juice. Then he'd driven home and had tried to go to sleep, but the caffeine had done the trick. He'd stayed up until eight o'clock drinking water, trying to replenish his dehydrated system. Finally he'd succumbed to sleep and tumbled into bed.

He glanced at the clock on the nightstand by his

bed. It was two-thirty p.m. It couldn't be Carol; he told her he wouldn't be getting back till six p.m. this evening. He picked the receiver up and brought it slowly to his ear, rubbing his eyes as he raised himself off the bed on his elbow. "Yeah?"

"What the fuck happened?" It was Bernard. He sounded more than angry; he sounded righteously pissed.

An elevator dropped in Mark's stomach. He had completely forgotten the phone rendezvous. "What are you talking about?"

"I'm talking about why the *hell* didn't you *kill* George *Fielding*!" Bernard yelled. "Jesus Fucking *Christ*, you fucked this one up, Mark."

Mark's heart raced. His veins were filled with ice. "That's impossible."

"Believe it. It's not only possible, but it has created a whole fuckload of trouble on my end. Goddamn, *fuck*!" Mark could picture Bernard dressed in a silk dressing gown throwing a temper tantrum in his comfy beachfront home.

"He can't be alive," Mark said, his voice shaking. "I crushed his skull . . . I . . ."

"Well, he is," Bernard said, his voice loud and angry again. "And I am holding you personally responsible if he comes out of it. He comes out of this and lives and you are *fucked*."

"He's in a hospital?"

"Yeah, he's in a fucking hospital. He's in a goddamned coma, but he's alive."

Mark didn't realize he was holding his breath until he exhaled. He sat up in bed, his nerves on edge. "He's in a coma. . . ."

"Yeah, he's in a coma. What the fuck's the matter with you? Can't you fucking hear what I'm saying?"

"I hear you," Mark said. His mind was trying to track on how it could have happened. But he already knew how it had happened; his drinking, his reluctance to go through with another murder. What had happened with George Fielding had been inevitable.

"Did George Fielding see you?"

"No," Mark said, a little too quickly.

"Bullshit!"

"He didn't see me, I'm telling you—"

"Don't fucking bullshit me! You broke his back patio door and gained entrance to his home that way; you probably jumped the fence. If a neighbor didn't see you, George certainly did when you encountered him on the stairs."

Mark was nervous. His hands were shaking as he sat up in bed, his feet on the floor. "L-look," he said. "When George came out onto the landing he surprised me. He put up a fight, I admit, but I got him. I—"

"I don't know what the fuck happened there, but whatever it was it's your death warrant. I'm told the police found a bunch of clues, one of which is the pool of puke you left on the hallway rug."

Mark felt his stomach lurch again at the mention of his sickness. "Shit . . ."

"What the fuck happened to you back there?" Bernard exclaimed, his tone pleading. "Talk to me, Mark. What the fuck happened?"

"I . . . I don't know . . . I . . . thought I got him."

"Christ."

Mark waited, his breath coming in fast and hard.

It sounded like Bernard was trying to control his anger on the other end of the line; he could hear the man pacing the floor. "Look, Bernard . . ."

"For your sake, you better fucking pray that George dies. You got me?"

Mark nodded, shuddering at the tone of George's voice. "He's gonna die, Bernard. Trust me, I . . . I crushed his skull. . . ." Mark winced at the sound of his voice; it was pleading and groveling. He felt pathetic and ashamed of himself.

"I should kill you now," Bernard growled.

"Listen, Bernard," Mark stammered. "It-it's going to be okay. He didn't see much, and what he did see, if he tells anybody they ain't gonna believe him."

"You better fucking hope," Bernard said, and hung up.

Mark held the receiver to his ear, the dial tone echoing. His stomach felt full of lead. He slowly replaced the receiver.

Fuck, what am I gonna do? The question went unanswered as he sat on the bed dressed in his underwear, the blinds shut to block out the sun. His body still felt like it had been put through the ringer.

With a heavy feeling of dread, Mark Wiseman stood up on shaky legs and wobbled to the bathroom where he was sick again.

Chapter Eighteen

Mark was just getting out of the shower when the phone rang again.

He let it ring. It was probably Bernard Roberts calling again to chew him out. He towel-dried his hair and peered into the mirror, noting his gaunt features and his red eyes. He had gotten rid of the beard a few months ago but he hadn't shaved in a few days; stubble graced his cheeks and jaw line. Despite the shower he still felt like shit.

The answering machine picked up; he heard his outgoing message and then there was a click. Carol's voice came through the answering machine speaker. "Hi Mark, it's me. Listen, I know you're probably still gone, but I wanted to call so you'd get this message when you come home." Mark started heading toward the phone. "I've been doing a lot of thinking and—"

Mark picked up the phone. "I'm here."

"Mark?" Carol sounded surprised. "I wasn't expecting you back this early. Have—"

"Can you come over?"

Carol seemed to notice the tension in his voice. "Well, yeah . . . is anything wrong?"

"I can't explain over the phone," Mark said, trying to keep his voice level and calm. "Just come over."

"I'll be there in twenty minutes."

Twenty minutes later Mark was dressed in a fresh pair of jeans and a flannel shirt, his hair halfway dry, the tips lying wetly against his shoulders. He ushered Carol in and swept her up in a hug. Carol laughed and hugged him back. "Mmmm, I'm glad to see you too."

Mark kissed her and when the kiss ended he gazed into her eyes a moment. He had been thinking about what he was going to tell her for the last twenty minutes and while he didn't have a particular script in mind, he knew he was going to finally do it. He had to. She had to know the possible danger she was in. "Come in," he said, leading her by the hand to his sofa. "We've got to talk."

Carol's expression turned to concern as he led her to the couch. "You okay, Mark? What's wrong?"

Mark sat down beside her and took her hands in his. "I need us to be completely honest with each other, Carol. What I have to say may be difficult for you to believe, but . . . well, before I tell you I have to know everything about Bernard. Everything that you even suspect about him. It will help you understand what I'm about to tell you."

Carol's face went ashen, as if she had just received news that her parents had both died. "What do you want to know?"

"You know, or suspect, that Bernard is involved in embezzling Free State. Do you think he has *anything* to do with the deaths of the board members over the past few months?"

Carol looked like she had just been slapped. "How . . . how do you know about those?"

"I know. Now *please* answer my question. Do you think Bernard has anything to do at all with those deaths?"

Carol looked too afraid to answer, but she nodded. She licked her lips. "Yes, I . . . I don't have proof, but I've been suspecting it."

"What do you suspect?"

Carol shrugged. "I don't know. Just that . . . after the second . . . death, Bernard's mood changed. Before, he had been very worried about the merger. He would constantly rave to me about the board and the decisions they made. And while he never came right out and explained why he felt that way, I began suspecting it had something to do with those funds. If they merged they would demand an audit and his fraud would be exposed. He could be arrested, face prison." Carol looked down at the floor, squeezed his hands, then resumed. "Mind you, this is all based on observation. I saw a lot and he told me more than most people at Free State know."

"You never let on to him what you thought?"

Carol shook her head. "Not on your life."

The next question was going to be hard on both of them. "How . . . how did you suspect that Bernard might have something to do with the deaths of the board members, especially concerning the way they were killed?"

Carol was silent for a moment, but Mark could sense that she was struggling for an answer. She sighed and looked at him. "I don't know. It's just . . . a gut feeling I have. Each time there was another . . . death . . . Bernard reacted . . . differently than I would have expected. It was almost like he didn't care. I mean, under normal circumstances I could understand why; after all, his job was in danger of being eliminated. But . . . well, he just seemed *different*. As if he knew what was going on. It was just something I could sense about him."

"Your feelings about this are correct," Mark said. He felt flushed; his hands were trembling.

"What do you mean?" Carol asked, her eyes growing wide. "Do you know more than you're telling me, Mark?"

Mark took a deep breath. "There was another incident . . . an attempted murder." Carol gasped. Mark nodded. "Another board member. A guy named George Fielding from Las Vegas."

"*When?*" Carol asked, her hands darting up to her mouth in shock.

"Yesterday . . . last night," Mark said, avoiding her gaze. He could feel Carol's demeanor change.

"You know what you know because you had something to do with it," Carol said, her face blank with shock. "You killed them didn't you?"

Mark avoided the question. He reached for Carol's hands again. "Before I tell you what I know, I want to tell you that I love you very much." His voice threatened to break. He forced himself to look at her, and he could feel tears springing to his eyes. "I've never felt this way about anyone before. I've never loved anybody the way I love you. You mean so much to me, more than you can ever imagine. I don't want to lose you."

His words seemed to have the right effect. Carol's expression softened. "Oh Mark, I love you too." She swept him up in a hug and for a moment they held each other, taking comfort in each other. Mark held her close with such ferocity he felt if he let her go he would lose her. Carol kissed his cheek, his earlobe. "You're the most incredible man I've ever met," she whispered.

Mark gently extracted himself from her embrace. He took her hands again, and her eyes met his. "I would do anything for you, Carol. I want you to know that. I would do anything for us."

Carol kissed him. "So would I."

"What I have to tell you is about Bernard," he began. "You'll find yourself believing it. He is an utterly evil man, Carol. Utterly evil."

"I know," Carol whispered.

"The other thing I have to tell you is . . . how I've come to know about this . . . my role in it. All I ask is that you remember three things: I love you very much, Bernard set me up, and . . . I haven't been totally honest with you about my past . . ."

It took forty minutes to tell her and through it all she remained entranced by the story, her eyes growing wide in horror and shock at Mark's revelations. He started at the beginning, when he was a seventeen-year-old kid, the only son of two brutal alcoholics, the living hell he had endured both at home and away from it. He told her about the brutal murders of his parents. He told her that he was suspected in their deaths even though evidence clearly pointed at them being attacked by a wolf. He told her about being cleared and his proclamations of innocence. He didn't dare tell her about the curse; he was going to, but decided not to at the last minute. It would be hard enough for her to accept the fact that he had killed people for Bernard.

He told her that despite a lack of physical and circumstantial evidence, he was still a suspect in his parents' deaths. "They could never charge me," he said. "There was no way I could have done it. I wasn't even at the cabin that weekend. I had stayed home. I hated them, but I could never have killed them. Their deaths were devastating to me, but . . . of course they would believe I did it. After all, I had reported them both for domestic abuse, and the neighbors . . . they had known what was going on for years. Of course it was simple to think that I killed them." He looked up at her, wide eyed. "But I didn't. Honest to God, I didn't." He said that with as straight a face as possible; he knew that was only partially true.

He concluded with Bernard's entrapment of blackmail, his threats, and what the executive had told Mark. "I don't know how he found out about my past, but he did," Mark said. "And that's what gave him leverage. Either I do what he told me to do, or he will provide enough planted evidence to tie me to my parents' deaths. There was no way I could get out of it; if I were to go to the authorities, he would kill me. And if I left town . . ." He shuddered. "Whatever information he had would be released to the authorities."

"I still don't understand," she said. At the confession of murder, Carol had withdrawn slightly; she had released her grip on him and settled back, her eyes a little wary. Mark noticed—his heart broke at the sight of it—but made no move to compensate for the damage done. "If what you're telling me is correct—that he's doing this to eliminate influence on the board so the secret of his crimes can remain hidden—why didn't he just hire a professional hit man?"

"The marks of a professional hit man would be obvious," Mark said. He rose from the couch and began pacing the floor. "I . . . I can't go into it anymore than that Carol, but the bottom line is he knew I'd be capable of it. And he knew about my past troubles. He blackmailed me, pure and simple."

"Did you even try going to the police?"

"I . . . yeah, once," Mark lied, running a hand through his still damp hair. "Bernard found out and . . . well, he had a gun. He came over here and threatened me. Said he'd kill me if I talked to the police again." He looked at her pleadingly. "You've got to believe me, Carol. I didn't want to do it. I didn't want to get involved with him, but he . . ." His voice rose to a cry and it cracked as he stifled a sob. His throat hurt. He turned away from her, his breath hitching. "I just kept hoping he would go away, that he . . . he would be found out, that . . . I don't know, that something would happen. It was . . . it was so *horrible* every time I had to . . . go and . . . do this for him. It . . ."

"How did you do it?" Carol asked. She appeared to have regained her composure. She was looking up at him with an open expression, her features calm.

"The official police reports all said that they had been mauled by animals."

Mark's mind raced. "That's how Bernard knew I would be capable of it," he said, quickly. "I . . . don't want to go into it." He turned to her. "Let's just say that . . . I have certain . . . certain . . ."

"Connections?" Carol looked at him curiously. "What did you do? Borrow a wolf or a mountain lion from the Santa Ana Zoo for the night?"

Mark didn't know how to answer that. He turned and walked toward the kitchen.

Carol stood up and walked toward him. Mark was afraid to turn around and face her, afraid of what he might find. His body trembled as she approached him tentatively, and then it erupted into gooseflesh as he felt her arms encircle him from behind. "You're telling me the truth?"

Mark grasped her hands. "Yes."

She was silent for a moment. He thought he could sense her holding back tears. Then: "You know, if it was anybody else I would be out the door in a second."

"What's keeping you here?"

"You," Carol said. Her grip around his waist tightened. Mark felt the tenseness that had developed between them dissipate. "And the fact that what you said sounds like something Bernard would be capable of."

He turned around. "Then you believe me?"

Carol nodded and Mark put his arms around her. She still looked a trifle apprehensive. "Believe me, Mark, I'm very . . . very scared about what you told me. I mean . . . you murdered three people in cold blood."

"I know." He swallowed a dry lump in his throat.

"I know you probably felt trapped by Bernard's blackmail," she continued. "But . . . there had to have been a way out. No matter what the circumstances, there had to have been another way to deal with this."

"I wish there had been," Mark whispered. "But there wasn't. There *still* isn't."

She looked up at him. "You said that . . . this latest one . . . George whatever . . ."

"George Fielding."

"Yes. You said that he was mauled? He's expected to live?"

Mark sighed. "I don't know. Bernard called me over an hour ago and told me. He was pretty pissed."

"I can imagine," Carol said, her lips pressed in a tight grimace. "I've seen him when he doesn't get his own way. He acts like a spoiled child."

"He practically threw a tantrum over the phone," Mark said. "Said that if George Fielding lived that he would kill me."

Carol's gaze never left his face. Mark looked down at her and she melted into his arms. She shuddered in his embrace. "You're afraid of him, aren't you?"

"Yes," Mark said, trying to suppress the chill racing through him.

"So am I," Carol said, her right cheek pressed against his upper chest. "I know what he can be capable of."

They were silent for a moment. They stood in the dark living room of Mark's apartment, holding each other. Finally, Carol said, "What are you going to do?"

"The only thing I can do. Pack up and get the hell out of here. I want you to come with me."

Carol looked up at him, her eyes wide with surprise. "You mean it?"

"Yes." Mark looked down at her. "I want to leave tonight. Just take some clothes and a few things. If George dies, Bernard isn't even going to tell me. He's going to come straight here first and kill me."

Carol kissed him suddenly. "Not if I can help it," she said. "I'm not going to let that bastard do anything to hurt you."

Mark smiled. It felt good to hear Carol suddenly rally behind him. Any other woman would have been aghast at what he had done, but there was something about Carol that was different. It could be her unique perspective on Bernard, gained from both her position behind the secretarial desk and as his mistress, but he also felt that she might perceive both of them as underdogs. She could have empathized with his story due to the way other people at Free State perceived her. Part of the reason Mark initially felt such a strong bond with her was because of her underdog status; he wanted to protect her from further harm by the gossiping and the mistreatment she had suffered at the hands of Bernard. She obviously felt some of the same toward him.

"When are we leaving?" she asked.

"Soon as I get some stuff." He headed toward the bedroom. "Hang out here a bit with me, and then when I'm done we'll go to your place and get your things; then we'll split."

"Okay." She followed him into the bedroom and helped him gather a week's worth of clothes and toiletries in one large duffel bag. "Don't worry about money, either." He pulled out the manila envelope from beneath his mattress and stuck it into the duffel bag. "I've got enough to keep us going for awhile."

"Is that—" She didn't finish the sentence.

Mark nodded. "Yeah. Blood money. But fuck it, what else are we going to do? We can't go to the bank and withdraw our own money or use our credit cards. He'll find us if we do that."

Carol nodded in agreement. Mark donned his black leather jacket and with Carol in tow, they left the apartment together and headed to her place.

Chapter Nineteen

Las Vegas Police Detective Peter Coverdale was just returning to the station when a uniformed officer met him out in the lobby. "Detective Coverdale, there's a private dick waiting at your desk."

"A private dick?" Peter Coverdale was curious. "What's he want?"

"Don't know, but he wouldn't leave a message. He insisted on meeting you personally. He's over there."

Detective Coverdale headed into the bullpen and saw the man immediately. Sitting at a chair by his desk was a tall, slightly overweight man with thinning, sandy blond hair. He was sitting with his back turned to the entrance of the bullpen. "Thanks," Detective Coverdale said. He headed toward his desk.

Detective Peter Coverdale didn't have a lot of time to go chasing after missing persons today—every time a private dick came to see him, it had to do with a missing person. He used to do what he could to assist in such investigations, but spreading himself so thin between his work at the station, and his volunteer time helping with private cases had cost him dearly. Mainly, three wives, and the various property squabbles that came with it. And those had led to a bleeding ulcer at the age of thirty-eight. He had put all that behind him ten years ago and now he tried to take it easy. He came to work, he did his nine to five, he went home. No sweat. And he never did remarry. He wanted to keep his stomach ulcer free.

The private dick stood up at Detective Coverdale's approach. He was dressed in dark slacks and a dark coat. "Detective Coverdale?"

"Officer Smith said you wanted to see me?"

"That's correct." He took out a billfold and presented his credentials. Detective Coverdale gave them a glance. The private dick's name was Allen Frey.

"Have a seat." Detective Coverdale crossed over to his desk and sat down. "What can I do for you, Mr. Fray?"

"It's pronounced Frey," Allen said. "As in french fry."

Detective Coverdale smiled. "Sorry."

"No apologies needed. It's not a common name."

Detective Coverdale nodded. "So what brings you here, Mr. Frey?"

"I'm told that you were just handed a case concerning the mauling of a man named George Fielding," Allen Frey said. "Is that correct?"

Detective Coverdale regarded Allen curiously. It was true, that case had just been opened, although God knew why. The doctors were all saying that

George Fielding had been attacked by a wayward dog that had been crazy enough to smash through the plate glass window of his home. The forensic guys had retrieved a couple of hairs that turned out to be of canine origin, but his superiors still wanted an investigation on the case. Apparently Fielding was on the Board of Directors of a pretty big corporation and there was concern that this might have been some kind of weird assassination attempt. "It's true that I'm working on the Fielding case. What interest is it of yours?"

Allen Frey reached down to a black leather briefcase that had been resting by the legs of his chair. He opened the briefcase and took out a large folder stuffed with papers. He leaned forward as he handed the file over. "You might want to read these. I've been hired by a private party to investigate the deaths of three businessmen, all of whom sat on the same board Mr. Fielding sits on: Free State Insurance Corporation."

Detective Coverdale started in surprise. "Really? Do tell."

"The short end of it is that they weren't officially classified as murders," Allen Frey continued. "All three were killed and two of them partially devoured by animals."

"Animals? What kind?"

"Officially, I don't know," Allen said. He looked excited. "But . . . off the record . . . in all three deaths the animals were noted as local; mountain lions, coyotes, bears, but in reality the coroner couldn't come up with an accurate description of the animal that had killed them. One of them retrieved several hairs that he identified as canine, but . . ." He smiled a sick smile. "If you had asked me that question when I was a kid, I would have told you a werewolf killed them."

Detective Coverdale smiled back. Surely this was too crazy to be a coincidence. "A werewolf, eh? You better not be fucking with me, Mr. Frey."

"Obviously, it can't be a *real* werewolf," Allen Frey said, remembering his interview with Joe Tripp and Kelly Baker the past summer. "But then . . . think about this: When was Mr. Fielding attacked?"

"Two nights ago," Detective Coverdale said.

"Two nights ago was the first night of the lunar cycle."

Detective Coverdale frowned. "Okay . . ."

"The other three murders were also committed on the first night of the lunar cycle. The full moon." Allen Frey leaned closer to the detective, his voice a whisper. "Somebody, for whatever reason they have, is killing the board members of Free State Insurance Corporation. And it's my belief that whoever is doing it . . . *thinks* he's a werewolf."

The two men looked at each other, their gazes unyielding. Detective Coverdale felt a slow feeling of intuition rise in him. As much as he didn't want to believe it, a part of him felt that the private dick was telling him the truth.

The phone ringing on his desk interrupted his thoughts.

"One moment," he said, picking up the receiver. "Coverdale here."

"Detective Coverdale, it's Officer Block, over at St. Luke's." St. Luke's Hospital was where George Fielding was receiving medical care; because of the ongoing investigation, the Las Vegas Police Department had an officer at the hospital in the hopes that Mr. Fielding would be able to talk when—or if—he emerged from his coma.

"What's happening?"

"George Fielding is doing okay. He came out of his coma about an hour ago. It's hard for him to talk, but he's talking. And he says that he can provide an accurate description of the suspect that attacked him."

Detective Coverdale's heart raced. "I'll be right there." He hung up the phone. "Looks like we're in luck. George Fielding just woke up."

"Is he talking?" Allen Frey asked, rising to his feet.

Detective Coverdale stood up and put on his coat. "Yeah. In fact, I want you to come with me and tell me more about this case. I want to know *everything*."

Bernard Roberts was sitting in his study at home, the lights dark, the shades drawn, when the phone rang.

He looked at it for a moment as it sat there on his desk. It rang four times before he picked it up. "Yes?"

He listened for a moment. Then: "Christ . . . No, no, I'm glad he's okay, it's just that . . . Yes, yes, Wednesday morning, the boardroom . . . Yes, yes, I'll be there . . . Tell Ellen that I'm glad George pulled through." Ellen Brite was George Fielding's ex-wife; they had been divorced for the past fifteen years but were still close friends.

Bernard Roberts replaced the receiver in its cradle and rested his chin in his hands, staring at the blackness in front of him. He had been preparing himself for this news, hoping that it wouldn't happen.

His mind went over the possible scenarios that might take place because of this new development. The first, and the one he secretly hoped for, was that George had been too traumatized by the incident to remember it. If that was the case, he would probably take a permanent leave of absence from the board, thus bringing everything back on track. As long as his memory of the incident remained fragmented, Bernard was safe.

The second scenario, and the one that he feared, was the one that he was going to have to prepare for *now*. That scenario was that George Fielding remembered everything that happened to him. Closely related to that scenario was the possibility that George got a good look at Mark Wiseman during the attack. During the past few days since receiving news of the bungled attack and talking to that dipshit Mark Wiseman on the phone, he was drawing the conclusion that there was a strong possibility that Mark had been in partial human form during the attack. He might also have been in human form at some point while in the house. If that was the case, it was possible that George Fielding saw Mark. If he merely saw Mark in his wolfish state, well, then they were still safe. If he were to describe what he saw, his rantings would be dismissed as hallucinations resulting from his trauma.

But if he saw Mark in his human form . . . if he was able to provide a good description . . . if, by that description they were able to identify Mark by name . . .

Bernard Roberts opened the right drawer of his desk and took out the Beretta and a full clip. He snapped the clip in place and set the weapon down on the desk. He took a deep breath and closed his eyes, gathering his thoughts.

He tried to retrace his steps over the past six months. He was fairly confident that he hadn't been seen with Mark; all of their meetings had been private, arranged via public pay phones. His mind went back to that night when he first saw Mark change in the security video camera. He remembered heading back upstairs to find out what the hell it was he had just seen. He remembered Mark's surprised look when he ran into him outside the bathroom, the look of guilt on his face. He remembered the research he had done, being excited at what he had found. He remembered paying the private detective he had found to do some snooping on Mark Wiseman, the information he had been able to dig up on Mark's parents, the background of abuse and neglect Mark had suffered at their hands. He remembered the excitement he felt when he had connected all those strange, unsolved deaths to Mark. And he remembered the look on Mark's face when he had called him up to that first meeting in his office, how pleased he had been with himself that his hunch had played off.

He frowned. That first meeting. There was something about it . . .

It suddenly hit him. He visualized in his mind Mark walking into the executive suite, stopping at Carol's desk to say that he had received a call that Bernard wanted to see him. He had told her that he had called Mark to his office and that when he arrived that he was to come right in. She would be the only person he could think of that had seen the two of them together. The question was, would she remember?

Bernard frowned as he thought more about it. Carol had called in sick today and yesterday. He hadn't spoken to her personally, but Barbara Holmes, the secretary who sat at another desk in the executive suite, had taken the call. He hadn't thought much of it, but now it suddenly seemed significant.

Because he had overheard a conversation in the cafeteria this afternoon among Mark's coworkers that Mark had called in sick today and the day before as well.

Surely it had to be a coincidence. There was no way they could possibly know each other. They worked on separate floors, associated with different people. There was no way that—

But Carol had been acting different lately. She had been evasive when he called her at home, she hardly talked to him at work, and her demeanor was different. She had that look that suggested that she was preoccupied with something. While she had given him the cold shoulder, there was something about her that seemed light and bubbly and happy. As if she—

His mind flashed back to what she told him last week. That she couldn't see him anymore because she didn't think it was a good idea, that she had met another man.

No way! It couldn't be!

As hard as he tried to deny it, the more another part of him whispered that it was true. Somehow, against all odds, Mark Wiseman and Carol Emrich had met and gotten involved romantically. How much Mark might have told Carol he was afraid to think about, but it must have been plenty. After all, she had been calling in sick to work the past few days just like Mark, and—

Bernard reached for the phone and punched in Carol's number from memory. It rang five times, then went into her answering machine. He hung up.

He glanced at his desk clock. The dial read eight-fifteen.

He picked up his phone again and dialed Mark's number, again from memory. He waited until the phone rang into Mark's answering machine; then he hung up.

Bad idea. Phone records can be traced . . .

It was too much of a coincidence. It just couldn't be happening.

There was no way they could be together. There was no way they could have met, fallen in love, conspired against him.

There was no way they could have skipped town on him.

But somehow, Bernard was afraid they had.

Bernard picked up the Beretta and caressed it lovingly. He remained that way for a long time, sitting in the dark thinking and holding the firearm.

Thinking . . .

Chapter Twenty

He remembered Pueblo, California from six years back when he had been angry at the world for the curse that had fallen upon him. He had spent a lot of time driving through the Southwest, and had fallen in love with the desert. The California desert was lonely, desolate country, but it could also be quite beautiful. Mark Wiseman used to think that he would like to retire in this part of the state; buy a small house in a small town, live out the rest of his life in this beautiful, peaceful community.

He never thought he would have to hide out in Pueblo. It made a poor town to hide out in. For one, it wasn't much of town; it consisted of two main streets with a gas station, a convenience store, a motel, and a small tourist center on another corner. Five hundred yards in either direction were small trailers, with large satellite dishes. Pueblo was barely a dot on the map. It was forty miles west of Needles and wasn't much to look at.

They drove nonstop from Newport Beach to the outskirts of Barstow that first night. They found a Motel 6 and checked in under their own names—they were still too stunned by all the driving and the sudden change of events—and slept for ten hours; exhaustion just wouldn't permit them to drive further. They left the following morning, heading further east.

There was no clear destination in mind. Their only purpose had been to gain as much distance between them and Bernard Roberts. They stumbled on Pueblo the next morning quite by accident, but the minute they crossed into the town Mark insisted they pull over and stay. "I've been here," he had said, as Carol swung her Camaro into a motel parking lot. "It's so beautiful out here."

Once checked in they had breakfast at a roadside diner. They were ravenous. They spoke little during their meal—pancakes, eggs, and hashbrowns for Carol, French toast, eggs, sausage and English muffins for Mark—and when they had finished they found a small motel and checked in.

They spent most of the day in their room with the blinds closed. They napped, watched the small television in silence. As the afternoon bled into evening Carol turned the water on in the bathtub and let a bath run. Mark lounged on the lumpy king-sized bed and watched the news. When the bathtub was filled, Carol stripped off her clothes, told Mark she was taking a bath, and stepped into the bathroom.

Mark watched the news for a minute, then took his clothes off and joined her.

Once in the tub he kissed her softly. "I love you," he whispered, nuzzling her ear.

"I love you, too," she said.

Their foreplay began in the bathtub and wound its way into the bedroom. They made love slowly, languidly. She hugged him tightly as he moved within her, and when release came Carol bit his shoulder, stifling her cries. They lay in each others arms for a long time afterward, Mark's penis shrinking inside her.

Carol snuggled up close to him. "That was wonderful . . ."

"But . . . ?"

Carol paused. "I sensed you were . . . holding back something."

Mark sighed. He had been fighting the curse the past three days; tomorrow was the last night of the full moon, and while the lunar effect was losing its strength, it still had a strong hold on Mark. Because of his mental state and the influence that alcohol had on his system three nights ago, he hadn't been able to let the beast run free completely. Now it was struggling to burst free.

Carol touched his face gently. "What is it, sweetie?"

Mark shook his head. He drew her close to him. He wanted to tell her about it, but he didn't want to lose her. If he could just fight the curse off for another day. "It's nothing," he said.

"Are you sure?"

"Yes."

"It doesn't seem like nothing to me."

He turned to her. Her blue eyes were staring into

his, deep and penetrating. Her hair lay wetly against the bed sheets. Her fingers traced lines across his chest. "I love you, Mark. And I will do anything for you. You mean more than anything to me, and I would never leave you. If you want to tell me something, you can."

Mark's heart swelled, and he pulled Carol close to him and kissed her. "I know, honey. I just . . ." It trailed off. He had no idea what he could say to her. How do you tell somebody that the full moon has an effect on you that most people regard as superstitious hogwash?

"Just what?"

"Nothing."

Carol frowned. He could sense the tension build between them. He didn't want to fight with her, but then he didn't want to put her in any danger, either. He just had one more night of the lunar cycle and then—

The pain in his stomach blossomed suddenly out of nowhere. It doubled him up so suddenly and forcefully that his elbow hit Carol's head as he lurched off the bed. "Oh, Christ!" Mark cried. He doubled over, hands clutching his stomach. He felt his skin grow suddenly warm and he gritted his teeth and tried to fight it off. Oh God, not now, not now, *not now!*

Carol sprang up, her hands clutching his shoulders, her features etched with worry. "Mark, what is it? What's wrong?"

Mark shook her hands off him. He scrambled off the bed, falling to the floor as another bolt of pain ripped through him. He moaned, his teeth clenched so tightly that they scraped together.

"Mark, what's *happening*?" Carol sounded panicked. "Oh God, Mark . . . let me call the front desk, get a doctor—"

"No!" It came out of Mark's throat like a snarl. He gritted his teeth and tried to fight it as his body went into convulsions.

Carol stood by helplessly, her eyes growing wide in horror. She knelt down beside Mark hesitantly. "Mark, I'm going to call 911, okay? Just hang on—"

"Don't call anybody!" With a great amount of mental determination, Mark fought down the curse. He lurched to his feet and headed toward the front door. He stopped at the door, leaning against it with his head bowed down, as if he were fighting off a migraine headache. His eyes were closed tight. "I'll be okay."

"Are you sure? You don't look okay, you look like you were . . . having some sort of . . . of *seizure*."

"I'm fine." Mark took a deep breath and raised his face to hers. The smile he mustered was a cruel caricature. "I'm fine, I just . . . need to get out of here for awhile." He opened the front door. "I need some fresh air."

"Mark, *wait*, you *can't*—"

But he wasn't listening. He exited the room and began running through the parking lot toward the desert that lay beyond. "I'll be okay," he called out. "I'll be right back." And then he couldn't say anything more because he could feel it returning. He ignored her cries of protest that followed as he made a mad dash for the desert. He barely felt the sting of sand and rocks as his bare feet hit the desert floor and then he was putting distance between himself and the motel. The last vestiges of his rational mind were thinking *I must look pretty foolish to Carol right now, sprinting out into the night stark naked.* His primal self paid it no heed: he was reacting on pure instinct, under the power of the moon and the curse.

He was barely aware of the physical metamorphoses his body was undergoing as he made his way farther and farther into the desert.

Three minutes later, as Carol Emrich sat on the king-sized bed sobbing uncontrollably, the piercing howl of a wolf penetrated the din of her sorrow. She stopped crying and looked toward the window and the fear in her heart was the greatest she had ever felt in her life.

Chapter Twenty-one

On Wednesday morning, January 9, Allen Frey met with Detective Peter Coverdale of the Las Vegas Police Department at the office of the Federal Bureau of Investigation in Los Angeles, California.

They were in a conference room with three FBI agents, along with two detectives from the Costa Mesa Police Department. Also present was Frederick Johansen, the man who had hired Allen Frey last summer, and four members of the Board of Directors of Free State Insurance Corporation. The conference table was piled with papers, briefcases, and folders. They had been in a very animate discussion for the past forty-five minutes.

Frederick Johansen had been trying to place a call to Bernard Roberts for the past hour. Now he looked up at the circle of law enforcement men he was gathered with and replaced the receiver. "He isn't answering," he said, quietly. "His office said he hasn't even called in sick this morning and they're very curious; this just isn't like him."

The head FBI agent in the room, a man in his fifties with a barrel chest and steel gray hair named Paul Strong, turned to Frey and Coverdale. "I don't know . . . the description George Fielding gave us doesn't resemble Bernard at all."

"But it *does* resemble a Free State employee," Allen Frey pointed out. "It bears a strong resemblance to a Mark Wiseman, a computer tape librarian. According to his shift supervisor he called in sick Monday and Tuesday, and they haven't heard from him this morning."

Special Agent Strong was shaking his head. "That's still not enough for us to go on. There's no proof that Roberts knew Wiseman, no way to connect them . . ."

"But you *can* connect Roberts to Fielding, as well as the three board members who are now dead." Peter Coverdale sat back in his chair, appraising the agent with a steely gaze. "Myself and my colleagues have presented viable evidence that clearly shows that Bernard Roberts has, for the past seven years, been defrauding the company and using his position as a way to improperly influence others to commit illegal acts. Thanks to the help of Mr. Frey here, I've been able to uncover this. We wouldn't have discovered this for months if Frey hadn't suggested we comb through the business transactions of all Free State executives and board members. And as you can clearly see, we might not have discovered the indiscretion if the merger had been voted down. Had the merger gone through, Bernard Roberts would have not only been discovered, he would be facing criminal charges, which I'm sure you can use to press your case."

Special Agent Strong nodded. "It's true. This is enough to issue a warrant for Bernard Roberts's arrest on embezzlement. But you're going to have to do some more talking to convince me to charge him with murder."

"What about conspiracy to commit murder?" Allen Frey asked.

"It's not there," Special Agent Strong said. He picked up one of the files from the vast array of file folders and paperwork on the desk, put his reading glasses on, and perused the document. "According to your report, all you have to connect Mr. Roberts to these three deaths and the one attack on Mr. Fielding is circumstantial evidence. Mighty *flimsy* circumstantial evidence, I might add."

"What about the composite sketch of Mark Wiseman?" Allen Frey asked. This morning he had faxed a copy of Mark's photograph to the Houston PD, who had taken it over to Kelly Baker and Joe Tripp. They had identified the person in the photo as the man they had seen at David Samuels's lakeside cabin the night he was murdered.

Agent Strong sighed. He picked up the photo of Mark Wiseman and looked at it. He set it down with a sigh. "It's not strong enough. Mr. Tripp and Ms. Baker were under the influence of narcotics the night they claimed they witnessed Mr. Samuels's death. The man they saw that night was probably a figment of their imagination."

"Okay, granted you can't connect Mark Wiseman to any of these deaths, or the attack on Mr. Fielding." Detective Peter Coverdale was growing annoyed at the bureaucracy of this meeting. "You *did* say that you could issue a warrant for Mr. Roberts's arrest, correct?"

Agent Strong nodded. "I'll get the request down to the courthouse this morning."

"Fine." Detective Coverdale, Allen Frey, and the other men stood up. They shook hands. Coverdale handed Strong his business card. "Give me a call when you get him."

"Will do."

Detective Coverdale, Allen Frey and Frederick Johansen left the FBI office and said little as they made their way outside.

Once in the parking lot, Johansen turned to the other two men. "I don't care what the feds say, I have a feeling that this Wiseman character is in on this."

Coverdale seconded the motion. "Unfortunately, Agent Strong is right. Everything we've presented them with is purely circumstantial."

"What do you believe?" Johansen asked.

The detective shrugged. "Beats the hell out of me."

Johansen turned to Frey. "I'd like you to find out everything you can about Mark Wiseman. I want to know where he lives, shits, and eats. I also want to know his present whereabouts and what he was doing on the nights Fielding, Samuels, John, and Krueger were attacked. And I want to know if there is any connection between him and Roberts."

"Sure thing," Allen said, squinting. The day was cool, but bright and sunny. "Might take a few days though."

"A few days is fine," Frederick said. "By then maybe the feds will have caught Bernard."

"We can only hope," Allen Frey said.

His body bore scratches and cuts from his foray into the desert. Unlike previous excursions within the past few months, he'd had no control this time. There was a four-hour block of time in which he remembered nothing. It wasn't until the early morning hours that he became aware of anything, but even then he couldn't will the change back. His lupine instinct was still strong; it prevailed over all else.

When he became aware of himself the first thing he noticed was the taste of jackrabbit in his mouth. He licked his lips; there was dried blood on his teeth. His stomach rumbled, but he felt somewhat satiated. He didn't remember making the kill, but apparently somewhere along the way he had. He looked out across the vast open desert and breathed in the desert air. A multitude of scents came to him: scrub brush, jasmine, cacti, different flowers, animal spoors, rodents. The smell of diesel was faint, coming from a slight breeze that blew from the east. He wasn't that far from the highway and the motel. He began heading toward it, keeping to the shadows.

He had to wait until dawn was approaching to venture closer to the highway. Far off in the distance he could see Pueblo illuminated in the few streetlights the town fathers were able to afford, still sleepy as the sky turned from black to a dark gray as the sun began to struggle to its ascent. As the sun's rays grew stronger, the lunar influence weakened, and finally as the sky began growing lighter he was able to will the change back. He gritted his teeth and fought the pain as his body went through the transformation. A moment later he stood in the still, California desert, shivering in the cold, his teeth chattering.

He crept out from behind a rock and eyed the town. There was no sign that anybody was awake. He looked around carefully until he saw the motel. He couldn't tell if Carol's Camaro was still parked in the lot, and at this point he didn't care. He had to get to shelter—either his room at the motel, or another one, preferably a vacant room. He had to get some clothes.

He made his way to the motel quickly, scampering over rocks and bushes. The motel parking lot and the highway was devoid of people. He quickly dashed across the parking lot and headed toward the door of the room they had checked into. His hands grasped the doorknob and twisted it; it was locked.

Shivering in the cold, Mark rapped on the door. He hugged himself, his body shaking. He knocked again and suddenly the door was open and Carol was standing there. He didn't even look at her; he pushed his way inside and headed toward the bathroom.

"What the fuck happened to you, goddamit?" Carol shouted. She was crying again. She had changed into jeans and a sweater. He could hear the tread of her footsteps as she trudged after him. He headed toward the shower and turned on the faucet to HOT.

"I'm talking to you!" Carol was in the bathroom now. He stepped into the shower, not even bothering to close the shower curtain. The water was lukewarm, but it was better than the chill his body felt from the cold desert night. He shivered uncontrol-

lably as he turned the water on full blast, rubbing his hands over his arms and body. Carol was crying uncontrollably. "You motherfucker, you had me *worried*! What the *hell happened*? *Why did you run out like that*?"

"It's okay," Mark said, the chill easing somewhat as the water grew warmer. He stepped into the spray and sighed as the water turned hot and he closed his eyes, letting it wash the dirt and grime away. He ducked his head in the spray, the hot water instantly waking him up. The more the water warmed up, the longer he stayed in, the more the chill was beaten down. "Everything's okay."

"No, everything is *not* okay!" Carol was trying to control her crying, and her voice was filled with anger. "Everything is not fucking okay until you start telling me the truth. What the *fuck* happened to you that made you run out of here so suddenly?"

"In a minute," Mark said, his body feeling better as he washed himself clean. He was no longer shivering. "I promise I'll tell you everything. Just let me clean up."

"You mother*fucker*!" Carol stomped into the bedroom. Her sobs came back to him, heavy with anger.

Mark's skin tingled under the water. He turned the water temperature to a more tolerable level and settled back, letting the water soothe his aching body. Carol's sobbing came to him loud and clear from the bedroom and his heart was heavy with sadness. He felt bad for not being completely honest and telling her everything, but what could he have done? She never would have believed it if he'd told her about the curse. In hindsight, he hoped perhaps that what had happened last night was for the best.

Now that she had seen what had happened to him, it might be easier to convince her of his condition.

He wanted to shower completely, but Carol's sorrow beckoned. When his body temperature returned to normal, he shut the water off and reached for a white towel resting over the toilet. He patted himself dry and stepped out of the shower. His wet hair clung to his skull and his upper back, dripping water on the floor. Wrapping the towel around his waist, he stepped into the bedroom.

Carol was sitting on the bed near the window, her back to him. Her face was buried in her hands as she sobbed. Mark approached her warily. "Carol," he said softly.

If she heard him she made no indication. Her sobs were heavy with emotion. Mark stepped behind her and nervously touched her shoulder. Her skin tingled, as if recoiling from something slimy. *"What?"* She jumped up suddenly, eyes and face red and wet with tears. "Oh, now you decide to come back and play the nice, sensitive caring boyfriend? After . . . pulling what you pulled last night . . . running out into . . . the fucking desert without your fucking *clothes* . . ." Her voice hitched with the sobs as she spit her dialog out. "I thought there was something *wrong* with you!"

"There is," Mark said, reaching to embrace her.

Carol moved away from him, her eyes angry and hurt. "No *shit*, there's something wrong with you!" She made a feeble attempt at slapping him and he grabbed her hand. She beat at his chest with her fists and collapsed against him, sobbing anew. "You motherfucker . . ."

Mark held her, his right hand stroking her hair. He

cooed meaningless words in an attempt to soothe her, but they only proved to make her cry harder. She struggled feebly in an attempt to break away but then gave up, her body completely exhausted. He held her and kept whispering, "It's okay now, it's okay now." In time her sobs trickled down.

When she gained control of herself Mark eased her down onto the bed gently. He sat down beside her. "I'm sorry about what happened," he began, speaking slowly. "But . . . what happened to me last night was something I couldn't control. It just came over me so suddenly—"

"It looked like you were having . . . *convulsions*," Carol said, sniffling. She looked at him wide eyed with an expression that suggested she wanted to trust him. "I didn't know what to think . . . and I was so scared when you ran out like that—"

"I know," Mark said, taking her hands. "I know it must have really scared you, and I am so sorry. If I had only . . . known it would have happened—"

"You could have *told* me about this," Carol said. "If you had only told me it wouldn't have scared me so bad."

"You might not have believed me if I had told you before."

Carol looked confused. "What are you saying? Of course I would have believed you. I mean . . . I saw what happened last night—"

"What do you think happened to me last night, Carol?" Mark regarded her seriously, his features set.

Carol looked at him, puzzled. "I . . . I don't know. It looked like you were having a . . . seizure or some-thing. I thought you were embarrassed to tell me about it. I sat here last night after you left driving myself crazy, wondering why you couldn't trust me enough to confide in me that you have some kind of neurological problem."

Mark nodded. Maybe she was on to something there. Maybe whatever had happened to him back on that first dark day had been the manifestation of some neurological problem that had suddenly sprung full-blown. That was what the rational part of him suggested; he had seen too much and lived through too much to believe it to be the truth.

"That's a good assessment," he said. "But unfortunately . . . it's the farthest thing from the truth."

"Well then what is it?"

"I'm sorry, Carol." Mark touched her face lightly with the back of his hand. "I didn't mean to lie to you, to hide the truth from you. But I was so damn scared, I was afraid that if you found out that I would lose you."

"You'll never lose me." Carol took his hand and kissed his fingers one by one. She held his hand to her cheek, nuzzling it. "No matter what is wrong with you, baby, you'll never lose me."

He was just about to say *you'll believe otherwise after you hear this*, but wisely decided not to. Now was not the time to bait her. It was better to let her hear his story in full so she could decide for herself.

Taking a deep breath, Mark took her back to those dark days when he lived in a violent household; from there the story segued easily into the day the curse manifested itself without warning.

From there it became easy. He told her everything. Carol sat next to him, eyes wide with amazement, horror, and a sort of wonder. She didn't say a word as Mark spun the story out. At times her breath was held as if in rapt suspense.

It didn't take long to tell her. She already knew about his role in the board member killings, his relationship with Bernard Roberts, and the card the executive was holding on his life. The part about his curse fit in neatly, like the missing piece of a long lost puzzle. That's how Mark saw it.

When he finished he was afraid to look at her, but he did. Her features were riddled with conflicting emotions: fear, rage, revulsion, and pity. She had released her grip on his hands and had inched back as he told his story, and now that he was finished she drew into herself. Her eyes darted around the room nervously, as if seeking escape. Mark had been expecting this and he told her, "I knew you would react this way. You think I'm crazy, that there's something wrong with me mentally."

"No, I don't think that at all," Carol protested. "It's just . . ."

"Just what?"

Carol regarded him silently. She appeared to be fighting the fear and revulsion she had exhibited. "It's just that . . ."

"It's unbelievable, isn't it?"

Carol nodded.

"I know. But trust me, Carol, it's real."

Carol opened her mouth as if to say something, closed it, then shook her head. She appeared to be struggling with something. Finally she spit it out: "What you're suggesting is . . . well, it's—"

"I thought you already used the word 'crazy'?"

"Crazy wasn't the word I was going for," Carol said. She seemed to be in more control of herself, especially since Mark apparently wasn't going to sprout fangs and fur and turn into a werewolf right before her eyes. "I guess the closest thing I can think of is that what you're describing is pure superstition."

"But don't you think that superstitions have some basis in fact? I mean, how else do they become superstitions in the first place?"

Carol shrugged and rubbed her shoulders. "I don't know. Walking under ladders, black cats crossing your path—"

"Ghosts, the Loch Ness monster, UFO's and alien abduction," Mark said. "Let's refer to some of them as urban legends, if you will."

"Okay."

"Let's take UFO's for instance. They seem to be the most popular right now. In fact, they seem to be just as popular an urban myth as werewolves and vampires were three hundred years ago. Why is that, do you think?"

Carol shrugged. Her shoulders looked less rigid, her face less strained. "People are less superstitious now?"

"Partly true. Another reason could be that technologically, we're more advanced now. Three hundred years ago we weren't and we relied more on folklore to help explain the things we didn't understand. When technology took off in the thirties and forties, new fears followed; nuclear war, the mysteries of space. We've long pondered the possibility of life on other planets and the more we learned about the solar system and the galaxy beyond, the more we began hearing stories of extraterrestrial visitors."

"If you're saying that folklore and urban legends are a result of mass hallucination, you're doing a terrible job of convincing me of your lycanthropic condition." Now Carol was becoming her old self again; strong, witty, and no-nonsense.

"Sorry. Didn't mean to lead you down that track, but this does eventually make sense." Mark paused briefly, leaned closer to Carol and continued. "I can't remember which pharaoh it was, but it had to have been the early 1920s when a particular tomb was unearthed in Egypt. It was estimated to be three thousand years old. Among the hieroglyphics engraved in the tomb that told that particular pharaoh's story, the archeologists discovered what could only be described as flying disks; in fact, that particular hieroglyph appeared to tell the story of beings from the outer stars who visited the Egyptians. Most of the hieroglyphics are still undecipherable, but it's the story that beings from another planet might have possibly visited the ancient Egyptians that continues to amaze UFO buffs to this day. Because here we have actual recorded evidence dating three thousand years before the UFO craze of the forties. There are various cultures around the world that have similar extraterrestrial folklore."

"So what are you saying?"

"What I'm saying is that if you believe that there is life on other planets, that it could have been very possible that extraterrestrials visited various primitive cultures thousands of years ago. And that those visits were what has resulted in UFO folklore to this day."

Carol was silent as she appeared to digest this information. "What about Roswell, then?"

"An anomaly," Mark said. "Of the thousands of reported sightings received every year, Roswell was probably the real thing."

"So in other words, most UFO sightings are bona fide fake."

"Right."

"And what about vampires and werewolves. You said before that their popularity was at its height three hundred years ago."

"Between the fifteenth and nineteenth century," Mark said. He ran his hand along his still wet hair. "And with each culture they had a different methodology to them. In some countries, somebody that died as a vampire came back as a werewolf. In some countries a vampire could only be killed by an oak stake through the heart; in others, it had to be decapitated as well, with garlic stuffed in its mouth. I could go on with the different myths for both, but the point is, the reason they were both extremely popular in their day and age was due to the scientific ignorance of the masses of that time, and religious hysteria. The church did a good job at convincing poor, uneducated peasants that crazy Simon who lived all by himself on the Moors—who, if a twentieth-century psychiatrist were to examine him today would diagnose paranoid schizophrenia—was really a demon-possessed werewolf."

"Okay, I can believe that," Carol said. "I'm sure there were serial killers back then just as well."

"Exactly!" Mark was feeling animated now, especially the more Carol warmed up to this theory.

"People like Ted Bundy have been around forever; it's only recently that we've been able to coin a phrase to describe people like that."

"A guy like Ted Bundy back then," Carol said, shaking her head. "Or Richard Chase—that vampire guy in Sacramento—would be prime for burning at the stake as a werewolf back in the Middle Ages."

"You're catching on," Mark said. "There's even evidence that suggests vampires and werewolves of the past were possible victims of a rare blood disease called *porphyria*. They may have attacked and drank the blood of fellow villagers in an attempt to get healthy hemoglobin into their systems."

Carol looked surprised. *"Porphyria?"*

Mark nodded. "It's a hereditary disease caused by a defect in the bone marrow. It lies dormant in the system until a stressful situation triggers it. One key symptom is an acute sensitivity to light. Sunlight may cause severe scarring and sores to erupt on the skin. Receding gums expose discolored reddish fang-like teeth. It's little wonder many victims of the disease stayed indoors during the day and only ventured out at night. There are ways to treat this condition now, but back in the 1500s? People like that were often scorned, they had to hide from fearful villagers who were afraid they would kill them."

"Hence the vampire and werewolf myths," Carol said.

"Precisely."

"That still doesn't explain what you just told me," Carol said. The fear and loathing had left her face only to be replaced by a stronger sense of pity. "In a sense, the part regarding *porphyria* rings true; your condition sprang suddenly during a stressful time of your life. But everything else . . . the . . . physical changing into a beast . . . it smacks right out of that movie *An American Werewolf in London*. You described being able to physically *change*. And that, to be painfully honest, smacks of something psychological."

Mark sighed. He knew very well that this is how it would sound to her, but there was no other way to tell her. He had to tell her everything, no holds barred. And he didn't want to will the change now in front of her for fear that he would lose control of the beast within. The thought of suddenly blacking out in the middle of the change and waking up to find her strewn bloodily across the room was something he didn't want to consider. "I don't know what it is," he said, his voice low. "All I know is . . . there is something within me that compels me to . . . to let the beast out every month during the lunar cycle. I used to be able to control it, but something happened last summer. It started getting out of control, taking a hold of me without warning. Bernard Roberts saw what happened to me that night in the tape library. He told me himself; he was standing by the security booth yakking it up with a security guard while the guy's back was turned. He saw me start to change in the camera, and he got a copy of the tape. That, and the research he did . . ." He let the sentence trail off. He shrugged. "He had me. I couldn't let him destroy me."

They were both silent for a moment. Outside the sun was up, casting morning light across the parking lot and through the closed curtains. Already the sound of trucks rolling across the motel's blacktop parking lot could be heard from outside. Mark sighed again and looked at Carol, trying not to let his grief show. He was going to lose her, he knew it. His throat constricted. "It looks like he's won, though. He's driven me from my home, he'll be after me, he'll get the police after me. But the most tragic thing is that he's turned you away from me."

"No, Mark—"

"If I hadn't told you the truth you would have left me anyway," Mark said, not paying heed to her denial. "You would have justifiably left me. I lied to you, I wasn't completely honest, so of course I wouldn't blame you if you left." He wiped a tear that threatened to spill from his left eye. "But *Christ*, I didn't want to lose you. You mean everything to me. I didn't want to lose you."

And then suddenly Carol was in his arms. "You're not going to lose me, Mark. You're not going to lose me."

Mark held her, breathing in her scent. He held her tight, as if he was afraid that she was going to be torn away from him. She held him just as tightly and a blossom of hope erupted in the pit of his belly. At first he tried to deny it, but it burned fiercely, igniting stronger until it suddenly flamed higher. She was telling him the truth. She wasn't going to leave him. Whether she believed him or not, that was for later debate.

She kissed him and looked into his eyes. What he saw there made him smile and feel good again. It was the face of the best friend he had ever had; she would never leave him. "I believe you," she said. "I don't understand it, but I believe you."

And for now, that was all Mark Wiseman needed in his life. For somebody to believe him and be on his side.

Chapter Twenty-two

Bernard Roberts's black Mercedes purred contentedly as it chewed up asphalt on Interstate 5 heading north.

He hadn't packed much for the trip; an overnight bag with a few days' change of clothes, toiletries, and not much else. The important stuff was in the leather case sitting on the seat beside him.

Along with the Beretta he had also packed a high-powered .32 Colt rifle. He had shot it before on target ranges and had become quite good at it. The rifle had to be assembled, but where he was going it would be safe to assume that he could assemble the rifle and keep it assembled for some time. After all, he was going hunting.

Also in the briefcase were ten cases of .32 shells, with one of them specially made. They had been melted down from the silver his mother had given him and Olivia when they had gotten married. Olivia had wanted the silver in the divorce settlement, but Bernard had fought stubbornly for it. He didn't know why, but at the time he wanted that silver set if it was the last thing he got out. He had won that particular battle and two months later he had no idea why he had fought so vigorously for it. After all, they were just a bunch of plates and silverware for Christsakes. In hindsight, he felt glad that he fought so hard for them.

They had melted down and made quite nice silver bullets.

The only stupid thing he had done was head to Mark Wiseman's apartment. He had been seething mad and was determined to kill the lying bastard the minute he opened the door. But Mark hadn't answered his repeated knocks and it confirmed Bernard's suspicions. Mark had split for places unknown with his prize, Carol Emrich. He had driven by Carol's condominium, but repeated calls to her went unanswered. There was nowhere else to go but follow his hunches and those were telling him that the two had run off together.

So he had gone home and cooled his anger off with a couple of drinks. The bourbon had calmed his nerves and he was actually able to sleep. When he woke up the next day it was with a new perspective and a fresh revelation. Suddenly inspired, he had checked on some things to confirm his hunch, then packed hurriedly and exited the house just as the morning rush-hour traffic was gaining full steam.

He had dressed casually for the trip and spent two hours that morning having breakfast and reading the morning paper at a Denny's in Whittier. By the time he hit the road again it was after ten and the freeway had cleared up considerably, but it was still stop-and-go in some parts. He didn't reach the Los Angeles County limits until after twelve. By the time he reached Bakersfield he was hungry again, so he pulled over at a roadside diner filled with eighteen-wheel semi tractor-trailers. For the first time in seven years—since making the presidency of Free State Insurance—he felt anonymous.

He got back on the road a little after two-thirty and continued north. He estimated that he should reach his destination in a little under three hours. It would be dark by the time he arrived and his first order of business was to drive by the place he felt Carol and Mark were going to be hiding. If it appeared that the coast was clear, then he would implement phase two of his hastily arranged plan.

Thanks to Carol at least he *had* a plan.

It never failed for Carol to make some feeble attempt at conversation whenever they got together. She had never gotten it through her thick skull that Bernard wasn't interested in her as a friend, or somebody to talk to. The only thing he had been interested in was fucking her. Plain and simple. It didn't matter where they were—his home, her condominium, his office, their hotel room at whatever vacation resort he took her to. The first things that he had noticed when he ushered her into his office for her interview were her spectacular tits (36D, and all natural), then her legs ending in a shapely, perfect ass, and then her face, framed by gorgeous, shimmering blonde hair. True, she hadn't been as airheaded as he was expecting, and that was good for business, but it also proved to be a hindrance in their relationship. They had started off casually, with a few lunch dates being the scope of their working relationship. That had quickly accelerated to Carol staying late at the office to take dictation from him for board meetings, to helping him out at his place on the weekends for some function or another. All perfectly legit business. It wasn't until one night, six months into their working relationship as they were finishing work that things heated up.

Carol had commented that her shoulders were aching. Bernard had stepped behind her as she sat at his glass dining room table in front of the laptop computer and began massaging her shoulders. She had moaned sensuously, tilting her head back. The vibes floating between them seemed appropriate, so Bernard had leaned forward and kissed her neck. She turned her face toward him and they came together in a lip-locking kiss that had melted him like candle wax. That had been the beginning of a nine-month affair that, for Bernard, was rooted in sex.

The first few weeks of the affair Carol was all the nymphomaniac. She had been demanding and hungry in bed. She had been a physically satisfying lover, one whose energy was boundless. She was good at playing instigator as well, and was easily equally the aggressor as Bernard.

Except one night in mid-spring during the time he began doing all that work at the office late at night, burning the midnight oil, she had stayed to help him out on a particular project. Most of the brown-nosers in the office had already gone home and he was taking her out to dinner; then they were going to meet up at his place. Bernard was sitting at Carol's desk, waiting for her to make adjustments to her makeup in the bathroom when out of curiosity he'd opened her desk drawer and begun sifting through it. Nothing too unusual in the top drawer; just assorted pens, pencils, paper clips, rubber bands, keys to an overhead bin, a nail file, a pack of chewing gum. Usual mishmash of personal and office items. He closed the drawer and opened the next one. More of the same, as well as storage space for mailing labels and envelopes. He opened the bottom drawer, which was deeper. Aside from the space at the rear of the drawer where she most likely kept her purse, the front contained half a dozen files. He flipped through them. All of them were empty. Except one.

He had pulled the file out and opened it. Glossy travel brochures rested within. He fingered through them, pausing to examine one that had been written in her familiar script. The name of a motel had been circled in red ink, along with a date—July 17–29. Those were the days that coincided with the two weeks' vacation she'd put in for and which she'd later taken, a vacation she hadn't revealed too much about. All she would say was that she'd taken off somewhere up north for some much needed rest and relaxation. He looked at the brochure and at first the name of the little town didn't register with him. All he remembered about it later was that it had the word 'Three' in it—Three Lakes, Three Rivers, Three Streams, something to that effect—and that it was near Sequoia National Park.

So when it became apparent that Carol had skipped town with Mark Wiseman, Bernard had quickly put two and two together. The question was, where did they go?

He had wracked his brain trying to think. With the money he had paid out to Mark, they could have gone anywhere. They could have boarded a flight out of the country. Carol could easily get out of the country, but Bernard wasn't sure if Mark had a passport. If he didn't, that meant they would have to lay low for a few days until they could get one. And where would they go to hide out for a few days?

He had spent all last night thinking about this when it had suddenly hit him. His mind reflected back on the brochures he had found in Carol's desk. He had gone into his office and consulted a California travel book until he found a listing for Sequoia National Park. He had scanned the list of hotels in the area and his heart skipped a beat when he found it, everything dovetailing perfectly in his mind.

Three Rivers, California.

And there was even a Three Rivers Lodge!

It was obvious that Three Rivers was Carol's own little private retreat, a place she liked to keep secret. No wonder she hadn't told him much about her vacation.

Destination: Three Rivers, California.

Bernard grinned. The road ran before him like a long, black tongue. The land all around him was farmland. Once he was past it he would begin to ascend some more hilly country until he was in the foothills. By then it would be closing in on darkness. It had been cold outside when he had stopped for lunch, and it would no doubt be snowy weather in Three Rivers. There would be some gas stations up ahead where he could pull over and buy tire chains, then it was back on the road. It would be dark by the time he began ascending the mountain range into

Three Rivers. Then it was a quick check-in at the first hotel he came across. Weather permitting, a quick trip to the Three Rivers Lodge to see if the parking lot contained a white Camaro was next on the agenda. Depending on the outcome, the evening could go in one of several different ways.

One, the Camaro might not be there. Which could mean that either Carol and Mark weren't there, or they were smarter than he thought they were and they had switched cars at some point. But Bernard didn't believe that to be the case. He was fairly confident that Carol and Mark falsely believed that they had conducted their affair under the unsuspecting noses of everybody at Free State. That was partly true. What they hadn't counted on was Bernard figuring out what they were up to. No doubt Mark was the kind of fuckwad to fall for Carol's "talking" bullshit and would have been more than willing to agree to head up to Three Rivers to hide out. They could hole up there and "talk" all they wanted. Or at least until Bernard found out where they were and blew them both to hell.

The second scenario was that the Camaro was in the parking lot. If it was, then Bernard would creep down and make sure it was the right vehicle. If it was, surveillance was needed to find out what room they were hiding out in. Once that information was gained, Bernard would burst into the room that evening quickly and—*bam bam!*—one dead bitch and one dead werewolf.

The third scenario was that Carol and Mark weren't even at the Three Rivers Lodge. Which meant he would worry about that if it happened.

Bernard gripped the steering wheel tightly as he drove. Static wafted softly through the radio and he hit the remote scan until he found Bruce Springsteen singing about Atlantic City. He turned it up and grinned. If he knew Carol, she would be in Three Rivers. That much was evident. Mark would have gone crying to her the minute Bernard got off the phone with him last night and if she didn't already know about the board murders, she would know by now. Knowing Carol the way he knew her, she wouldn't be the least bit repulsed by Mark's story of murder, nor of Bernard's involvement of it. In fact, she would probably expect Bernard's involvement if she hadn't suspected it already. Bernard doubted Mark would tell Carol about his ability to sprout fur, claws, and fangs during the full moon, but he would tell her the rest. And the reason Carol wouldn't be afraid of Mark's admission to murder was because he had been honest with her and had "talked" to her. That would turn her on.

Bernard laughed. Mark Wiseman and Carol Emrich may have been sneaking around behind his back, but if Mark had "talked" to her, he was going to get more pussy from that innocent act than Bernard had gotten from her in the nine months he had been fucking her.

No problem, Bernard thought as he drove on. *He can have that bitch. I hope he has as much fun fucking her as I did.*

The speedometer read sixty-five miles per hour; he had three-quarters of a tank. That would be more than enough to get him to his destination. Prince replaced the Boss, followed by Rod Stewart. Nice, but not what Bernard wanted. He scanned more stations, passing country, rock, disco, rap, gospel, and talk radio. Nothing. Then he saw a tape lying in the side dish that Carol had left there one evening after they had returned from a record store. Bernard fingered it, one eye on the road. He grinned. It was a Metallica tape, the cover showing a hammer with the silhouette of a hand gripping it, blood staining the white surface. The title of the album was *Kill 'Em All*. Bernard laughed. What a fitting title!

He extracted the tape and inserted it in his tape deck. The heaviest heavy metal he had ever heard cranked the speakers and Bernard turned it up. The music thundered and pumped the Mercedes's interior. The song currently blaring forth was another fitting title: "Seek and Destroy."

Seek and Destroy, indeed.

Bernard drove the remainder of the one hundred and eighteen miles to Three Rivers with Metallica's *Kill 'Em All* blaring from the speakers. By the time he reached the city limits he was thoroughly pumped to see this mission to its conclusion.

Seek and Destroy.

Chapter Twenty-three

He didn't remember ever seeing them before, but the two men standing in George Fielding's private hospital room assured him that they had spoken before, although only briefly. "You probably don't remember much of it," a tall, stocky man who identified himself as Allen Frey said. "You were pretty out of it."

"I should say," George said. He was in bed, the backrest up to a comfortable reclining position. His throat was still sore from the breathing tube they had stuck down his windpipe. His left arm was hooked up to an IV, his right index finger connected to a pulse monitor. An automatic blood pressure gauge was wrapped around his right bicep. When the anesthetic began to wear off late last night the sound of its timely inflation had scared the shit out of him. Now it merely served as background noise, along with the constant stream of oxygen coursing through the tubes in his nose. At least he could speak.

"You look good," the second man said. He had

identified himself as Detective Peter Coverdale from the Las Vegas Police Department. George didn't remember meeting him last night, either. "Considering what you've been through."

"Thank you," George said. "You said that we were going to be joined by an FBI agent. Where is he?"

"Agent Strong should be here any minute," Detective Coverdale said. "The local field office is routing him in from John Wayne in Irvine."

"Hmmpphh." George picked up a cup of Sprite that the nurse had poured for him and took a sip. It helped his throat. "Feels better. Despite the extent of my other injuries, it's the goddamn breathing tube they stick down your throat to provide you with oxygen during surgery that hurts like a sonofabitch when you come out of it."

Detective Coverdale and Allen Frey, the private detective, nodded. Whether they had ever been under the knife before was of no concern to George Fielding. The fact that he had been under the knife for approximately four hours Saturday night, and another two hours Monday morning, meant a great deal to George. All told, he had suffered a broken skull, a broken nose, a broken right wrist, numerous gashes requiring stitches, and one mother of a gash that ran from his lower right neck, to his shoulder. It might be safe to say that a whole chunk of meat had been torn from that section of his body. There was also the massive blood loss that had resulted from this injury; they'd had to run three blood transfusions on him during surgery.

"So what did you want to see me about?"

"We were hoping to talk to you more about the man that attacked you," Detective Coverdale said.

"Ah, yes. Of course."

Allen Frey extracted a photograph from a manila folder and held it up for George to see. George took the photograph and squinted. He motioned toward the nightstand. "Can you hand me my glasses, please?"

Allen handed him his glasses and George put them on, blinking. He took another look at the photograph and tried to stifle the surprised gasp. He wasn't aware of it, but his heart monitor accelerated slightly. "That's him."

Frey and Coverdale traded glances. "You're sure about that?" Detective Coverdale asked.

"Positive." Fielding handed the photo back. "I recognized him instantly even though he was all fucked up."

"That's what currently has us puzzled, Mr. Fielding."

"What's that?"

"The description of events you gave us the day after the attack."

"What's there to be confused about? The guy in that photo broke into my house and he was . . . well, he appeared severely deformed at first. His back was all misshapen, his hands had grown huge, he had hair all over him, his face was . . ." He gestured for the right word. "His face was just mutated. The lower portion was pushed out slightly like this." He indicated his nose and jaw with his hands. "Like the snout of an animal, but not quite all the way. It was still very humanlike."

"And the man you claim broke into your home

looked like the man in this photo?" Coverdale asked. He sounded like he didn't believe George.

"Not looked like. *Was*."

"Come now, Mr. Fielding! Surely you don't expect us to believe that?"

"The man who broke into my home and attacked me was naked," George said, his voice strong and controlled. "He had a tattoo of the cartoon character Wile E. Coyote on the underside of his left forearm." He patted his own left forearm, as if to indicate the limb. "The man in that photo, Mark Wiseman, I've seen him. He sticks out at Free State like a sore thumb, so it's hard not to miss him. He's the only guy at that place with shoulder-length hair. One day as myself, Bernard, and a couple of the board members were on our way back from lunch, we rode up in the elevator with him. He was wearing a nice pair of jeans and a white, short-sleeved shirt. I was standing right next to him and noticed the tattoo." He looked from Detective Coverdale to Allen Frey. "The man that burst into my house last week had the same tattoo and with the exception of his fucked-up face, had the same facial features, the same hair. It was the same guy."

Coverdale looked flustered. Frey had the faint hint of a smile on his face, but wasn't yielding to it. Footsteps approaching from the corridor outside made Allen turn around and another man stepped into the room. He was middle-aged, slightly portly, with graying hair. He was wearing a three-piece dark suit. Detective Coverdale said, "Agent Strong. Glad you could make it."

Agent Strong regarded George Fielding. "Hello, Mr. Fielding."

"Greetings, Agent Strong." He held out his hand. "You can call me George."

"You can call me Paul." Agent Strong acknowledged Allen Frey with a nod, then walked over to the windows that overlooked the front of the hospital. "I got here as quick as I could, gentlemen. There's a private plane waiting for me at the airport, so let's make this quick."

Coverdale turned to George Fielding. "Why don't we skip what happened to you at your house that night and just tell us what you told me over the phone yesterday?"

"Sure." George Fielding took a sip of Sprite. He looked at Coverdale and Frey. "What I have to tell you relates to what happened to me, though."

"That's fine. Just tell us so Agent Strong can hear it."

George Fielding regarded the two law enforcement officers and one private detective, took another sip of Sprite and launched into his narrative. "Like I said, I noticed the man right away at Free State. He stuck out like a sore thumb."

"So you've positively identified the man in the photo—Mark Wiseman—as the man who attacked you?" Agent Strong asked.

"Yes." No use in launching into what he had really seen. He already knew that what he had described was being tacked up as a hallucination from the traumatic experience. "I noticed him at Free State's Corporate Headquarters. This was in November. The next month I was back in town again at Free State for another round of meetings. I ended up having to wait in Bernard Roberts's lobby to wait for a meeting and wound up talking to his secretary. A nice, pretty girl named Carol Emrich."

"Yes, we're aware of Miss Emrich," Agent Strong said.

"Mr. Fielding was made aware that Miss Emrich is missing," Detective Coverdale informed Agent Strong.

"Oh hell," Strong said, looking gruff. "You guys tell him?"

"My personal assistant told me this morning," George Fielding said. "Doug called me this morning with the news. Apparently her parents are in quite a distress."

Agent Strong waved the matter aside. "Okay, she's missing. That much you know. But let's cut to the chase. Detective Coverdale and Allen Frey told me last night that you believe Mark Wiseman was the man responsible for the attack on you, and that Bernard Roberts ordered it. I'd like to hear this."

"Of course." George Fielding took a long pull off his Sprite. He would have to ring the nurse for another one pretty soon. "Let me resume. Like I said, I wound up waiting in Bernard's lobby for a meeting and struck up a conversation with Carol. She looked radiant; bubbly, you might say. This struck me as somewhat odd, since in the previous eight or nine months she had seemed, oh . . . morose, I guess. I had seen the interplay between her and Bernard and knew that the two of them were involved in an affair. Bernard didn't volunteer information, nor did I inquire. Let's just say it was obvious. But when I walked into the lobby that day Carol was a completely changed woman. She was happy, smiling, vivacious—more so than usual. We struck up a conversation and she made frequent mentions of a boyfriend she was seeing. When I inquired who it was, she quickly assured me that it was nobody I would know."

"The guy she was seeing could have been anybody," Agent Strong said. "So what?"

"I'll get to that in a minute," George Fielding said, holding up his hand. "Bernard became free and we had our meeting. As fate would have it, the topic of the meeting turned to the potential takeover. We were going over possible cuts in the budget and Bernard became very combative. He emphasized over and over that he thought the merger was a wrong idea—this despite all the legwork we had done to prove to the executive staff of Free State that it would be better for their financial status—and that he was against it all the way. I didn't think about this conversation until much later—yesterday, in fact—when I thought about John, Samuels, and Krueger and how they had met their end. I realized then that I had almost met a similar fate and that's when it occurred to me that Bernard had been behind this."

"Because Bernard was so *against* the merger and yourself and the other three gentlemen that were killed were all *for* the merger," Detective Coverdale said. "Is that correct, Mr. Fielding?"

George nodded. "It's a silly notion, I know. I don't know who ordered the investigation on Bernard, but—"

"That would have been your colleague, Fred Johansen," Allen said. "He hired me back in August to investigate Samuels's death."

"Yes. Thanks goodness he did. And thanks to your hard work and perseverance, you've been able to find what Bernard has been up to the past seven years."

"I can buy corporate fraud," Agent Strong said, looking exasperated. "I still don't see how that can tie Bernard with conspiracy to commit murder."

"I think I may have the final two pieces to convince you," George said quietly. He looked up at the three men and made a weak attempt at a smile. He sipped at his Sprite; almost gone. "The evening of our meeting I asked Bernard if he would accompany me to dinner. He politely turned me down and said he had another engagement. I wound up taking dinner by myself at a nice restaurant in Newport Beach called Calavan's. On my way out I saw a young couple in an embrace, and they were quite passionate about it, I might add. As I got to my car I gave them another look and recognized them instantly as Carol Emrich and Mark Wiseman."

The three men glanced at each other, then back at George. Frey was nodding his smile appearing to say *this is just what I thought*. George ignored their reactions and continued. "The next morning I had another meeting with Bernard and some other board members. I saw Carol again, but I didn't reveal what I had seen to either of them. I did, however, inquire with Carol on how her evening had gone and the girl literally blushed. She was entirely smitten with Mr. Wiseman and it showed in the way she reacted. She said, 'I had a wonderful evening, Mr. Fielding. Simply wonderful.' I asked if she had gone out with her boyfriend last night, she said she had and we left it at that. That confirmed it for me. She and Mark Wiseman were romantically involved and she was keeping it under wraps, I imagine to hide it from Bernard."

He paused. The Sprite can was empty and he picked up the CALL button. "Will you excuse me please? I'd like to get a refill."

"By all means," Agent Strong said. Fielding smiled and rang for the nurse. When she came he asked for a refill and she returned with it a few minutes later.

"Bernard reiterated his position at the meeting that afternoon," George related, pausing between sips of Sprite. "The entire board and executive staff was present at that meeting, including Fred Johansen. Again, I didn't find anything out of the ordinary regarding Bernard's position. A few of the other executive staff members and senior management personnel were against the move. The meeting adjourned briefly for lunch and as myself and a few of my colleagues were heading toward the parking lot to drive to a restaurant, I noticed Mark Wiseman again. He walked past us, just as normal as can be. It was a nice day, and he was dressed casually, but not sloppy. Business casual is a more appropriate term.

"Anyway, as he passed us one of the people with us, a woman who is vice president of Claims made an aside about the tattoo Mark had on his arm. She found it to be rather, well, cute. One of the members of my party asked her if she knew him and she replied that his name was Mark Wiseman, that he was a computer tape librarian who had just moved over from swing shift to the day shift. Then somebody else commented rather sarcastically that perhaps Mark should have remained working nights—that to look the way Mark looked with his long hair was perhaps a risk to the business health of Free State." He chuckled and took a sip of Sprite. "I've always hated such elitist bullshit myself. Anyway, we had our lunch, then came back and resumed our meeting.

"The meeting didn't officially adjourn for the day until six p.m. I accompanied Bernard back to his office and waited for him at Carol's desk while he prepared to leave; this time we were going to go out for dinner. Carol and the rest of the executive and support staff had left for the evening, so Bernard and I were the only ones in the suite. I sat at Carol's desk and leafed through her appointment book, which she had left sitting on her desk."

"Was this her personal appointment book?" Detective Coverdale asked.

"No. It was an appointment book secretaries keep for those they support. It consisted of Bernard's business schedule."

Detective Coverdale nodded and traded a glance with Allen Frey, who remained stony faced, yet optimistic. George Fielding took a sip of Sprite, licked his lips, and continued. "I was just casually leafing through it, not really paying much attention to what was on it, until I came to the month of June. And it was there, penciled in for an appointment at four-thirty p.m.—which date I couldn't tell you now, but it would have had to have been June 7 or 8, I think—was Mark Wiseman's name."

The two detectives and FBI agent were silent for a

minute, as if analyzing this bit of information. Frey got the significance before the other two. "Mark Wiseman's name was in his appointment book almost one full week before Martin John was killed," he said. "It also provides a connection between Bernard and Mark."

The two detectives and FBI agent were silent as they appeared to mull this over. Agent Strong sighed. "I must admit, George, that does sound rather convincing. Not strong enough to stand up in court, mind you, but it's something we may be able to go on."

George smiled. "That's what I thought."

Agent Strong traded a glance with the two detectives and turned back to George. "Would you have any idea where Bernard may have disappeared to?"

"None, I'm afraid."

"A vacation spot he may have mentioned? The city or state where friends or family may live?"

"Bernard had exotic tastes in vacation spots. I know he has a sister who lives in the Bay Area, but I doubt he'd hide out there. From what he told me he and his sister don't get along very well."

"He might have headed off for whatever exotic location he likes to vacation," Allen Frey said. "Guys like him, the minute they go on the lam they head to somewhere nice and exotic. To go underground and live like a fugitive, they have to do it in class."

Detective Coverdale nodded. "That's right. We might want to start there."

"In that case you're looking at places like the Virgin Islands, Baja, the Cayman Islands, Hawaii,"

George said from his hospital bed. "He liked Cancun a bit, too."

"What about Carol Emrich?" Agent Strong asked. "It's safe to assume that Mark Wiseman is with her. Since you don't seem to know much about Mark, is there anything you know about Carol that might shed some light on where she might have gone?"

George pursed his lips in contemplation and shook his head. "I don't know. Bernard used to take her everywhere with him. I would say she had the same tastes in vacation spots as he—"

"I doubt she and Mark would have headed to the Cayman Islands to hide out," Allen said. "I think it would be safe to say that the attack on you didn't go as planned and that Bernard is quite pissed off. Mark and Carol probably took off for points unknown out of fear of retribution from Bernard, rather than fear from the law."

"And Bernard?" George asked, eyebrows raised questionably.

"Either he has a sense that the noose is tightening around his own neck due to the bungled attempt on your life, or he took off to try to hunt down Mark," Allen said. "He's only been missing for a day. He must know by now that Mark and Carol skipped out on him."

"True," George said, nodding. "In that case I'm afraid I can't offer you much. They could have gone anywhere."

"You don't think she would have gone to Nebraska where her parents live?" Coverdale asked.

"Well, anything's possible," George said. "But I

would think if she was afraid that Bernard would be coming after her and Mark to kill them, her parents' house would be the last place she would go. Besides, her parents are frantic, so it's obvious she hasn't contacted them."

"What about Mark?" Agent Strong asked the two detectives.

"We don't know too much about him," Detective Coverdale said. "We're doing a background check on him now."

"Well, let's get something over the wire about them," Agent Strong said. "We can pull their photos from DMV. Hopefully we can find them before Bernard does."

As the men were preparing to leave, George nodded at each of them. Detective Coverdale nodded back. "Don't worry. We'll get them."

"Thank you, Detective," George said.

Allen Frey shook George's hand. "I hope you recover quickly."

"So do I," George said.

Chapter Twenty-four

They pulled into the Three Rivers city limits a little before midnight on Thursday, January 13.

The decision to hole up for awhile at Three Rivers had been made Wednesday morning by Carol. She'd suggested it to Mark the morning after returning from the desert and his revelation to her. "I know the area very well and it's remote. Nobody will ever think of looking for us there."

"I should think so," Mark had said. "Nobody will think of looking for us there because they haven't heard of it."

After breakfasting at a Pueblo diner attached to the motel and checking out of their room, they headed west. Mark navigated the first part of the trip while Carol drove. They hooked up with Interstate 58 to Bakersfield, and then Interstate 65 into Three Rivers.

They got a late start. Mark was exhausted from his ordeal in the desert, and he slept. By the time they gathered their things and checked out, it was late afternoon. By the time they reached Bakersfield it was closing in on nine o'clock in the evening. "We've got another two hours or so," Carol said from the passenger seat as Mark drove. "You want to keep going?"

"Might as well."

They had called ahead to the Three Rivers Lodge and booked a room during a stop in Needles. They stopped in a small town at the foothills of the Sierra Nevadas and bought tire chains. "Storm dumped six inches of snow two weeks ago and the streets might still be a bit slushy," the attendant told Mark as he made the purchase inside. "Another storm is expected to hit in a few days though. You planning on staying up there long?"

"We might," Mark said as he took the chains. "You think I'll need to put these on now?"

"How far up you going?"

"Three Rivers."

"You won't need them if that's how far you're going. Long as you get up there in the next few hours. We're supposed to have snow flurries later this evening."

The drive up the winding mountain road took a little over an hour. It had been over three years since Mark had made a drive like this through the mountains and he was a little nervous as he piloted the car through turn after turn. The Camaro's heater was on, and the interior of the car was warm and cozy. When they passed the sign that told them they were entering the city limits, Carol told him to be on the lookout for the sign that would lead them to the lodge. "It'll be on the left," she said.

They reached the motel a few minutes later. There were only three other cars in the parking lot. Mark scrutinized them closely as they circled and parked. There were two Range Rovers and one station wagon. Not a black Mercedes to be seen. Mark smiled weakly at Carol. "Guess this place is as safe as any."

"Of course it is," Carol said, getting her purse. "Why wouldn't it be?"

"I don't know. Guess I'm just paranoid."

Carol leaned over and kissed him. "It'll be fine. Bernard will never think of looking for us here. Besides, he doesn't even know we're together. He has no idea you're with me."

I hope you're right, Mark thought, as he followed Carol outside to the front desk to check in for the night.

They were just about to bed down for the night when there was a light knock on the door.

Mark was dressed in a pair of sweat pants and a T-shirt. Carol was in the bathroom brushing her teeth. They had turned the heater on in the room and it was now at a nice, toasty level. Mark's heart leaped in his chest at the sound of the knock and he quickly backed up toward the bathroom. "Turn the water off!" he whispered.

Carol looked over at him, foamy toothpaste in her mouth as she brushed her teeth. "Huh?"

Mark leaned over and turned the water off. "Somebody just knocked on the door," he whispered.

Carol spit out the toothpaste, her eyes suddenly wide with fear. "Are you sure? Maybe it's just—"

The knocking came again. Three light raps.

They both froze. Mark's heart was pounding. "Stay here," he whispered. He crept slowly toward the door, his senses on full alert. Something told him that he shouldn't go right up to the door and peer out the peephole because whatever was on the other side was dangerous; whoever was on the other side was hunting them. He hung back, sniffing the air and he picked up the scent right away: the sharp, metallic scent of madness. "Bernard," he whispered.

Carol had ventured a step into the room but she hung back, afraid. Mark retreated, the hairs along his arms rising. "It's Bernard," he whispered.

"Bernard? How—"

The door shuddered with a heavy thud as something slammed against it from the other side. The sound of it startled them and they jumped back. Mark grabbed Carol's hand and pulled her into the bathroom. The door shuddered again and this time there was a splintering crack; it would only take a few more slams before it splintered open.

"Stay here!" Mark headed back into the bedroom, his adrenaline surging.

"Mark, don't go out there!" She followed him out, trying to pull at him and he shoved her back into the bathroom. Whoever was slamming against the door wasn't doing a very good job of it; the door was barely splintered and the more he slammed against it, the more noise he made. Which meant it had to be Bernard. A man with an Ivy League education and who lived an upwardly mobile professional life wouldn't know how to bust a door down if his life depended on it.

Mark positioned himself by the north wall, which

would be out of the line of sight for whoever was trying to break in. The door splintered more as Bernard—or whoever the hell it was—kept throwing himself against it. Mark could now hear the grunts of the person on the other side and he caught their scent, too. It was definitely Bernard.

"*Get down!*" Mark yelled to Carol.

Carol ducked down behind the bed and the door finally gave on Bernard's last blow, snapping open with the splintering of wood.

Mark got a brief glimpse of Bernard as he stumbled into the room; even after all the work it had taken to break the door down his clothes didn't look the least bit rumpled. He looked around the room wildly, his right hand clutching a handgun. Mark sprang at him, slamming into the bigger man. As their bodies hit the floor he heard the loud report of the gun as a shot went off.

Mark's anger exploded. He pinned the hand that held the handgun to the floor and grunted as he tried to hold Bernard down. Bernard's left hand shot up and struck Mark in the face. Mark barely felt it; already he could feel instinct taking over and he silently tried to empty himself out to allow the change to occur. The last eight months of murderous, hateful emotions that he had harbored toward Bernard Roberts were all coming to the surface and they manifested themselves in a fighting rage. Bernard hit Mark twice, once in the face, the second blow glanced off his chest. Mark barely felt them. A growl rose deep in his chest and he squeezed the hand that held the gun. Bernard grimaced in pain. "*I'm going to kill you,*" Bernard hissed.

"It's going to be the other way around," Mark growled. His left hand locked around Bernard's throat.

Bernard struggled wildly, almost throwing Mark off. He struggled to get his hand free, but Mark applied a vice-like pressure to it. Mark grimaced, sweat running down his brow as he tried to will the change to come over him.

Suddenly Carol was looming over them both. She stepped down on the gun and tried to take it from Bernard's fingers. "Give it up, Bernard!"

"*Fuck you!*" Bernard's mad eyes rolled up at her with blinding hate.

Mark locked his fingers around Bernard's windpipe and pressed down.

Bernard gave one last burst of energy as he struggled. His mouth opened as he tried to suck in air and failed. He went limp suddenly, his eyes closing. Mark tightened his grip around Bernard's throat.

"Mark, let go," Carol said. She reached down and pulled the gun from Bernard's grip, which had loosened with Bernard's unconsciousness. She threw the firearm on the bed.

The last eight months flashed before Mark's eyes; Bernard's threats, sitting in his office watching himself on the security video as he tried to fight the change; Bernard showing him the gun and the silver bullets, telling him what he would do if he didn't follow his orders.

"*Mark! Stop it, you're going to kill him!*"

All those months of living with the shame of knowing that he had been made a slave to this man.

The shame he felt in being manipulated, in having his curse used against him . . .

"*Mark!*"

He felt her hands grab his and try to pry his fingers off of Bernard's throat. He felt himself breaking down, the anger shattering his emotions.

"Mark, honey, you've got to let him go." Carol's voice finally cut through the din. The fog cleared from his mind and suddenly he was on the floor hunched over Bernard's prone body, his left hand clutched around the executive's throat. Carol was beside him, crying, trying to loosen his grip from Bernard's throat.

Mark released his grasp with a strangled cry. He fell back, panic suddenly taking center stage. "Oh my God," he moaned.

"Come on, Mark, we've got to get out of here." Carol dragged Mark away and tried to get him to stand on his feet. Bernard didn't move; he was a large, lifeless lump on the motel room floor.

An excited voice coming from outside cut through the fog. Mark blinked and looked down at Bernard's body, then looked around the room. The front door to their motel room was leaning against the wall, the frame cracked. Although the air blowing in from outside was freezing cold, Mark could barely feel it. He felt warm with the rush of adrenaline. Sweat dotted his brow.

"Mark, we've got to get out of here!" It was Carol, leaning next to him, gripping his shoulders firmly.

Mark looked at her and nodded. They stood up together, his arms reaching out to hold her.

A big bearded man who resembled a lumberjack leaned in the room. His eyes widened when he saw the carnage and Bernard's body on the floor. "Jesus Christ, what the hell happened?"

"This guy just broke in and tried to kill us," Mark said, heading to where his and Carol's suitcases still lay unpacked.

"Call the police," Carol said, her voice breaking.

The guy gave a quick nod and disappeared.

Mark slammed his suitcase closed and turned to Carol. "You okay?"

"Of course," she said, the sobbing tone in her voice gone. "The minute men hear the sound of a woman breaking down, especially when they tell them to call the police, they head off to do exactly as they're told." She grinned.

Mark hefted his suitcase up and handed Carol hers. "Let's get the fuck out of here."

They headed straight outside to the car, not even glancing around to see if anybody—the night manager, other motel guests—were poking their heads outside to see what the commotion was all about. Carol unlocked the doors and they threw their baggage into the backseat. Carol started the car and peeled out of the driveway the minute Mark slammed the passenger car door shut, and they turned right, heading south down Route 11. The faint sounds of sirens emerged from the north as they headed back down the hills, away from the Three Rivers Lodge.

PART THREE

Chapter Twenty-five

Frederick Johansen was staying in the Executive Suite of the Marriott in Newport Beach. It was by far his favorite hotel when he stayed in Orange County for business; it was right on the bustling harbor, and in the summer there were plenty of attractive women to ogle as they walked down the boardwalk. The area around the harbor itself sported fine seafood restaurants, quaint little gift shops, and a nice country club. A mile or so down the 55 Freeway was the South Coast Plaza, and not far from that was the Orange County Opera House. John Wayne Airport in Irvine was a quick hop, skip, and jump away, and not two blocks from the airport was where Elaine Brewer, a high-class call girl that Fred often hired to accompany him to social mixers when he was in town, kept a condo. In fact, he had just called Elaine and had arranged a date with her for tonight at her usual fee—fifteen hundred dollars. That fee would get him the enjoyment of her company for dinner, a stroll around Crystal Court, a massage and a bath in his room, and then a night of making love to that fabulous body. Fred really saw nothing wrong with employing Elaine's services. After all, he wasn't married anymore, and he didn't have the patience, nor the time it took, to cultivate new relationships. Plus, he could afford it. The only time he disapproved of employing the services of an escort was when you were married, like David Samuels had been. And look what had happened to *him*.

Fred frowned. He knew that David hadn't been killed because he had been screwing around behind his wife's back with a similar woman, one that he kept as a mistress. David had been killed because Bernard Roberts saw it in his sick, twisted mind to eliminate him due to David's position on the Free State merger. Infidelity, and the bad karma it produced, had nothing to do with it.

Fred glanced at his watch. Elaine was scheduled to show up at the hotel in forty minutes. He had just showered, shaved, and changed into evening clothes—black slacks, white shirt, black tie, and a black jacket. He had sat down on the bed to pull on his socks when he had slipped into this introspective funk. He was here in Newport Beach because Agent Strong wanted him to be in the area when they caught Bernard. Fred had complied, and had checked into the Marriott for the week. He had a few meetings and miscellaneous business to take care of in Orange County, and thanks to Federal Express, and fax machines, he could conduct his other business interests in the comfort of his room.

At first, Fred wasn't going to go out at all. It was

Friday evening and the weather forecast said rain by Saturday night. Fred had been in Orange County for the past few days and he hadn't seen Elaine since his arrival. He hadn't called her for fear of having those plans dashed if Agent Strong called with the news. When Thursday rolled around and no news followed, Fred had broken down and called her, arranging a date for tonight. Then what happens but Agent Strong calls him this morning to tell him the news that Bernard Roberts had been caught.

"Three Rivers PD picked him up at the Three Rivers Lodge late last night," Agent Strong said. "Motherfucker was slicker than we thought. He knew *exactly* where to find them and he was one step ahead of us. They're extraditing him to Orange County today."

Fred had wanted to know what the hell had happened and Agent Strong gave it to him in a nutshell: Bernard had driven up to Three Rivers and had checked into a motel down the road from the Three Rivers Lodge. Last night he had gone to the lodge and when he saw Carol Emrich's car in the parking lot, he had gone to the front desk and told the clerk that he was supposed to meet some friends there, a young couple named Mark Wiseman and Carol Emrich. The clerk had told him they were in room 17. He had broken the door down, only Mark must have been lying in wait because he tackled Bernard. The gun had gone off, there was a struggle, and somehow Bernard was choked into unconsciousness. "Carol Emrich and Mark Wiseman fled immediately after. Bernard was just regaining consciousness when the Three Rivers PD showed up and since they found a gun in the room they placed Bernard in custody. Of course, by then we had it over the wire that he was wanted for questioning and they held him for us."

It was that *wanted for questioning* thing that bothered Fred. *What is this wanted for questioning crap? I thought Agent Strong said that there's enough evidence to nail the bastard on fraud and embezzling?*

Agent Strong wouldn't comment further when Fred asked him about the charges. He only said he would call him later and then he had hung up.

That one phone call had ruined Fred's whole day. He had been planning on catching up on some other business in his room, but instead he had gone down to the hotel bar and had a few drinks. Whenever something distressing emerged in his life, Fred always sought solace by retreating to the nearest bar—not to drown his misery in alcohol, but to surround himself with people, to lose himself in his thoughts as the normal bustle of bar life floated behind him. It was his way of chilling out.

After a few drinks he had taken a walk along the boardwalk, then had gone back to his room. There were no messages on his voice mail. The afternoon had zipped by and he supposed the best thing to do was just shower and get ready for his evening with Elaine. He doubted Agent Strong would call again today anyway, and if he did he wouldn't meet with the man until tomorrow.

Frederick Johansen sighed and slipped into a pair of Tony Llama boots. He rose to his feet and inspected himself in a full-length mirror. His steel gray hair was combed and styled perfectly, the lines on his face only serving to accentuate his ruggedness. Women had always told him he was attractive as hell, and Fred had never really understood why. He was neither overweight nor skinny, nor was he built of rippling muscle. But now that he had attained the ripe old age of fifty-five, he supposed that he had gotten better looking with age, like a fine wine. He grinned at himself. The skinny, gawky kid that used to stare back at him from the mirror in high school had changed into quite a good-looking man, if he didn't say so himself. After almost forty years he was finally beginning to see that.

His thoughts were interrupted by the ringing of the telephone. He picked it up. "Yeah."

"Fred, Agent Strong here."

"What's up, Strong?"

There was a hint of hesitancy in Agent Strong's voice and Fred caught it immediately. His stomach tightened. "This better not be what I think it is."

"We had to release him."

Although Fred was expecting this, hearing it was still stunning. He released a sigh. "What happened?"

"There wasn't enough evidence to hold him on the embezzling charge," Agent Strong said, sounding disappointed. "It's going to take a few months to go through all his records and make a thorough investigation. In the meantime, the most he could be charged with at the motel was simple breaking and entering. He posted bail and was released this morning."

"Goddammit!"

"I'm sorry, Fred," Agent Strong said. He sounded defeated. "But . . . well, legally we couldn't just hold him pending the investigation. The minute he was placed in custody he got on the phone with his lawyer. He was pretty much released the minute he reached Orange County."

Fred closed his eyes and rubbed the bridge of his nose, gripping the receiver tight in his other hand. "Okay," he said, opening his eyes. "He's out. Now what?"

"All we can do is proceed to gather evidence against him for the embezzling, but that's going to be tougher now. His lawyer is already on to us and is preparing to file an injunction in court against the investigation."

"Can he do that?"

"Sure. Won't do much, though. Bernard obviously knows this. He's doing it to stall for time."

"How long do you think it will take to get the evidence you need?"

"With your help, hopefully a month."

"And with this lawyer around to fuck things up?"

Agent Strong sighed. "I don't know. Three, four months maybe."

"Shit!"

"We have to find Carol Emrich and Mark Wiseman."

"No shit you've got to find them. Any news on where they might have gone?"

"None." Embarrassment crept into Agent Strong's voice again. "I'm afraid that ... well ... it wasn't properly conveyed to the Three Rivers officials that Mark and Carol were wanted for questioning. They just about creamed their pants when they slapped the cuffs on Bernard. Small town cops like that . . . they hardly ever deal with federal cases."

"So after Bernard bursts in there and tries killing Mark, they overpower him, then hightail it the hell out of there and nobody bothered to follow up on where they might have gone?"

Agent Strong paused for a moment. "I'm afraid so."

Shit! Fred steeled himself against the anger that threatened to come out, fighting it down. "You did issue an APB on Carol Emrich and Mark Wiseman, right?"

"Yes, we did."

"And?"

"Nothing so far. We know they ditched their car not far from the Three Rivers Lodge. A stolen car report came in early this morning, not far from where Carol's Camaro was found. We think they got away in a 1988 Toyota Celica. They could be anywhere by now."

"I want them found. I don't care if you *can't* pin murder charges on Mark; they can be sought as material witnesses against Bernard Roberts."

"We're working on it," Agent Strong said. His voice sounded less nervous now, more in control. "We have people looking for them."

"What's the next step regarding Bernard?"

"That would be up to your board members, I guess," Agent Strong replied. "Legally we can't do anything except gather evidence and build our case. I would think that with suspicion of embezzling you could have him fired."

"I'll arrange a phone conference on that as soon as possible," Fred said. "In the meantime, call me as soon as you get any news." He told the agent that he would be at the hotel for another two days and could be reached at his home in Phoenix afterward, and hung up.

He felt drained, as if the suddenness of the news had zapped all his energy. He had been afraid this was going to happen. He'd hoped it wouldn't come to that but it had, and now they had to deal with it. He picked up the phone again and was just about to dial William Rose's number to talk strategy when he stopped. Why go through all this now? Bernard Roberts obviously knew that the events of the past week were grounds for his immediate termination; he would know that the board was made aware of the investigation into his embezzling. And besides, it was nearing five p.m. on a Friday evening; he might not be able to reach everybody on the board tonight. He could leave messages with them this weekend.

There was a knock on the door to his suite. He turned toward it, smiling. Besides, there were other immediate needs to be taken care of.

Feeling relaxed, pushing the latest problems to the back of his mind, Frederick Johansen answered his door and greeted Elaine Brewer with a hug and kiss that made her wonder what he was so happy about.

Chapter Twenty-six

When they pulled out of the Three Rivers Lodge, Carol had to resist the temptation to put the pedal to the metal. Surprisingly, Mark was calm throughout the ordeal and managed to coax Carol into slowing down and pulling onto a side road. They drove down the meandering road until Mark saw a turn-off; he directed Carol to it and saw that it wound into some brush.

"Let's park here and wait it out for a minute," he said.

Carol pulled in but was wary about turning the car off. "I don't think we should stay here for very long," she said, hugging herself. In their haste to leave they had neglected to dress in warmer clothes. Mark was still in his sweat pants and a T-shirt, and Carol was dressed in a sweatshirt and sweat pants. Their coats and heavy clothes were in the suitcases in the back seat. "It's cold out here," she said. "We should find somewhere else to stay."

"Once the police investigate they'll get our names from the front desk," Mark had said. "They'll be looking for us."

"So what are we going to do?"

Mark thought about it a minute, then donned some warmer clothes from what was in the suitcase and stepped outside. He wandered along the dirt road until he found a house sitting up on a small hill. The occupants of the home appeared to be fast asleep judging by the lack of lights in the house. More important were the two cars in the parking lot; a brand new 1991 Chevy Blazer and a 1988 Toyota Celica. Mark tried the Celica first and found it was unlocked. He didn't know how to hotwire a car, so he crept up to the house and tried the door. The stereotype was correct: people didn't lock their doors this far out in the boonies.

Using his animal stealth, Mark silently opened the door and crept inside the house. Despite the darkness he was able to see everything, and he found a set of keys within a minute. He pilfered them from a shelf near the front door and quietly let himself back out. Once at the car he tried them on the Celica: perfect fit. He released the emergency brake, put the car in neutral, and coasted it down the driveway. When it was a goodly distance from the house, he started the engine and drove it to the clearing they had parked in.

They quickly transferred all their belongings to the Celica and were heading back to the main highway within minutes. By the time they reached Bakersfield it was nearing two a.m. Carol suggested pulling over somewhere and catching some sleep for a few hours, but Mark vetoed that; he was so wired now that he wouldn't be able to sleep. What he wanted to do was get out of the state as soon as possible.

Once in Bakersfield they retraced their way to Interstate 10. They followed the 10 all the way to the California/Arizona border. Carol fell asleep and got a good two hours' worth between Palm Springs and Needles. She woke up around six and by then Mark was getting tired. They switched driving roles at a truck stop just past the California border and continued on until they reached another truck stop a few hours later, literally in the middle of the desert. Mark had dozed lightly and woke up when they reached the truck stop. Already the sun was struggling to rise.

"Pull over here," he said, motioning to the motel/diner off the interstate. A full service gas station was across the way, and both lots were full of eighteen-wheel tractor-trailers. "We'll be fine here."

Carol pulled in and Mark checked them in to a room at the motel. Once in the room they crashed. They didn't wake up until four o'clock that afternoon.

They left the Toyota in the lot the following day and hitched a ride with a trucker to El Paso, Texas. From there they went over the border to Juarez, Mexico, where they bought a Chevy Suburban for four grand. Mark paid for the vehicle with some of the cash in the manila envelope and they drove over the border without even having to sign ownership papers. The vehicle had Texas plates, which the seller had switched with a pair of plates from Oklahoma to play it safe. "These will be better," he said, his grin gap-toothed. "You'll go far with this."

Thank God for shady used-car dealers who were experts in rubbing down vehicle identification numbers and switching plates, doing everything they could to erase all identity of a stolen car. By the end of the day they were heading north in the Suburban toward Oklahoma. They stayed in Carlsbad, New Mexico that night, then drove on to Oklahoma, then through Kansas into Missouri. They stopped in Florence four days after they fled Three Rivers because a strong winter storm was starting to dump snow along the highway and the Missouri State Highway Patrol was setting up roadblocks.

"Better for you to pull over if you can," one patrolman said when they pulled up to a checkpoint; they had been heading east on Interstate 63. "The road ahead is going to be pretty rough going. We're expecting twenty inches of snow in the next day."

So they pulled over and meandered down a secondary road until they found a little town called Florence and found the Star Motor Lodge. Their first week there had been spent virtually snowbound. The storm dumped forty inches of snow and the wind chill dipped down to eighteen below zero. Mark and Carol spent much of that time huddled in their room keeping each other warm and keeping their fears at bay.

When the storm abated a few days later, Mark suggested they stay for a while. "At least until we can think of what to do," he said. Despite having enough cash to carry them through for awhile, Mark suggested they get jobs so they wouldn't attract attention. "People might think we're drug dealers or something. Might as well blend in as much as we can."

Blending in was more difficult than they thought it would be. They landed jobs at a small diner in the main drag of town—if you could call the two intersecting streets that comprised Florence, Missouri the main drag. The diner's clientele consisted of farmers who showed up mainly for their morning breakfast of eggs and hashbrowns.

Despite easily landing jobs at the diner, the patrons immediately picked them out as city folks. Carol came up with a safe alibi; they were both from Omaha, Nebraska, and were hoping to get away from the hustle and bustle of the big city and settle into a rural area. Mark kept mostly silent as Carol knew Nebraska well enough to successfully field the questions that would come up when offering bits and pieces of their new background. For the most part, Mark thought they were doing all right as far as escaping the scrutiny of the locals. Within a few weeks they were hardly being paid a second glance. Just as long as Mark was able to prepare the orders fast enough and Carol was able to serve with a smile, they were doing okay.

And through it all they tried to keep up with the news in Orange County as best as they could. No matter how many newspapers they read, or how many times they watched the news, there was simply no news on the arrest of Bernard Roberts for anything—attempted murder, embezzling, or otherwise.

A month later, Carol Emrich finally cracked under the strain. It was a cold day, the sky spitting snow, and Carol was due to leave for work in thirty minutes. She had just put her waitress uniform on and suddenly stumbled out of the bathroom, crying. "I can't take it anymore!"

Mark took Carol in his arms as she sobbed and she leaned against him. He held her, her sobs more of tiredness and frustration than hurt. The four days it had taken them to drive across the country had been wrought with fear that they were going to be pulled over; or worse, that Bernard Roberts was dogging their every step. In the weeks that passed they lived with the fear that Bernard would appear on their doorstep.

Carol's sobbing dwindled. Mark held her, rubbing her back. "I'm so tired," she said between sniffles.

"I know," Mark said.

Carol stood up and walked to the dresser, wiping the tears from her eyes with a Kleenex. "I'm tired and I'm scared and I don't know how long I can live like this."

Mark didn't know how to respond to that. He sat on the bed silent.

"Mark?"

"What?"

Carol turned around. There were dark circles under her eyes. She was no longer wearing makeup the way she had when he had known her in Orange County; she was a pretty woman, but without the makeup her face looked tired, worn down. She didn't even look like the same woman he had met and fallen in love with. "How long are we going to keep living like this?"

"It's only been a month," Mark said. "If you want we can move somewhere else. Maybe a bigger town, like Sedalia, or head east to St. Louis. In a bigger city we might be able to blend back in with the same standard of living we had before."

He knew that Carol was going to suggest that they give themselves up; she hadn't said it yet, but he could tell. She had been hinting around it. The past week she had suggested going back to Orange County, or calling their friends to tell them they were okay. Mark had nixed both swiftly, countering them with, "If we turn ourselves in we're in deep shit. Bernard will find a way to kill us both." Now she brought it up again and Mark quickly vetoed it.

"For all we know Bernard might be in custody now," Carol argued. "After all, it's been a month. Don't you think the cops would have done some checking when they picked him up in Three Rivers?"

"I just don't want to risk it," Mark said, rubbing Carol's shoulders. "If he is in custody, he's already spilled the beans about my involvement. That will be enough for the authorities to begin linking me with all three murders, as well as the attempted murder of George Fielding. There's also the matter of my parents. And then there's the tape."

"Nobody's going to believe what they're seeing on that tape!" Carol said, animated now.

"Yeah, maybe not. But why risk it?"

Carol opened her mouth to say something, then closed it. She turned to the mirror and opened her makeup case. The subject appeared to be closed with her. "I don't want to argue about this anymore. If we do I'm just going to cry and I can't be late to work again."

Mark didn't say anything. They'd had a similar conversation the previous night and Carol had gotten so upset that she had been late to work at the diner. The diner's owner had chewed her out for her tardiness and that had only made her more upset. "I just hate what we've become," she said, applying eye shadow, trying hard to keep her voice from breaking.

"I know," Mark said. "We'll think of something."

"You said that last night." Carol touched up her other eye, then applied lipstick. She stood back, appraising herself in the mirror. "That's good enough for these country yokels."

As Carol gathered her jacket, boots, and purse, Mark remained seated on the bed. They had spent the last three weeks at the Star Motor Lodge, resisting the urge to move into the more spacious dwelling of a two-bedroom house in the sticks. As much as Mark wanted to settle down in one place, the urge to move someplace else was stronger. Moving to more permanent dwellings would only serve to put them closer in the crosshairs of those hunting for them.

"I get off at nine-thirty," Carol said, slinging her purse over her shoulder. "I would say that we'll talk when I get home, but obviously if the conversation is just going to go around in circles about us doing something about our situation, we might as well forget it."

"Carol—" Mark said, turning around to follow her out, but she wasn't hearing any of it. She strode past him and out the door into the cold, winter afternoon.

Mark stood at the foot of the bed as he heard the

engine of the Suburban start outside. The diner was only half a mile down the road, but with this weather and another storm due in the next eighteen hours, it was better that Carol drive to work. Mark had the evening off and the only thing on his agenda for the evening was chilling out and trying to think about what their next move should be.

But what should that next move be? Move to St. Louis? Maybe further east to Memphis, Tennessee? Out of the country altogether? Mark had toyed with the idea of getting new identities for the both of them, but he had no idea if that would work. They would eventually be caught anyway.

But they couldn't simply give themselves up. Even if Bernard was safe behind bars now, Mark would still be facing charges. He was damned if he was going to take the rap for Bernard, which he knew would end up happening.

Mark flopped down on the king-sized bed and closed his eyes. He felt a migraine coming on and he pinched the bridge of his nose. The headaches were coming on more regularly now, especially since they had been on the run. He was also tired and hadn't been getting much sleep. Maybe if he took a nap he would wake up with a fresh perspective on things. Maybe if that happened by the time Carol came home from work they could talk this problem through rationally and sensibly.

He felt the sandman come and he gave in to it. Within minutes he was fast asleep. And with sleep came the dream.

He was in Big Bear, six months after graduating from high school. He had remained home after that fateful day in mid-June, when he had joined the Gardena High School's Class of 1982 on the campus football field. It had been a typical June day; overcast and sullen. He didn't even know why he decided to show up for the ceremony, but show up he did, in cap and gown. He had paid for the cap and gown himself with money earned from a part-time job he'd gotten a few months before at a gas station. His parents surely weren't going to spring for them; it would only take away from the beer money.

Apparently attending their only child's high school graduation hadn't been worth the effort of blasting past the morning hangover, because neither parent had been present at the ceremony. Mark had taken the bus to a friend's house, had changed into his gown there, and had ridden along with his buddy's parents to the school. He had told his friend that his parents were coming from work, but as he sat out on the football field with the rest of his classmates, some of whom he'd known since kindergarten, he knew his parents weren't going to show up. He'd tried to push the thought out of his mind, instead concentrating on the milestone he was achieving with graduation. He was now a man. He was now finally, in the eyes of the rest of the world, an adult.

He had been right; his parents hadn't come to the ceremony. In fact, they had been pissed off at him when he'd come home later that evening, mildly intoxicated from an after-graduation celebratory bacchanal. The argument had tipped into violence when his father had struck him across the head with a spatula. Mark had almost felt the beast leap out of him right then, but instead he'd turned tail and headed out the door, hardly even aware that he was crying hot tears of anger and hurt.

He had spent that night at the Calvary Baptist Church day care center, just down the street from his home. He had slept in the day care's playground, and when he woke up the next morning he'd made his way silently back to the house. Both parents had found the motivation to get up early and truck their sorry asses to their respective jobs and Mark had sought the opportunity to dash inside for a shower, shave, and to gather a quick change of clothes. Then he had riffled through his parents' things, coming up with five hundred and eighty-three dollars. He'd packed all his stuff in one large duffel bag, then headed out. He never went back.

His friend Shane Peters had taken him in. Shane had lived in a small, two-room bungalow that sat adjacent to a larger home occupied by his parents, built on ten acres of land on the corner of Artesia Boulevard and Normandie. Shane's parents had owned and operated horse stables that they rented out to equestrians, and Mark eagerly accepted their offer of stable hand in exchange for free room and board. Mark spent the next six months cleaning stables, watering and feeding the horses, and making sure they got appropriate exercise by frequent walks or rides around the grounds. He also assisted Shane's mother, Michelle, with record keeping, as well as other odds and ends around the grounds. After a month of employment, Shane's parents raised his pay by an additional two hundred and fifty dollars a month; spending money that had been wisely used that summer in pursuit of the last vestiges of teenage wasteland.

He had called his parents a few days after fleeing for Shane's and told his father that he was living with a friend and not coming back. His father had yelled at him over the phone and called him a fucking moron. Mark hung up on him. He'd called back five minutes later and apologized. Dad told him when he got his hands on him he was going to wring his skinny neck. Mark had held his temper and told his dad that he wasn't coming home until he and Mom got help for their drinking. His father replied that he was going to rip off Mark's head and shit down his neck. Mark hung up again. As troubled as he had been by the conversation, he hadn't cried. He'd bottled up the emotions inside him, part of him telling himself that he should have expected it. They were never going to change.

Some small hope that they would change had remained and it was this hope that spurred him to call again in late November. Once again his father had answered the phone. And that time his father had sounded sober.

For the first time Mark could remember, father and son had a long talk. Mark had detected a sense of hesitancy in the older man's voice, and Mark had resisted the urge to steer the conversation toward the fights that had broken the family apart. Instead they had talked about the day-to-day things; work, current events, Mom's newly found interest in a bridge club. Mark had felt his spirits rise as he thought *maybe they've changed*. Those feelings had been verified when his dad invited him on a trip to Big Bear for the first weekend in December. A friend of his at the plant had a cabin there and maybe it would be good for the three of them to get out of the city for an extended weekend. Just hang out, not worry about the day-to-day things of life. Mark had immediately said yes.

In the days that followed, Mark and his parents talked every day on the phone. Mark had gotten the directions to the cabin and Shane had agreed to let Mark borrow his truck. He'd also gotten Friday and Monday off of work and on Thursday evening, December 4, he'd set off for Big Bear.

He'd arrived at the cabin a little after ten-thirty and his parents were already there. When Mark had walked in he'd met two strangers he had never seen before; both of his parents were cold sober. His mother had looked worn, but rested somewhat. She'd smiled and held out her arms to him. "Hello, son," she'd said.

Mark almost cried in relief as he hugged both parents. It was them, and they were sober. They were completely different people. The three of them had held onto each other as if they hadn't seen each other in years and then his dad had stepped back. "Let's go inside. Your mom's got some coffee brewing."

That night was the first time in Mark's life it almost felt he had a family. They'd sat up and talked and like that first conversation with his father, he'd gotten the impression that his parents were still a bit apprehensive about revisiting earlier times of dysfunction. *Fine*, Mark had thought. *Going back down that road might not be a good thing for them, yet. Let them get strength in their sobriety, and when they feel like they want to talk about it, they'll bring it up.*

They had stayed up to well past one o'clock and

when they'd turned in his mother had actually kissed him good night. "Maybe tomorrow we can do some sledding or something," his father had said.

Mark had nodded, still flushed with good vibes from the past few weeks. "Yeah. That sounds great."

They had gone to their rooms, and Mark had been elated as he'd changed into nightclothes and gotten into bed. He was so excited it had taken him an hour to fall asleep.

What had awakened him was the smell of gunpowder. It was coming from his parents' bedroom and he had opened his eyes, startled. Then he'd heard his mother's whispered voice: ". . . I think we've made a mistake, Hank. He's our son, he's not some—"

"Can it, Loretta," his father hissed in a whisper. "The kid's a fucking monster." Then came the sound of a cartridge being inserted into the chamber of a gun. "You know it and I know it. Just because we were fucking drunks this time last year doesn't mean we were hallucinating what we saw. You saw him that night as well as I did."

Mark had gotten up and crossed the room, his heart pounding. They had seen him! He didn't know how, but somehow his parents must have seen him one night coming back after he had changed, maybe even after he had—

"But *Hank*!" His mother's voice, louder.

The door to his parents' room had opened and Mark paused, hiding behind the doorway to his own room, already feeling the change taking place, fueled by his fear and his growing anger that they had led him up here for the singular purpose of killing him, their only son. They had raised him in a volatile environment, had beaten him time and time again, had neglected him, and they were still turning their backs on him in his time of need. Some fucking parents they were.

"Hank!" His mother wailed as his father opened the door and stepped into the room.

Blinded by his wolf-nature, Mark sprung.

The nightmare bled deep red.

When Carol Emrich returned from work Mark Wiseman was gone.

"Goddamn him," Carol muttered, shutting and locking the door behind her. She crossed the room and threw her purse on the table by the nightstand. She shrugged out of her coat and sat down on a chair to take off her boots. It was a quarter till ten. The minute a customer named Grant Forest had found out that Mark wasn't working tonight, he'd begun doing his best to put on what charm he had. The guy actually had gone out on a limb and not only asked her out, but he had grabbed her ass as she'd walked by him with a pot of coffee. It had taken all her willpower to resist dumping the pot's contents into his face. Instead she had smiled sweetly at him and told him that if he ever tried that again she would rip his arm off and stuff it up his ass.

Thanks to his country-hickness, the buttwad had complained to her boss, who had pulled her aside in his office and told her that "as a waitress you are not to insult or threaten my customers in any way. You do that again, and I'm firing your ass."

It had taken all her might to hold her tongue and the way he had told her this—in a condescending tone of voice—seemed to set the stage for the rest of the evening. For some reason the patrons that came to Jake's Diner that night were unusually demanding—"Can I have more ketchup?" "Can you send this back to the grill and have him do it a little more well done?" "I ordered the steak fries, not the onion rings"—and she began to feel that she was being treated as a slave. From Mark's insistence that they hide out from all of humanity by staying in this bug-fuck little town, to his clamming up and not talking to her when she explicitly told him that they needed to talk, to being pushed around at the diner, Carol felt that she was being taken advantage of. She was beginning to feel the way she'd felt when she was with Bernard. It was a feeling she had grown to hate and as the night wore on she told herself that she wasn't going to let it go on any longer. Tonight it ended.

Therefore she was extremely pissed when she arrived back at the motel and saw that Mark was gone. She changed out of her waitress uniform into a pair of sweat pants and a sweater, then pulled on a pair of thick socks. Her anger smoldered. Asshole probably went to the bar down the street. *I hope he gets his skinny little ass kicked by the local rednecks.*

Carol turned the TV on and reclined on the bed, mindlessly watching the news, then switching over to a sitcom. She briefly debated on changing into jeans and a sweater and braving the cold and heading over to Jason's Pool Hall and Roadhouse, but decided against it. She needed a drink, but putting up with drunk assholes she didn't want, or need.

So she sat in the room and let her anger smolder to

a simmer. By the time eleven-thirty rolled around, so did her fatigue from the day. Mark would be back soon enough; last week he had gone to Jason's for a few rounds of pool and a couple of beers and there had been no trouble. Perhaps tonight had been more of the same; maybe he just needed to break the monotony of staying at the motel room whenever they had a night off. Carol surely understood that; she had been wanting to break the monotony the minute they had checked in to the Star Motor Lodge.

When Carol finally succumbed to sleep she did so quietly. She turned the TV off with the remote control, placed it on the nightstand and turned off the bedside light. She was asleep within minutes of her head hitting the pillow.

Outside the moon was full, bloated and white. It shone like a beacon through sparse clouds.

In the dream he was roaming, a wolf in the night.

He ran through the thick copse of woods, weaving in and out of streams and thickets of brush. In the deep Missouri winter he felt warm and snug in his winter coat. His clawed feet padded along the well-packed snow, his nose picking out a million scents in the air. He steered clear of the scattered farm houses; the animals that resided on the farms all sensed him and they all took up bleats of fear. Better not to alert farmers that a wayward wolf was on the prowl.

He had stuck far enough away from farms, but deep enough in the woods to avoid detection. He wouldn't be able to for long. His hunger was strong and it propelled him closer to the outer periphery of the woods. Toward the edge of civilization.

He headed toward lights at the edge of the woods. The smells and sounds coming from them told him all he needed to know. He was near a bar, probably the one outside of town. The bar was packed with a drunk, rowdy crowd.

One lone man was exiting the bar, staggering toward his car.

Mark's nostrils flared with the scent of him. His stomach churned. He stepped slightly out of the trees and gestured, trying to get the man's attention. He did.

The man looked up and squinted. He took a shuffling step closer. "Hey, Bobby, that you, man?"

Mark stepped back into the shadows.

The man stumbled closer. "Hey, Travis, we were wonderin' what happened to ya. I mean, I know you got sick and all, but Bob ain't that mad at ya for throwin' up on his new boots."

The man stumbled closer, stepping past his car and into the woods. He was in his mid-twenties and would have been slim were it not for the beer fat that had settled into his stomach and jowls. He had a thick beard and wavy brown hair that fell around his ears. He was dressed in blue jeans, a blue flannel shirt, and a heavy leather jacket and black work boots. He stumbled into the woods, squinting. "Ya don't have to be fuckin' embarrassed, Travis. I mean, Christ, man—"

Mark sprang at the man. His teeth sank into his neck as he drove him down to the ground. As the taste of hot blood spurted into his mouth he lost all control and lost himself in his hunger—

Mark started awake, his breathing heavy. He

blinked; he was in their motel room, back at the Star Motor Lodge and it was still night outside.

Mark turned in bed. Carol slept soundly beside him.

Christ, that was a bad one, Mark thought, rubbing his hand over his sleep-tangled hair. *Worst fucking nightmare I've ever had.*

His mind spun with the suddenness of being woken suddenly. He swung his legs over the edge of the bed and sat down, rubbing his face with his hands. They came away sticky.

He looked at his hands. They were stained with something sticky and dark.

Then he tasted it in his mouth. He ran his tongue along his teeth and gums and the salty taste of blood came to him. His stomach roiled. It wasn't a dream. It had happened and it had happened so suddenly and was so strong that he hadn't even been aware of it.

Mark felt his chest hitch with a sob of frustration and he fought it down. He turned to Carol's sleeping form in bed. How long had he been in bed with her? Did she even know that he had come back with blood on his hands?

Who did I kill tonight?

He tried to remember as much of the dream as he could, tried to trace his doings over the last eight hours as the darkness slowly gave way to the light of morning.

Chapter Twenty-seven

"I hope you're right about this," Agent Strong said. He buckled his seatbelt as the private plane they had chartered in Orange County taxied for landing at the small Columbia, Missouri airport.

"Trust me on this," Allen Frey said. He reached for his carry-on bag. He hadn't packed much, just a change of clothes and a toothbrush. The minute he had heard the news from Frederick Johansen, he had called Agent Strong and told them that they would find Mark Wiseman and Carol Emrich in Florence, Missouri.

"You still haven't explained what this is all about," Agent Strong said, looking out the window as they approached the runway.

"The description of Samuels's killer that I got in Texas fits Mark Wiseman," Allen said. "Judging from the reports we got out of Missouri today, the young man killed yesterday is an exact match."

"An exact match of what?"

"An exact match of modus operandi. He was killed by the same person."

"By Mark Wiseman, you mean?"

Allen nodded. He didn't want to go into it further. He was surprised the agent had gone this far. On a hunch he had monitored all police activity in the country, or as much as he could with only a four person staff. He had been rewarded this morning with a report out of Florence, Missouri that a man exiting a roadhouse had been attacked and mauled by a wolf. Allen had placed a call himself to the Missouri Highway Patrol where he learned that the attack had been a surprise. "We don't get wolves this far south," the man he had talked to said. "I've heard about them coming down as far south as, oh, Moberly, but never this far down. And even then they normally don't venture this far into civilization. This one must have been mighty hungry."

Allen had learned two very important things from his conversation: one, they were treating the death of Travis Peary as an animal attack, and two, the media hadn't caught wind of it yet. "We'd rather keep it that way," the patrolman told him. "Don't want everybody up in arms about a goddamn wolf. We got the Missouri Department of Fish and Game tracking the critter now."

That gave Allen a window of opportunity. He had placed a call to Agent Strong and told him that he had evidence that Mark Wiseman and Carol Emrich were somewhere near Florence, Missouri. Agent Strong hadn't even asked how he knew this, or why he thought the two could be found there. He had simply arranged to meet Allen at John Wayne Airport.

The only thing Frey had told Agent Strong on the flight was that he had gotten his information from a source of his in the area. He had done some investigating and found out about the murder of Travis Peary this morning, and was able to connect it with the three deaths they were working on. And that was when things began unraveling.

"Those two dipshits you interviewed in Texas were loaded to the gills on dope," Agent Strong said. "I read a transcript of their interview myself. Worthless fucks claim that what killed Samuels was a werewolf."

"I'm sure in the dark Mark appeared to be a werewolf to them," Allen explained, hoping to satisfy the agent. "But the man they saw fit Mark's description *exactly*. It also fit the description George Fielding gave us."

"That's another thing I'm having trouble with." Agent Strong looked at Allen from across the aisle. The plane was now beginning its descent and they could hear the whine of the engine. "Fielding said this Mark Wiseman guy looked like some kind of half-human, half-monster thing. Said he had claws and long sharp teeth. What kind of shit is *that*?"

"That's what I hope to find out," Allen said. "And that's why I think that if we talk to some people in town, show them some pictures of Mark and Carol, and if we find out they're in town we may get some answers."

Agent Strong regarded Allen for a minute. "We'd better," he said, settling into his seat for the landing.

Allen Frey sat back in his seat, trying to suppress

the shit-eating grin that was trying to worm its way across his features. He felt somewhat vindicated that Agent Strong was trusting his investigation and his instinct. He just hoped that his suspicions paid off. If they didn't he might not get a second chance.

When the telephone rang in Bernard Roberts's private office at home he picked it up on the first ring. "Yeah?"

He listened carefully, his features dark and serious. "You're sure?" He listened some more, then picked up a pen and dragged a pad of paper toward him. He began writing on the pad. "Where the fuck is Florence, Missouri?" He listened some more, nodding. He jotted down some more notes, then began to grin. "This sounds like exactly what I'm looking for. Thanks Brian." He hung up.

He tore the scrap of paper off the pad and looked at it, leaning back in his chair. The private investigator he had hired eight months ago to perform the background check on Mark Wiseman had been instructed to keep a watch out for any unusual deaths in which a wild animal was the suspected culprit. "It doesn't matter," he had told Brian Keith last month. "Dogs, wolves, mountain lions, bears, alligators, whatever, as long as they're chewed up pretty bad, that's fine. I would like to find out within twenty-four hours of the attack and where it happened."

He had sent Brian off to work and for the next month had sat at home and followed all reports Brian gave him. He'd also followed all reports another private investigator was giving him; this investigator was working at trying to trace Mark

Wiseman's and Carol Emrich's steps after they had ambushed him and almost tried to kill him in that fleabag motel in Three Rivers. The trail had started off hot: Apparently Mark had stolen a car not far from the Three Rivers Lodge and it was dumped later at a truck stop in Arizona. A motel clerk at the truck stop recalled seeing a couple who matched their description, and a waitress at the diner the motel was connected to said she had served them breakfast one morning. A mechanic at the truck stop thought he saw a couple fitting their description climbing into the cab of an eighteen-wheel tractor-trailer, but he didn't remember what the trucker who gave them a ride looked like, or what state his rig was from. Smart move on their part; they could be anywhere.

Therefore he'd put Brian Keith to work monitoring all cases of animal attacks on humans. It would take another month or so until the next full moon, and once that happened that would be the giveaway. Mark Wiseman might have grown to loathe killing for Bernard, but forcing him to do his bidding had no doubt awakened the beast within him. He wouldn't be able to contain it the way he had in the past.

Bernard picked up the phone and dialed his travel agency. He asked for Marci and was put through almost immediately. "Marci, Bernard here. Listen, I was wondering if you could help me charter a flight from John Wayne Airport to Florence, Missouri, or a nearby hub." He listened as Marci consulted the computer. "Fine, Columbia will do. How far is it from Florence? Really? Great. Why don't you get me a car at the airport, as well. Yes, that's fine, thanks."

He gave Marci his American Express number, thanked her for her time and help, and hung up. Marci had booked him a flight on a private plane that could leave in four hours. Bernard rose from his desk and headed upstairs to pack.

There had been no hollow ringing sound over the phone lines during both calls, so he knew his lines weren't bugged. But, he was fairly confident that he was being tailed. That FBI guy, Agent Strong or whatever his name was, had told him that he was going to get him, that he was going to do whatever it took to build the evidence he needed to haul him back into custody. Bernard had politely told him to get stuffed. Then, after making the ten thousand dollars bail on the vandalism and suspected attempted assault charge in Three Rivers, he had gone straight to the office and began packing it up. There weren't many personal effects at the office, just a few photos framed and matted on the walls and his Rolodex. By the time he was finished two security guards were at his door along with Hank Owen, one of the senior board members. Hank had looked embarrassed. "I'm sorry, Bernard, but—"

"It's okay," Bernard had said, shouldering his way past him. "I'm going."

"It will only be temporary," Hank had said. "You know we have to do this, that we have to relieve you of your duties until a complete investigation is done. I hope that you—"

"Hank, it's all right." Bernard had turned to Hank and smiled, patting the older man's shoulder. He always had the impression that Hank saw him as a son; Hank had once sat on this same presidency seat when he was Bernard's age. "I intend to cooperate fully with the members of the board and law enforcement. We'll straighten this out, I promise you that."

Hank had been silent, looking at Bernard as if he didn't know him anymore. Bernard thought he detected a note of disappointment in those eyes. "I hope so, Bernard. I really hope so."

The minute he'd gotten home he'd placed a call to his lawyer, Jim Weinstein in Costa Mesa. He'd gotten Jim on the phone and explained the entire situation to him: The board had suspected Bernard of embezzling funds and had let him go pending an investigation, the FBI was investigating and it was a big fucking mess. Jim had questioned him, wanted to know the how's, why's and where's. Bernard had told him that somebody was out to frame him; he didn't know who, but he thought it might be one of the board members who was for the merger. Furthermore, he was certain whoever this board member was had somehow arranged for his three colleagues to be murdered, and a fourth to be almost murdered just recently in Las Vegas. And *still* furthermore, he was positive that this certain unknown board member had not only covered his or her tracks, but that they had successfully made it seem that it was *Bernard* that had ordered the hits and done the embezzling. "I have airtight alibis on the nights those men were murdered," he'd said. "They can go through my phone records if they want, they can check my database at home. Of course, I'd rather have you advise me on that, and—"

"Nobody is going to get a peek at your personal records until they go through me first," Jim had said, his tone gruff. "I don't even want you to make any comments to a meter reader unless I'm present, do you understand?"

"You bet."

"What's this about this assault and vandalism charge in Three Rivers you mentioned earlier?"

That was bullshit, he'd told Jim. He shouldn't have done it, but there had been no other way. His secretary, Carol Emrich, had been acting strangely lately and he'd begun to suspect that she was helping whoever it was that was trying to destroy him. He had told her too much about his opposition to the merger—they had been lovers, you see, and Carol had always been a gold digger anyway. Somebody must have gotten to her and now she was not only in the sack with this bigwig hot shot, she was helping them stick it to him. And furthermore, he was certain that she had seduced one of the hourly minions at the company, some computer tape librarian named Mark Wiseman, and had bribed him into making the actual hits. It would make sense, since he'd found out Mark was not working on the nights of the murders and he wasn't that well-off financially—"I mean for a guy who only makes twenty-seven thousand dollars a year, who the fuck could live off that in Orange County? Besides, if Carol had come along and shaken her tits at him the right way, the guy would have licked all the bathrooms in Grand Central Station to get a piece of that pussy. Shit, I've heard of real murder cases in which the woman successfully got the man to do all her dirty shit for her and then—"

"I get the picture," Jim had said. "And I'm on it."

The next few days had been spent in phone conference strategy sessions with Jim and his team of lawyers. A simple barrier was set up in Bernard's defense: Bernard had been unaware of any embezzling and they could prove that through his personal financial records. Bernard had been careful to go through all his legitimate records and handed them over to Jim, who went over them with a fine-toothed comb. All the records Bernard had funneled the money he had stolen were safe in a Cayman Island account that Jim and his cronies wouldn't dare look for. Half the board members themselves had dirty money in similar accounts and for them to go sniffing after him might bring down a whole truckload of shit on their heads as well. Therefore, he was fairly confident they weren't going to go snooping around after that end of the financial spectrum. As far as domestic accounts went, Bernard was clean.

He was also clean in other matters; Bernard had kept meticulous records of phone calls, bills, and receipts. Within a week they were able to comfortably place Bernard away from any charge of embezzlement. Therefore when the call came that detectives wanted to search his home, Jim had given them the okay.

Nothing had been found in Bernard's home. Jim had supervised the search himself and the detectives and FBI agents went through drawers, dressers, closets, file cabinets, all to no avail. They'd left with nothing, much like Jim had said they would.

That hadn't stopped them from trying to subpoena his bank records. Jim had filed an order to have the subpoena postponed and the request had been granted, giving Bernard and Jim ample time to document every transaction in Bernard's accounts. The investigators, upon hitting the brick wall in the form of Jim's brief, had tried to have it overturned and been denied. That had pushed the whole hearing on the matter back another month. Bernard laughed as he thought about it.

Fully packed now, Bernard picked up his suitcase and walked through the house. Everything was locked up and secure. He would call Jim on his cell phone on the drive to John Wayne Airport and tell him he was heading out of town to visit an old college buddy for a few days. Jim wouldn't need to know where he was going. The investigation had slowed down the last few days, anyway. Once he flew out to Missouri and got rid of Mark and Carol, he would be free and clear because soon after that the people doing the investigation would have to call it quits; they would have no proof and no witnesses. No witnesses meant no repercussions on him.

Grinning, Bernard got in his black Mercedes and backed slowly out of the driveway, then headed toward John Wayne Airport. Already the thrill of the hunt was pulsing through his veins.

Chapter Twenty-eight

They were in their room watching television when Carol Emrich turned to Mark. "What's wrong?"

Mark looked at her. "Nothing. Why?"

"There is something wrong and you're not telling me. What is it?"

"Nothing. Everything's fine."

"Mark, I don't want you to think we're going through what we went through last night—"

Last night had been the first time they had finally talked seriously about their predicament and Carol thought they had made some progress. When she had woken up that morning, she found that Mark had come home sometime during the middle of the night without managing to wake her up. She had awakened to the sound of the shower in the bathroom and when Mark came out he'd looked pale and tired. Her first instinct was that something was wrong, but then he had come to her naked and put his arms around her. "I'm sorry for the fight," he had said. "You were right; we do need to talk about what we're going to do."

Carol hadn't wanted to talk right then; she had been too stunned with emotion to summon up what she wanted to talk about. Instead she had drawn Mark into bed with her and wrapped herself into his embrace.

They had fallen asleep again, then woken up around noon. They'd showered together and for the first time in over a month they had made love in the shower and then again in bed. It had been like when they'd first met and fallen in love; they couldn't keep their hands off each other. All told, it had taken them two hours to shower and get dressed for supper, for which they had driven into Sedalia.

They had eaten dinner in Sedalia near the mall, then taken a walk. The weather had been crisp and cold, in the low forties with the nighttime temperatures expected to plunge into the low teens. They'd debated on going to the movies since it was their night off of work, but Mark had suggested heading back to the motel. Carol had agreed and they had headed back and immediately flopped back into bed.

Now Carol was trying to draw Mark out and find out what was bothering him so much. She could tell something had been on his mind all day and it seemed to weigh even heavier since they'd gotten home. He kept looking toward the curtained windows, as if expecting somebody to show up. "You are acting nervous and scared, honey. We've been meaning to talk about what we're going to do, what our next move is going to be and maybe that time should be now."

Mark nodded and glanced at the watch he had left by the nightstand. It was eight-fifteen. Carol thought he looked a trifle better, as if some tremendous weight had been taken off his shoulders. "We should be fine now. It's been night for a few hours and I've been fine."

It suddenly hit her like a sledgehammer. "Oh Christ, you mean it's—"

"The full moon?" Mark was looking at her apologetically. "Yeah, it is. Last night was the first night. I didn't want to scare you but—"

"That's why you weren't here," she said suddenly. "That's why you were gone when I came home." Her hands flew to her mouth as if to stifle a scream. *What happened?*

It looked like Mark didn't want to confess; he shifted uneasily on his side of the bed and looked at her with what seemed like shame on his face. "I went out last night," he said, quietly. "I changed. It just hit me so suddenly. I . . . I fell asleep and I started dreaming . . . I . . . I had this weird dream about my parents and . . . I . . . I don't remember much else."

Carol looked at him for a moment, too stunned to say anything. Finally: "Are you sure? *Think*, Mark. If you killed somebody, they might find out—"

"They're not going to find out."

"How do you know?" Carol's voice was raising in pitch as her emotions rose.

"They aren't going to know where we are," Mark said. "Even if . . . what I think happened last night did happen."

Carol looked at him with slow, dawning horror. "Oh my God, you *did* kill somebody last night didn't you?"

"Carol, I told you once before that when . . . when this happens to me, it's not me!" He was pleading with her to understand; she could detect it in the tone of his voice, but it also had a tinge of whining desperation in it. "It's like . . . somebody else occupies my body for the night and changes it. It makes me do things I wouldn't think of doing and—"

"If that's the case why are you fine now?" She motioned to him with a tilt of her head. "You *seem* fine now. I don't see you sprouting fangs and fur and it's a full moon right now. Why aren't you changing into a fucking monster *right now*?"

"I told you last month that I can usually control it. It's only when—"

"So why couldn't you control it last night? What happened?"

Mark took a deep breath. "If you would just listen to me instead of—"

"I *am* listening to you! You said the moon changes you, that it turns you into a werewolf. Why isn't—"

"*If I don't let it out every once in awhile it takes complete control over me!*" Mark yelled, suddenly looming over her. Carol fell back against the bed, her heart leaping in her throat. She made a mad scramble to get away from him and he came after her, not threateningly, but coming after her just the same. His eyes were wide, his expression one of anger. "I can only control it for so long, but it's always there. If I don't let it out, if I keep it bottled up, the pressure builds and then it just bursts out. It takes control of me and then I don't know what happens. I lose all control to it. It makes me do those things. Then when it's run its course it's easier to control . . . like tonight."

Carol stood there stiffly, not daring to move. For the first time in almost two months she felt afraid of Mark. A thought rose in her mind and she tried to bat it aside, but it refused to die. *He says he can't control it sometimes, that sometimes he just has to let it out. Suppose it had been me he had killed?*

She voiced this concern without even thinking. "Suppose it had been me, Mark? Suppose that this morning when you woke up, you woke up to me all torn up and strewn across this room. What then?"

Mark turned away from her. "That wouldn't have happened."

"Why not?" She was gaining some of her boldness back.

Mark looked away from her, refusing to meet her gaze. Her heart was beating hard in her ribcage. He didn't have to answer this question; she knew the answer just from the way he was behaving. *He wouldn't have been able to control it because it had taken control of him while he had been asleep.*

Carol stood over him, not quite knowing how to react. Part of her felt angry with him for initially hiding this part of himself, but she knew how she would have reacted upon first hearing it, too. She wouldn't have believed him; she would have dismissed him as a lunatic. Hell, she had a hard enough time believing it even after practically witnessing the metamorphosis last month. It was actually because of witnessing it that she had stayed with him; there was obviously something wrong with him and she loved him too much to desert him. It was obvious he couldn't control it. It was obvious that it was something he didn't want, that it was a crutch. That was why she had stayed with him.

Carol took a deep breath and tried to think things through. She wanted to turn the television on and see if there was anything on the news. She didn't remember passing any newspapers carrying the story, or hearing any conversation about the attack. Of course it might not have made the news yet; it had only happened last night. She tried to remember how many days there were in a typical full-moon cycle—was it four or five? She turned back to Mark, who was still sitting on the bed with his head bowed. "How do you feel now?" she asked softly.

Mark started sobbing quietly.

For a minute Carol was too stunned to react. Then she sat beside Mark and put her arms around him awkwardly, holding him close. He was trying to control his emotions and he wiped at his tears with the back of his hands. "I'm sorry," he said. "I didn't mean to . . . to break down like this, but—"

"It's okay," she said, brushing his hair back from his face. She kissed him. "It's okay."

"It's not okay," he sniffled. "It's my fault that we're both in this mess."

"No, it's not."

"Yes it is. If it wasn't for me, Bernard wouldn't have . . . wouldn't have come at me the way he did. He wouldn't have trapped me."

"It's not your fault," Carol said. She felt stupid saying that, but what else could she say? *I'm sorry you have this uncontrollable urge to change into a monster every month on the full moon and kill people, honey, but it's really not your fault that we're being hunted down by Bernard Roberts because you failed to kill one of the faceless suits on the Free State Board of Directors. Maybe if you had been a normal person instead of a werewolf he wouldn't have seen fit to wrangle you into this little mess.*

Carol changed the subject, hoping to get Mark's mind off of feeling sorry for himself. "You think we should pack up and head out?"

Mark had calmed down somewhat. His breathing was heavy as he sought control of his sobs and he nodded, wiping his eyes. "Yeah, maybe we should. Get the fuck out of Missouri, maybe head north into Illinois or Iowa or something."

"When do you want to leave?"

Mark looked up at her. "I don't know . . . tomorrow?"

"Tomorrow." She bent down and kissed his cheek. He seemed so vulnerable now and she realized that she couldn't baby him—Mark Wiseman wasn't that kind of man—but she felt the need to protect and nurture him. "I'll start packing some things. We'll leave first thing tomorrow morning."

Mark nodded. He pushed his hair back from his face. He appeared more in control of his emotions now. "Maybe I should turn on the TV. We should at least see if what happened last night made the news." He stood up and turned the TV on, flipping through the channels until he got the local news. He stood back and watched as Carol worked at packing their clothes together into the two suitcases. She listened as she worked and thought about what to do: pack their stuff up, turn in early, get up early, change, shower, head out to the diner to pick up their paychecks and formally quit, then hit the road.

The local news was broadcast from Kansas City and there was nothing reported about the surrounding areas; the closest anything came to that was the weather report when the anchorman warned motorists heading into Sedalia to be careful of snow drifts along US 70. There was no mention of anybody killed by anything, human or inhuman.

"Maybe they didn't find him," she said, putting the last piece of clothing in her suitcase. She had laid out clothes for tomorrow, but otherwise she was ready to go. She turned to Mark who sat back down on the bed, still looking up at the television. "I would think that anybody being attacked and killed by *anything* would have made the news."

"You would think," Mark said in a strange, flat voice. He turned to her and smiled, but Carol saw that it was forced. He was trying to put her at ease.

"You okay?"

Mark nodded. "Yeah. I'm fine."

"How do you feel? Do you feel the . . . you know . . . ?"

"It's there, but very slight. And I call it the curse." Mark smiled again, and this time it was slightly more genuine. "The closest way I can describe it is . . . well, like being hungry. It's like something natural that your body goes through. I can feel myself wanting to yield to it, to change. And when it's strong it's like you're starving. You know, you haven't eaten all day and the hunger suddenly comes on you so strong that you simply have to pull into the nearest Wendy's or Burger King and eat all the fried, greasy slop they serve simply to quench that hunger. When the curse comes on really strong, that's what it's like. To resist it is . . . well, it physically *hurts*."

Carol had come to the bed and sat down beside him as he explained this to her. For the first time she understood what he was going through; he had expressed what he physically went through so eloquently that it was stunning. She took his hands and squeezed them. "You won't have to worry about going through it alone like you used to, Mark. I'm here with you and I'm always going to be here. You can count on that."

Mark smiled. For the first time today he appeared happy. "You don't know how much that means to me."

But she did. And she expressed it that night as they lay together in bed, not making love, but just holding each other and keeping his demons at bay.

Chapter Twenty-nine

They made it into Springfield, Illinois by six p.m. the following night. There was a Motel Six just off the interstate and they checked in for the night, dragging their tired bodies and their luggage to their room and shutting the door to the outside world.

Outside it was cold and spitting snow.

Carol was exhausted. She flopped down on the queen-sized bed while Mark showered. It seemed like she could feel every aching muscle and tendon in her body. Even though the day had not been a physically active one, it had been tiring. She was still trying to puzzle why that was so; it wasn't like she had pulled an eight-hour shift and then had somehow found the time to drive four hundred miles today.

After rising early this morning they had checked out of the Star Motor Lodge and had made Jake's Grill their first stop. They told Jake Owens that they were quitting and he hadn't put up a fuss. He'd written out their checks on the spot in his office and when he'd handed them over his features were somewhat softer than they had been, as if he were seeing two of his own children off to college for the first time. "You people take care now, you hear?"

They had thanked him, then eaten a quick breakfast at the diner counter. Then they hit the road.

With a map of Missouri and Illinois spread out on the seat between them, they traced the most appropriate route: Route 52 to Sedalia, Route 63 to Interstate 70 into St. Louis, then north to Springfield, Illinois. Just before they had drifted off to sleep last night, Mark had suggested settling in Chicago. "It's a big city," he had said sleepily. "We've got enough bucks to get ourselves a place and we can get jobs there real easy. It'll be harder for somebody to pick us out there too; not like a small town where you stick out like a sore thumb."

Carol had thought about it and the more she'd thought about it, the more she liked it. Why the hell hadn't they gone to a big city right away? They had been so distraught during their initial flight to get out of California that getting out had meant going anywhere, even if it had meant hiding in a little roadside lodge in bumfuck Missouri.

So Chicago it was, then. They had left the diner at a little past ten o'clock on a cold, sunny morning. Mark had said he felt fine; the curse had hardly bugged him last night and now that the lunar cycle was on its downswing it would affect him less and less in the next few nights. On the drive out Carol had asked him what he would do next month when they were in a big city: how would he handle the curse then? "The same way I handled it in California," he'd said. "Hopefully head out of the city for at least one night and let it run its course. I've managed to survive the last eight years that way. I suppose I can survive the next eight in the Windy City the same way."

"Maybe once we're settled we can try to find a way to beat this thing," Carol had said. She had volunteered to drive the first few hours, and she'd kept the Suburban at a steady sixty miles per hour. The rays of sun had reflected off white landscapes of snow that had covered farmers' fields and the woods surrounding the interstate. "From what you described there has to be some way to cure it. I mean, you weren't bitten or attacked by a werewolf before this happened, right? Isn't that one of the ways you become a werewolf?"

"According to movies, yeah," Mark had said from the passenger side.

"What about, like, wolfsbane? Isn't that another way to become one?"

"Yeah, if the area I lived in had any growing around there," Mark had said, chuckling softly. "I hardly think that wolfsbane is growing wild in Gardena, California, though."

Carol nodded, her forehead creased in thought. "Well, we'll think of something. Don't worry, honey, we're in this together now. We'll find a way to beat this."

They made small talk for the rest of the drive. They'd stopped in St. Louis for lunch, then crossed the Mississippi River into Illinois around three. Mark had driven from there, giving Carol a chance to lean back in her seat and catnap as Mark drove, the radio turned to whatever rock station he'd found on the dial.

Now in their motel room Carol wanted to doze again, but tried to fight back the exhaustion as the shower trickled off. She sat up on the bed and rubbed her eyes. Maybe they should stay one more night in Springfield to give them a chance to catch up on all the sleep they had missed. Mark said he hadn't slept well last night himself and they could both use it. They might as well; they had all the time in the—

There was a thundering crash that startled Carol so badly she literally jumped off the bed. Her scream lodged in her throat at the suddenness of it and she whirled around as a sharp crack blasted through the quiet din, splintering the door to their room. She jumped back, her mind spinning. It was happening so fast that her whirling mind was having a hard time tracking the events; the sudden crash, the sharp report and the cracking, splintering door, then the door bursting open and a man staggering in with a large handgun gripped in his right fist. She looked up at the man and while she recognized him as Bernard Roberts, her mind refused to believe it. *We left him in the dust back in California! How the hell could he have—*

Bernard Roberts loomed over her, his once hand-some features now twisted by some insane evil. He grinned. "Step aside, bitch."

Now she found that she could act and she rose to her feet, the adrenaline suddenly hitting her. *"What the hell are you doing here? Get the fuck out—"*

"I said step aside!" Bernard yelled. He backhanded

her with the fist that held the gun and she felt the heaviness of the weapon behind the fist smack into her left cheek so hard that it knocked her onto the bed, then spilled her onto the floor. The blow sent her reeling, making her dizzy, and her legs were all scrambled. She fought the dizziness, tried to fight the pain as she attempted to lift herself up off the floor. She watched everything in a sort of bizarre slow-motion as Bernard lunged toward the rear of the motel room where the bathroom was; then Mark threw the bathroom door open and she caught a glimpse of his naked form for just a fraction of a second before all hell broke loose.

Mark stood there, his lips curling back from his teeth as Bernard smiled and advanced toward him. Mark looked beautiful standing there; his naked form pure and perfect in the harsh fluorescent of the bathroom light. He stood in the bathroom doorway as if guarding it from entry and then everything slowed down even more. She was able to witness everything clearly and concisely. It seemed to go slowly, as if it was being stretched out just to torture her, but when she later thought back on it she supposed it all really went down in a matter of seconds.

Bernard stepped closer to Mark and smiled. "Now it's time to send you to the hell you came from."

Mark's upper lip curled back to reveal a mouthful of teeth that should have come from the jaws of a large wolf. Then the snarl came from deep within his throat as his muscles twitched, his body primed to spring.

Bernard's face changed briefly; it bore a trace of remorse as he raised the weapon and pointed it at

Mark. "It was a pleasure working with you, Mark. For a while there, we made a great team."

Mark snarled—it was not the sound of a human being—and then he changed so fast that Carol barely had time to recover. He seemed to instantly change right before her eyes, to shimmer from human-form to wolf-form within seconds, changing effortlessly with no sign of the pain of transformation she had witnessed before. He changed so fast that he even took Bernard by surprise. He leaped at Bernard, who stepped back in surprise as the gun went off and the two crashed to the floor.

There was a yell amid snarls of rage and pain and then the gun went off three more times. More yelling, this time loud bellowing. Carol had been frozen in shock on the floor and now she sprang to her feet and rushed over to where they had come together. She almost stumbled over them. Bernard was pushing at Mark's prone form, trying to roll him over and yelling at the same time. Blood was rapidly spreading below them, staining the tan-colored carpet.

"Mark! Mark!" Carol was frantic. For a moment the scene was so chaotic that she didn't know what she was seeing. Mark's wolf-form lay on the floor, pinning Bernard to the ground as the executive struggled. Carol watched in a kind of numb fascination as blood spread rapidly along the carpet, staining it a deep crimson. Then, as abruptly as he had changed to his wolf form, Mark changed back; the thick fur along his back, arms, and legs retreated inward, the hunched muscles shrivelled, the arms and fingers shrank into themselves and the head reformed.

Leaving Mark's nude, prostrate body on the ground, gasping for breath.

"Mark!" Carol dropped to her knees, bending over Mark as he struggled to get up.

Bernard got to his feet. Carol wasn't even paying attention to him. If she had, she would have seen Bernard stand behind her and point the barrel of the pistol at the back of her head.

"Mark!" Carol sobbed, cradling his head in her arms. There were three large exit wounds on his back, one of them the size of her fist. Blood squished beneath her feet and knees as she bent over him. *"Mark . . . oh, my God, Mark . . ."*

Mark's eyes turned up to her. His mouth opened and through her blurred vision she thought he was trying to say something to her. Then he opened his mouth again and began taking deep breaths, as if he were hyperventilating. His right arm pawed wildly at her as she gently lifted him up and held him close, not even noticing the blood that spilled out of him and onto her jeans and blouse.

Behind her, Bernard said, "Say good-bye to your boyfriend, Carol."

Another voice cut through the din, but Carol wasn't listening. Her mind was whirling with a thousand memories as she held Mark and rocked him slowly back and forth. There was a loud, explosive *pop*, and then the sudden surge of running feet and angry voices. She was dimly aware of something going on around her, but she huddled over Mark, protecting him from the storm. *It's going to be okay, baby, it's going to be okay.* She cried harder, holding his broken form, not even aware that his life had already left him, leaving behind an empty shell with empty, brown eyes.

After that, things got even fuzzier. Even when the police came and tried to gently pry her away from Mark Wiseman, whom she still cradled in her arms.

Chapter Thirty

She had been thinking of a thousand ways to do it and finally settled on one that she felt fairly certain would go down painlessly, with little to no suffering.

She palmed the bottle of Valium in her left fist as she sat on her bed in her apartment, her mind wandering. Ever since Bernard's trial had ended, she had been inching closer and closer to this decision and now she had finally made it. It was a decision that would be permanent.

No turning back.

Carol Emrich stood up and walked into the living room. She turned her stereo on and then bent over to the CD rack that rested beside the stereo. She ran one finger along the spines of the CD's until she found the one she wanted to fall asleep listening to. She pulled it out and turned it over, her heart swelling with the memories this band's music had on her childhood.

The CD was *The Best of Sweet*, and it had all her favorite songs on it: "Little Willy," "Wig-Wam Bam," "The Ballroom Blitz," "Fox on the Run." She had been ten years old when she first saw them on some television show, it was either *Don Kirshner's Rock Concert*, or *Saturday Night Live*; she didn't remember which. But she knew the song they had played on the show—"Ballroom Blitz"—because they played it on the radio all the time in that long-ago summer of 1975. Sporting coifed, shoulder-length hair and flamboyant costumes, she'd fallen instantly into puppy-love with the band members. In an age when all her girlfriends were all either into David Cassidy, or the Bay City Rollers, or KC and the Sunshine Band, Sweet was both slightly bubblegum enough to win the respect of her girlfriends, but snotty enough in their lyrics to win the disdain of her parents, yet they weren't as threatening as, say, Alice Cooper or Black Sabbath, which her older brother Joey was into. She had had all of the band's albums and wore out the stylus on the turntable her parents got her so often that she'd had to retire it two years later. A few years later, Styx and Journey had taken Sweet's place, but they'd never entirely left that spot in her heart. They'd always remained in that one secret spot, a place she could visit again and again when the mood struck to reminisce.

Now she had this CD compilation, the only CD of the band's recordings she had. Weird to think she had been such a big fan of them when she was a kid—she'd had all their albums, all the magazine articles she could find, had even seen them on their 1978 world tour—but as an adult she was reduced to this one CD of their "greatest hits." How time flies.

She turned the CD player on and opened up the cradle that would hold the CD. She placed the disc in, pressed the button that retracted the cradle and set the compact disc into motion, then adjusted the volume. When the first song came on—"Little Willy"—she smiled and began to hum along with it. She stood there for a moment humming along, suddenly ten years old again and playing with her friends under a warm, Nebraska summer sun.

There were sixteen tracks on the CD, more than enough to provide the soundtrack for her send-off. She briefly debated on whether she should replace the CD with something else: Ozzy Osborne or Judas Priest perhaps? She had CDs of both artists. After all, how many people committed suicide while listening to bubblegum '70s glam rock?

She headed back to her bedroom and stopped for a moment, debating on whether or not she should change into something more comfortable. She frowned. She had read somewhere that when somebody dies that their sphincter muscle relaxes, voiding whatever is in the bowel. She didn't want to leave a big mess for whoever would come in to place her in the standard body bag, but then she supposed she shouldn't really care about that. After all, she would be dead. She surely wasn't going to be embarrassed by the fact that whoever picked her up off the bed was not only going to be dealing with picking up a rather attractive woman (and yes, she was attractive, she told herself this morning as she looked in the mirror and got ready; *I guess I'm really not so bad looking after all*), but they might have to be dealing with whatever she had involuntarily shit out of herself as she died. But again, she wouldn't be around to hear the complaints, or be embarrassed by it. She would be dead. End of story.

The decision to take her own life had been one she had wrestled with over the past fifteen months, ever since the evening of February 12, 1991, when Bernard Roberts had burst into their room just off the interstate in Springfield, Illinois and killed Mark Wiseman with four shots from a .38 revolver. Mark had died almost instantly, but he had still tried to fight Bernard off. He had fought bravely until the end, facing Bernard Roberts and the gun, lunging at him, taking him down as Bernard fired again and again into Mark's vulnerable belly.

Carol hated thinking about that. Thankfully most of the incident, and what had happened afterward, would soon be gone from her memory.

She remembered the endless questioning. She remembered being taken to Springfield, a two-hour drive, and being interrogated at the police department there. She'd later learned that since Mark's murder had occurred in rural Springfield County that the state police had to be involved, hence the drive to the state capital. She had been hysterical and a day later she had talked to somebody from the FBI, a guy named Agent Strong. She remembered him as being very kind, if not somewhat confused-looking and jumpy. He kept hedging around whether Mark and Bernard had known each other, if she knew of any possible criminal activity Mark might have been involved in. That had stopped her, made her evaluate her options. Her first instinct had been to deny that she knew anything, and she had done so right then and there. Agent Strong had asked her if she was sure. She'd said yes, nodding emphatically She had had no idea Mark and Bernard had known each other.

If that was the case, why would Bernard Roberts come two thousand miles just to kill him? Agent Strong had asked.

Carol had tried to come up with an answer, but Agent Strong had beaten her to the punch. *I'm sure you don't want to be accused as an accessory to the murders of Mr. Samuels, John, and Krueger, nor to the attempted murder of Mr. Fielding. Because that's what this is shaping up to be, Miss Emrich. Frankly, I don't want to have to hold this over your head, but we need your cooperation. Mark Wiseman must have told you something, and if he did and you didn't do anything about it, that's called accessory after-the-fact. That could mean a ten-year prison term, Miss Emrich. So I think you should think long and hard before you answer any of my questions. We don't really want to give you any trouble, but we do need your help in helping to connect Mark Wiseman with the crimes that Bernard Roberts is being accused of in California. You do want him put away for a long time, don't you?*

He had looked at her with a questioning gaze and she had been stiff with fear, her heart beating hard in her ribcage. She'd nodded. Agent Strong had smiled and patted her hands. *Good. Thankfully, we have him on first-degree murder. That's pretty much open and shut. But if we can get him on the other murders, say as the mastermind behind them, we can put him away for a very long, long time, Miss Emrich. Surely you would like to see that, wouldn't you?*

Carol had nodded again because she wanted to see that. She wanted Bernard Roberts to suffer for what he had done. That was when she had become the crucial witness in two cases: the State of Illinois versus Bernard Roberts in the first-degree murder of Mark Wiseman; and the State of California versus Bernard Roberts in embezzling, fraud, conspiracy to commit fraud, conspiracy to embezzle from a corporation, and conspiracy to commit murder.

Carol went to the closet and opened it. She decided she would slip into her nightgown. As long as she was going to go to sleep, she might as well dress comfy. She pulled out a red satin nightgown and laid it on the bed. Then she slipped out of her faded blue jeans, her white blouse, her bra, and her white cotton panties. She put the bra and panties in her laundry basket and then she folded the clothes and placed those at the foot of her bed. She went into the master bathroom and took out her earrings; then she slipped the one ring she wore off her right ring finger and placed it on the bathroom counter. She combed her hair and brushed her teeth, capping it off with a gargle of mint-flavored Listerine. She briefly debated on whether she should take a shower, but decided not to. She had taken a shower this morning and she hadn't really done enough to work up a sweat to justify a shower. Instead, she applied another layer of deodorant on her underarms and dabbed some perfume along the nape of her neck, between her breasts, and behind each ear. Just a touch. She stepped back from the bathroom mirror and smiled. She looked and smelled just fine. Of course that wouldn't matter if she was found two weeks from now and she smelled like rotting meat, but she was hoping that wouldn't happen. But then, why worry about it? She would be dead.

Sweet was blasting through "The Ballroom Blitz." Carol breezed back into the bedroom and slipped into the red satin nightgown. Then she went into the kitchen and got a glass of water. She returned to the bedroom and sat down on the edge of the bed and picked up the bottle of Valium. She had gotten the prescription from her psychiatrist; she had been going for the last four months, and the Valium had been prescribed to help her sleep and to steady her nerves. She hadn't been able to sleep the past six months, especially during the trial. The Valium had proven to be a godsend.

She opened the bottle and shook a handful out. She stared at them in the palm of her hand, then looked up at the bureau and the large mirror mounted above it. She wondered if she should pee first before embarking on this last trip. Sometimes when she went to bed without going to the bathroom her bladder woke her up, even if she only had to pee a drop. She had to get out of bed and shuck over to the bathroom and squat on the toilet and let that one drop trickle out before she could drift off to sleep. Otherwise her fucking bladder wouldn't let her sleep.

She got up and went to the bathroom. Might as well have one last pee before the journey.

When she was finished she flushed the toilet, then came back and sat down on the edge of the bed. "Teenage Rampage" was coming out of the speakers now and Carol listened to the song for a moment, letting the memory of youth carry her away.

She had talked to Agent Strong that day at the Illinois State Police Headquarters in Springfield. She hadn't been sure if he would believe most of it, so she'd left out the bit about Mark's curse—there was no way he would believe *that*. She'd told him what she knew; that Mark had only told her about his involvement with Bernard in early January. She'd told him that Bernard had blackmailed Mark into committing the murders, that Mark had felt trapped. She'd mentioned the level of suspicion Mark had been under when his parents were murdered (of course, she didn't tell him that she believed Mark had killed his parents and if anybody had deserved to be killed more than Bernard, it was Mark's folks; they had been real bastards). Bernard had told Mark that he would fix it so that he would be arrested for the deaths of his parents despite the anatomical evidence that had showed they were killed by some wild animal. Mark had buckled; that had been a touchy subject for him, and furthermore, Bernard had made it clear that if he found out Mark had gone to the police he would have him killed.

Agent Strong had listened to her calmly, stroking his chin with his fingers. *So he felt trapped*, Agent Strong had said.

Carol had nodded. Trapped. That was the perfect word for it. Mark had felt trapped, with no one to turn to. He'd believed that Bernard had him on all corners, so he had given in. He'd thought that if he went through with it that Bernard would keep his end of the bargain, that he would destroy whatever circumstantial evidence he had dug up on his parents and that would be the end of it.

She'd told him the reason Mark had bungled the hit on George Fielding was because his conscience was getting the better of him, and that when Bernard had found out he had called Mark, threatening to kill him. She had told him of Mark calling her at her apartment and her coming over and hearing this for the first time. Of course she had suspected something was going wrong with Bernard for some time, but that only served to justify those feelings. She'd told Agent Strong about their flight to Three Rivers, how Bernard had somehow tracked them there, how Mark had ambushed him and managed to knock him out. How they'd fled before the police had arrived. She'd told the agent about her confusion during this time, the conflicting emotions of fear and love tearing her apart. But most important had been an overriding feeling that she'd had to help Mark, that she'd had to keep him safe.

Why was that? Agent Strong had asked.

Carol had shrugged. I don't know, she'd said. Of course, deep down inside she'd known, but she hadn't been about to tell him that. Agent Strong had looked at her for a moment, as if trying to read her thoughts, then had nodded for her to continue.

There hadn't been much else to tell; he'd known the rest. They had settled in Florence, Missouri and hidden out there for a month, then decided to head to Chicago. They had stopped at the Motel Six in Springfield for the night and somehow Bernard Roberts had tracked them. How, she didn't know, but he had, and now Mark was dead, and would he please just leave her the fuck alone?

He had left her alone that night, in a motel room with a guard posted outside her door. The next morning she had been interviewed by a couple of detectives, mostly about what had happened back at the motel. She'd begun to wonder if she would need a lawyer, but Agent Strong had assured her that she wouldn't face charges. *As long as we have our understanding*, he'd said, smiling.

Bernard Roberts had been held in Illinois on no bond. Meanwhile, prosecutors had wanted to extradite him to California so they could charge him with the conspiracy charges, but it appeared that Illinois wanted to hold him there until he'd been tried first. Meanwhile, Carol had been flown back to Orange County for interrogation by law enforcement personnel about her knowledge of Bernard's criminal activities in Orange County. *As long as we have our understanding*, Agent Strong's voice had whispered in her mind, reminding her.

She had lost her apartment upon fleeing with Mark, but with the help of her parents, who had been supportive during the ordeal, she'd found a new place in Huntington Beach. She'd cooperated fully with the FBI on the fraud and embezzling charges and also in the three murder-for-hire plots, as well as the attempted murder-for-hire on George Fielding. She'd been interviewed and interrogated so much that she'd soon lost count. With the help of her parents and the salary from a job she'd started six months later at a small computer firm, she'd retained a good lawyer who had sat in with her on several interrogations. As the months had drawn on, the lawyer had been able to arrange a deal with prosecutors: Carol Emrich would reveal all she knew as their star witness; she would testify against Bernard Roberts in both trials. In return, she would get full immunity. The deal had been struck and even after the documents were signed Carol had still felt troubled.

Bernard hadn't budged in questioning. All the evidence gathered against him in the fraud and embezzling had been largely based on circumstantial evidence and testimony from Carol, based on the nine months she had been dating him. They had still been debating on whether to admit into evidence the private conversations between Mark Wiseman and Carol about his involvement in the killings and Bernard's confessions to Mark, when Bernard's murder trial had come up in Illinois.

It had been a three-week trial, held at the Springfield County Courthouse. Bernard had been represented by a lawyer from Mission Viejo, a criminal defense lawyer named Jim Weinstein who had worn big flashy gold rings on his fingers and a large gold chain around his wrist. The defense had tried to paint the picture that Bernard was a spurned lover, that Carol had dumped him for Mark, and that Bernard had travelled brokenhearted to Illinois to try to patch things up and had been attacked by Mark. "My client may very well have been stalking Mark Wiseman for the better part of two months," Jim had said during closing arguments. "I admit, he was acting like a lovesick kid. He was devastated by the break-up between he and Ms. Emrich. But he was also scared for her, because he suspected that Mark harbored a violent streak and he feared Carol was in danger. That's why he was armed the day he went to their motel room in Springfield. He didn't go armed with the intent to kill, but to protect himself from the possibility of Mark turning violent. And unfortunately, that's what happened."

It had been the most ludicrous piece of owlshit she had ever heard. The jury hadn't bought it either, and after deliberating for two days they'd found Bernard Roberts guilty of murder in the first degree. As the penalty phase of the trial had gotten under way, Carol had found herself besieged with media inquiries. The stress had been too much and that was when the urge to check out had started to clamor. She hadn't been able to get away from the images she'd seen on TV and magazines: The defense had painted her as she had been painted during her employment at Free State, as a castrating, money-hungry bitch; she had not only sent Mark Wiseman to his grave, but she had ruined the career of a brilliant businessman. Carol had almost committed suicide in the two weeks during the penalty phase of the trial, but couldn't. She'd had to see it through; she'd needed closure. Vengeance.

The jury had voted for life without the possibility of parole, striking down a possible death sentence. The judge had sealed the jury's decision with the pounding of the gavel and the case had been closed, pending appeals. Bernard hadn't even looked at

Carol as he'd been led by a bailiff toward the rear of
the court that took him down a long hallway to a
waiting car, where he'd been transported back to the
county jail. From there he had been transferred to
Joliet State Prison where he shared lodgings with
such masterminds of crime as serial killer John
Wayne Gacy. And all because he'd wanted to cover
up his evidence of fraud and embezzling.

Carol looked down at the pills in her hand, then
took a deep breath. She looked around the room and
smiled. Then she popped the first two pills in her
mouth and chased them with the water. Against the
soundtrack of "Fox on the Run," she fed the pills to
herself one by one, chasing them with the water until she emptied the bottle. Almost thirty-five pills.
She set the empty glass down on the nightstand
along with the empty bottle. Then she settled back
on the bed and lay down, closing her eyes, listening
to the music.

Somehow the people at her new job had gotten
wind of what had happened and it wasn't long before the rumors had begun plaguing her there, too.
She'd tried to dodge it, tried to simply keep her head
down and do her job, but it had been so hard. Accusations had flown, hurtful, hateful words had plagued
her, and she'd been forced to quit and look for another job. The recession had been running deep and
she'd taken temp jobs. She'd thought that she could
be anonymous at the companies the temp agencies
sent her to. But for some reason the men that she
worked with had all begun to sniff around her like
hungry wolves. She had batted down their advances

while trying to focus on her job. Then the accusations had come again: cold bitch, cock-teasing cunt, then—*Hey, isn't she the chick that testified in that murder trial, the one where the guy she was dating, some CEO, killed her boyfriend because she had dumped him?*

Yeah, that's the one. I heard she fucked her way up to that job and that she fucked him, too. Claimed to love him and everything. Then she dumped him. Went after some other guy and the guy she dumped just went ape-shit. He had proposed marriage to her, bought her a big engagement ring, bought her all kinds of shit. Fucking gold-digging bitch is what she is. And now he's doing time for killing that crazy boyfriend of hers because he attacked him when he tried to talk to her. That sucks.

The accusations had chased her from job to job and then Bernard's trial for conspiracy to commit murder and embezzling had come up. Once again, Carol had been the prosecution's star witness. The prosecutors had told her that with her testimony they had an open and shut case. They had the support of the surviving board members, Bernard's colleagues in the executive suite at Free State, and her testimony, not to mention the paper trail they had been able to wrestle out of the Cayman Island accounts, a paper trail that led right back to the Free State coffers.

So Bernard had been flown out to Orange County and stood trial for conspiracy to commit murder and embezzling in the Santa Ana Courthouse. Two weeks later he had been convicted on all counts and a month later he was sentenced to three life terms, plus seventy-five years with no possibility of parole. Once again, he hadn't even looked at her as he was led out of the courtroom by the bailiff.

During that trial she'd been treated coldly by the people she had known; former coworkers who had come to the trial to either testify, or to watch the proceedings. She had almost gotten the feeling that they were silently blaming her for the mess, that if she hadn't gotten involved with Bernard—and Mark for that matter—it wouldn't have happened. The only two people who hadn't snubbed her were two board members, Frederick Johansen, who had given a good, strong testimony, and George Fielding, healed up fully from his attack. Both men had approached her separately to offer their condolences and to express their sorrow for what had happened. Frederick Johansen had even said that if she ever needed anything—*and I mean anything*—to give him a call. He could help her get a job at one of the companies he owned, no sweat. He had given her his card and she had taken it, smiling. She'd thanked them both, then went home alone.

And now she was home alone again with the music of Sweet blasting through her speakers. It was all over and soon all the grief and hurt and guilt she felt over Mark's death would be gone, too. Soon she would be with Mark Wiseman again; it was all she dreamed of. It was what had kept her going these past fifteen months. To make sure that he was avenged.

She felt the dark pall of sleep come over her and she smiled, welcoming it. The music she most loved as a child was playing in the background and she tried to conjure up visions of that long-ago time, when the world had seemed so bright and innocent, when she had been unmarred by the harsh cruelties of the world. She was ten years old again and playing in the warm, Nebraska sun. It was late afternoon and her friends were somewhere—she didn't know where—and she was in her front yard playing with her Barbies and her tea set, her portable turntable on the front porch, "Little Willy" blaring out of the tiny speakers. It was a beautiful day, the sun warm, a nice cool breeze blowing from the north, and the shadows were long on the sidewalks and the front lawn, which was a deep green. She played, humming the song under her breath and when she heard Mark call her name she looked up and smiled, surprised to see him. He was standing at the bottom step that led up to the front porch and he was smiling, looking like he had when she'd first met him at that night club, his hair combed back and resting on his shoulders, his face clean-shaven. He smiled at her and held out his hand and she reached her hand out to him and suddenly she wasn't ten years old anymore, she was twenty-eight again, but she was still in that world of her childhood, where her childhood memories gave her the warm, comforting feeling of home.

Epilogue

He had been exercising in the yard by himself now for the past three years. He preferred it. It gave him time to think.

He couldn't think in the bullpen of the Joliet State Prison. He couldn't think because the bullpen was loud, ringing with the voices of the three hundred plus men in the wing where he was imprisoned. Men that were serving time for grand theft, bank robbery, aggravated assault, rape, first- and second-degree murder. Between the hours of one and three p.m., they were out of their cells and congregating in the recreation area, or they were watching television, or they were in their cells writing letters, or they were lined up at the pay phones talking to loved ones. Those that were on some sort of work duty were slaving away in the laundry, or in the prison library, or in the factory making license plates. And between the hours of two-thirty and three, Bernard Roberts was allowed thirty minutes of exercise in the yard by himself. It had to be this way; he was a danger to others and he was often the target of danger.

Bernard Roberts grinned slightly and looked up at the blue sky, clouds dotting the horizon. It was hard to believe that he had been behind bars now for nine years, but it was true. How time flies. When he'd first come to Joliet to serve his term he had still been lean and handsome, with hardly a speck of gray in his hair. Now he had put on eighty pounds, especially around the midsection and the hair along the crown of his head had completely fallen out. It had gone gray around the temples and he now wore glasses to correct his vision. But his mind was still sharp; he supposed it always would be.

Three years was a long time to have solitary exercise duties, but it had come at a price. He had been offering a fellow con financial advice, which had been passed on to the con's family on the outside. The market had taken a downturn and the man's family had lost twenty thousand dollars. The con—who was serving a life sentence for killing three people in a robbery—had gone after Bernard in the yard. The fight hadn't been that bad; the guards had broken it up, but the worst had come three weeks later after they'd both come out of solitary.

It was pretty much common knowledge that Bernard was serving time for first-degree murder and that he had been convicted in California for a bunch of embezzling and conspiracy-to-murder shit. Only in the day following his and Bruce Taylor's— the guy he had fought with in the yard—release from solitary, Bruce had let the word leak that there was one charge the DA in California hadn't been able to pin on Bernard: child molestation. Bernard didn't know how Bruce had been able to success-fully convince the twelve or so cronies he hung with that he had almost been tried on seven counts of sexual molestation of a child, but somehow he had. The rumor had gotten around. It was dismissed in most circles; everybody was trying to fuck every-body else in prison, so those cons that were sea-soned veterans had picked up on the lie. However, there were others that hadn't dismissed it so easily. Many of these men were those with children them-selves, but not all. Men who weren't above a little torture themselves.

A big lunkhead named Jaime Wills had tried it first, coming at Bernard one morning at breakfast. He'd come at Bernard with a shiv and Bernard had been fast enough to bring Jaime to the ground, twist the shiv out of his hand and stab the motherfucker in the back. He'd spent another two weeks in soli-tary for that, but when he'd gotten out there was more waiting for him.

The first time Bernard had been gang raped in prison had been two weeks after he'd first arrived at Joliet. It had happened in the shower. Bernard had been apprehensive about showering when he'd first arrived at Joliet, but then he'd seen that not much re-ally happened. All the stories he had heard about gang rapes in prison showers must have been bull-shit, because they surely didn't happen at Joliet. For one, there were guards all over the place. That seemed to be the main deterrent. Bernard had started chalking that one up as an urban myth, but then it had happened to him.

He had been in the shower and for awhile everything had been normal. Then he'd suddenly noticed that the showers had emptied out. The minute he'd realized that two things had happened: the first, he'd noticed that the guards had all suddenly vanished; the second, he'd felt something long and hard probe between his buttocks from behind. He'd started and was about to turn around when a hand had clamped around his neck. "I been wantin' to fuck yo ass since I laid eyes on you, homey," a rough voice had whispered in his ear. The hand around his throat had clamped down harder and then everything had become a blur.

He had been beaten and raped by four hardened men, gang members, real hardasses. All of them big and muscular and one of them with a violent fetish for sexual torture. Bernard had spent a week on his stomach in the infirmary after that, with the prison doctors telling him that another attack could permanently damage his rectum. Therefore, when he'd gotten out of the infirmary he'd changed his tactics; he'd begun hanging out with the Aryan Nations assholes that he had always hated, and because Bernard had a keen business mind they'd begun using him as a resource for their activities outside. They'd also protected him. He would never be raped by another gang of niggers and wetbacks again.

Instead he had gotten it from an Aryan Nations skin, one of the new leaders of the gang inside the prison. Two days after being sprung from solitary after stabbing Jaime, this skin had come into his cell, flanked by two blond men with crew cuts and multiple tattoos on their arms and shoulders. The skin,

Doug Simpson, had grinned and his beady little eyes had gleamed with a hollow stupidity. "Didn't know you liked to butt-fuck little girls, Bernard. If we had known that fourteen years ago, your ass would have been dead a long time ago."

The beating that he'd received in his cell was almost fatal. One of the cronies Doug had brought with him had had a piece of lead pipe in his fist, and that was what had fractured his skull and crushed his nose—he still had nasal problems because of it. He'd also received two broken ribs, a ruptured spleen which was removed in surgery, a shattered right eardrum which had led to complete deafness in that ear, and a massive concussion. Oh, yeah, and he had also had to rely on a colostomy bag for doing his business, too. It seemed that Doug Simpson was hung like a horse—twelve inches long and three inches thick—and they'd stopped beating him just shy of blacking out so Doug could make sure Bernard had felt every inch of that huge cock plow up his nether regions. It had been the worst pain he had ever felt, so bad that he had finally blacked out from the sheer intensity of it.

When he'd come to they were still there, standing over him, grinning. Then they'd beaten him again. The last thing he remembered them saying was "This is what we do to fucking child molesters!"

He'd spent nearly a month in the infirmary.

When he was healed he'd been placed in a different cell block at the request of his lawyer and with much pressure. The cell block he was put in was for prisoners under protective custody. He spent most of his days in his cell reading quietly, or writing in his journal. He also got to use of one of the computers in the prison library, and he surfed the Internet, perusing the various law sites in his never-ending quest to have his sentence overturned. His appeals had gone all the way to the Federal Supreme Court, which had turned him down, refusing to hear the case. Still, he was undaunted. He would persevere.

Now, three years after the vicious beating and rape that had almost taken his life, he was simply trying to get by. At fifty-five years of age he looked ten years older. On cold nights he sometimes got headaches and the joints in his hip sometimes hurt, but he was alive. At least he was alive.

Bernard coughed lightly and began heading toward the southeastern corner of the yard. He walked with a slight limp due to the injury to his rectum—he suppose he would be walking bowlegged for the rest of his life due to that fuck Doug Simpson—but at least he could walk. Despite what he had feared, there was actually no feeling down there at all anymore. He later found out that in addition to being raped by Doug Simpson's monster cock, they had used a piece of lead pipe on him too; that was what had caused the permanent damage to his rectum and the sphincter damage. The nerves had been damaged during surgery to remove his rectum and lower colon, so Bernard could sit down quite normally and not feel any pain. He just couldn't take a dump like a normal man anymore.

It was a cool, crisp afternoon and the leaves beyond the high, chain-link fence of the yard were turning brown on the trees. It was late October and it was already cooling down, with a cold wind blowing briskly. Bernard had always liked the fall the best, in fact—

"Bernard."

The voice was a whisper, but he heard it loud and clear. It was behind him and he whirled around. Standing in front of him was a naked man who appeared to be in his late sixties or early seventies, his belly a paunch, his gray hair longish and wispy around his head. He had a small goatee and he smiled. "Don't you recognize me, Bernard? It's your old boardroom buddy. George Fielding."

Bernard blinked, recognition setting in. It *was* George Fielding. Nine years older, and looking it, too. But what the fuck was he doing naked here in the yard? And how the fuck had he gotten over the fence and *inside* the yard for that matter?

Bernard opened his mouth to say something: *What the hell are you doing here?* would have been appropriate. George Fielding stopped him by putting his finger to his lips, silencing him. He grinned. Bernard blinked again, not really believing this was happening. The guards would have noticed an elderly, naked man trying to get over the fence in a heartbeat, they would have been rushing him before he even got to the fence, *they would have fucking shot him, for Chrissakes!* Bernard glanced quickly at the guard tower—the one guard was looking out over the north side of the yard, away from him. *Either he hasn't noticed or this is a setup, this is a fucking setup and—*

"Can you keep a secret, Bernard?" George asked, moving forward like smoke billowing from a fire. "You aren't going to believe what happened to me.

You aren't going to believe what you have inadvertently done to me, you son-of-a-bitch."

Bernard took another involuntary step back. "What?" It came out as a strangled croak.

"This." George grinned and the change was so immediate that for a moment Bernard thought he was hallucinating. It was like watching one of those action-adventure movies they let them watch in the entertainment room inside, the way motion-picture special effects had graduated to improve computer-morphing of people into monsters. That was what was happening with George; he was morphing seamlessly into something bigger, something hideous and animal-like and monstrous and—

The change fully complete, the wolf-creature opened its mouth, seeming to grin a mouthful of fanged teeth. The implication of what George had said hit Bernard fully now as he took another fumbling step back, his throat trying to unlock so he could scream. *Oh God, why didn't I think of that before, George Fielding lived through the attack, he lived through the attack of a fucking werewolf and what was one of the ways you become a werewolf, you had to survive a werewolf's bite, holy shit—*

George Fielding interrupted Bernard's thoughts by lunging quickly and silently at him, his elongated, wolfish snout snaking in and ripping Bernard's throat out with one vicious rip. Blood flew outward in an arterial spray, drenching George's grayish coat and the grass.

George gulped down the bloody mass of Bernard's throat and stood back, his brown eyes narrowed in canine slits as he watched Bernard wobble on his feet, hands clutching his ruined throat, his head flopping on what remained of his neck, his eyes growing wide as all the color drained out of his face, turning him a pasty gray. He opened his mouth as if to scream and then fell forward, landing on his face on the blood-soaked grass. George stepped back and dropped to all fours; if the guard had turned around, he would have seen what looked to be a large dog or wolf straddling the body of Bernard Roberts. But the guard wouldn't glance this way at all; George had spent the past two weeks watching the movements of the guard. The guard had the same routine every day. And the routine was that he looked out across the Illinois landscape as he stood at the top of the guard tower while Bernard was free to smoke, read, exercise, or jack off. Bernard wouldn't have had the time to make an escape and if he did the sensors along the fence would alert him to it.

It took under twenty seconds for Bernard Roberts to die. When he was dead, George headed toward the corner Bernard had been walking to before George had snuck up on him. He wriggled his way through the trench he had dug under the chain-link fence, his lithe wolf body not even touching the bottom of the fence. Once on the other side he trotted off toward the woods that lined the outer perimeter of the prison.

The guard saw him retreat into the woods and thought to himself that there was nothing more beautiful than seeing a wolf running free in this part of the country again.

From Horror's greatest talents comes

THE NEW FACE OF FEAR.

Terrifying, sexy, dangerous and deadly.

And they are hunting for YOU...

WEREWOLVES

SHAPESHIFTER by J. F. GONZALEZ
JANUARY 2008

THE NIGHTWALKER by THOMAS TESSIER
FEBRUARY 2008

RAVENOUS by RAY GARTON
APRIL 2008

BRIAN KEENE

Something very strange is happening in LeHorn's Hollow. Eerie, piping music is heard late at night, and mysterious fires have been spotted deep in the woods. Women are vanishing without a trace overnight, leaving behind husbands and families. When up-and-coming novelist Adam Senft stumbles upon an unearthly scene, it plunges him and the entire town into an ancient nightmare. Folks say the woods in LeHorn's Hollow are haunted, but what waits there is far worse than any ghost. It has been summoned...and now it demands to be satisfied.

DARK HOLLOW

ISBN 13: 978-0-8439-5861-4